We hope you enjoy this book. Please return or renew it by the due date.

You can renew it at www.norfolk.gov.uk/libraries or by using our free library app.

Otherwise you can phone 0344 800 8020 - please have your library card and PIN ready.

You can sign up for email reminders too.

D1340709

NORFOLK ITEM

30129 085 951 839

NORFOLK COUNTY COUNCIL
LIBRARY AND INFORMATION SERVICE

ALMA CLASSICS

ALMA CLASSICS
an imprint of

ALMA BOOKS LTD
3 Castle Yard
Richmond
Surrey TW10 6TF
United Kingdom
www.almaclassics.com

This collection first published by Alma Books Ltd in 2014. Repr. 2019

Extra Material © Richard Parker

Printed and bound by CPI Group (UK) Ltd, Croydon, CR0 4YY

ISBN: 978-1-84749-380-4

Contents

Other books by F. SCOTT FITZGERALD
published by Alma Classics

F. Scott Fitzgerald (1896–1940)

Edward Fitzgerald,
Fitzgerald's father

Mary McQuillan Fitzgerald,
Fitzgerald's mother

Ginevra King

Zelda Fitzgerald

The Fitzgeralds' house in Montgomery, Alabama

The Fitzgeralds' grave in Rockville, Maryland,
inscribed with the closing line from *The Great Gatsby*

The first page of 'Babylon Revisited', as it first
appeared in the *Saturday Evening Post* in 1931

Babylon Revisited

and Other Stories

Babylon Revisited

1

" $\mathbf{A}$ ND WHERE'S MR CAMPBELL?" Charlie asked.
"Gone to Switzerland. Mr Campbell's a pretty sick man, Mr Wales."

"I'm sorry to hear that. And George Hardt?" Charlie enquired.

"Back in America, gone to work."

"And where is the Snow Bird?"

"He was in here last week. Anyway, his friend, Mr Schaeffer, is in Paris."

Two familiar names from the long list of a year and a half ago. Charlie scribbled an address in his notebook and tore out the page.

"If you see Mr Schaeffer, give him this," he said. "It's my brother-in-law's address. I haven't settled on a hotel yet."

He was not really disappointed to find Paris was so empty. But the stillness in the Ritz bar was strange and portentous. It was not an American bar any more – he felt polite in it, and not as if he owned it. It had gone back into France. He felt the stillness from the moment he got out of the taxi and saw the doorman, usually in a frenzy of activity at this hour, gossiping with a *chasseur** by the servants' entrance.

Passing through the corridor, he heard only a single, bored voice in the once clamorous women's room. When he turned into the bar he travelled the twenty feet of green carpet with his eyes fixed straight ahead by old habit; and then, with his foot firmly on the rail, he turned and surveyed the room, encountering only a single pair of eyes that fluttered up from a newspaper in the corner. Charlie asked for the head barman,

3

Paul, who in the latter days of the bull market had come to work in his own custom-built car – disembarking, however, with due nicety at the nearest corner. But Paul was at his country house today and Alix giving him information.

"No, no more," Charlie said, "I'm going slow these days."

Alix congratulated him: "You were going pretty strong a couple of years ago."

"I'll stick to it all right," Charlie assured him. "I've stuck to it for over a year and a half now."

"How do you find conditions in America?"

"I haven't been to America for months. I'm in business in Prague, representing a couple of concerns there. They don't know about me down there."

Alix smiled.

"Remember the night of George Hardt's bachelor dinner here?" said Charlie. "By the way, what's become of Claude Fessenden?"

Alix lowered his voice confidentially: "He's in Paris, but he doesn't come here any more. Paul doesn't allow it. He ran up a bill of thirty thousand francs, charging all his drinks and his lunches, and usually his dinner, for more than a year. And when Paul finally told him he had to pay, he gave him a bad cheque."

Alix shook his head sadly.

"I don't understand it, such a dandy fellow. Now he's all bloated up..." He made a plump apple of his hands.

Charlie watched a group of strident queens installing themselves in a corner.

"Nothing affects them," he thought. "Stocks rise and fall, people loaf or work, but they go on for ever." The place oppressed him. He called for the dice and shook with Alix for the drink.

"Here for long, Mr Wales?"

"I'm here for four or five days to see my little girl."

"Oh-h! You have a little girl?"

Outside, the fire-red, gas-blue, ghost-green signs shone smokily through the tranquil rain. It was late afternoon and the streets were in movement; the *bistros* gleamed. At the corner of the Boulevard des Capucines he took a taxi. The Place de la Concorde moved by in pink majesty; they crossed the logical Seine, and Charlie felt the sudden provincial quality of the Left Bank.

Charlie directed his taxi to the Avenue de l'Opéra, which was out of his way. But he wanted to see the blue hour spread over the magnificent façade, and imagine that the cab horns, playing endlessly the first few bars of 'La plus que lente',* were the trumpets of the Second Empire. They were closing the iron grille in front of Brentano's bookstore, and people were already at dinner behind the trim little bourgeois hedge of Duval's. He had never eaten at a really cheap restaurant in Paris. Five-course dinner, four francs fifty, eighteen cents, wine included. For some odd reason he wished that he had.

As they rolled on to the Left Bank and he felt its sudden provincialism, he thought, "I spoilt this city for myself. I didn't realize it, but the days came along one after another, and then two years were gone, and everything was gone, and I was gone."

He was thirty-five, and good to look at. The Irish mobility of his face was sobered by a deep wrinkle between his eyes. As he rang his brother-in-law's bell in the Rue Palatine, the wrinkle deepened till it pulled down his brows; he felt a cramping sensation in his belly. From behind the maid who opened the door darted a lovely little girl of nine who shrieked "Daddy!" and flew up, struggling like a fish, into his arms. She pulled his head around by one ear and set her cheek against his.

"My old pie," he said.

"Oh, Daddy, Daddy, Daddy, Daddy, Dads, Dads, Dads!"

She drew him into the salon, where the family waited, a boy and girl his daughter's age, his sister-in-law and her husband. He greeted Marion with his voice pitched carefully to avoid either feigned enthusiasm or dislike, but her response was more frankly tepid, though she minimized her expression of unalterable distrust by directing her regard towards his child. The two men clasped hands in a friendly way, and Lincoln Peters rested his for a moment on Charlie's shoulder.

The room was warm and comfortably American. The three children moved intimately about, playing through the yellow oblongs that led to other rooms; the cheer of six o'clock spoke in the eager smacks of the fire and the sounds of French activity in the kitchen. But Charlie did not relax; his heart sat up rigidly in his body and he drew confidence from his daughter, who from time to time came close to him, holding in her arms the doll he had brought.

"Really extremely well," he declared in answer to Lincoln's question. "There's a lot of business there that isn't moving at all, but we're doing even better than ever. In fact, damn well. I'm bringing my sister over from America next month to keep house for me. My income last year was bigger than it was when I had money. You see, the Czechs…"

His boasting was for a specific purpose, but after a moment, seeing a faint restiveness in Lincoln's eye, he changed the subject.

"Those are fine children of yours, well brought up, good manners."

"We think Honoria's a great little girl too."

Marion Peters came back from the kitchen. She was a tall woman with worried eyes, who had once possessed a fresh American loveliness. Charlie had never been sensitive to it and was always surprised when people spoke of how pretty she had been. From the first there had been an instinctive antipathy between them.

"Well, how do you find Honoria?" she asked.

"Wonderful. I was astonished how much she's grown in ten months. All the children are looking well."

"We haven't had a doctor for a year. How do you like being back in Paris?"

"It seems very funny to see so few Americans around."

"I'm delighted," Marion said vehemently. "Now at least you can go into a store without their assuming you're a millionaire. We've suffered like everybody, but on the whole it's a good deal pleasanter."

"But it was nice while it lasted," Charlie said. "We were a sort of royalty, almost infallible, with a sort of magic around us. In the bar this afternoon" – he stumbled, seeing his mistake – "there wasn't a man I knew."

She looked at him keenly. "I should think you'd have had enough of bars."

"I only stayed a minute. I take one drink every afternoon, and no more."

"Don't you want a cocktail before dinner?" Lincoln asked.

"I take only one drink every afternoon, and I've had that."

"I hope you keep to it," said Marion.

Her dislike was evident in the coldness with which she spoke, but Charlie only smiled; he had larger plans. Her very aggressiveness gave him an advantage, and he knew enough to wait. He wanted them to initiate the discussion of what they knew had brought him to Paris.

At dinner he couldn't decide whether Honoria was most like him or her mother. Fortunate if she didn't combine the traits of both that had brought them to disaster. A great wave of protectiveness went over him. He thought he knew what to do for her. He believed in character; he wanted to jump back a whole generation and trust in character again as the eternally valuable element. Everything wore out.

He left soon after dinner, but not to go home. He was curious to see Paris by night with clearer and more judicious eyes than those of other days. He bought a *strapontin** for the Casino and watched Josephine Baker* go through her chocolate arabesques.

After an hour he left and strolled towards Montmartre, up the Rue Pigalle into the Place Blanche. The rain had stopped and there were a few people in evening clothes disembarking from taxis in front of cabarets, and *cocottes* prowling singly or in pairs, and many Negroes. He passed a lighted door from which issued music, and stopped with the sense of familiarity; it was Bricktop's, where he had parted with so many hours and so much money. A few doors farther on he found another ancient rendezvous and incautiously put his head inside. Immediately an eager orchestra burst into sound, a pair of professional dancers leapt to their feet and a maître d'hôtel swooped towards him, crying, "Crowd just arriving, sir!" But he withdrew quickly.

"You have to be damn drunk," he thought.

Zelli's was closed, the bleak and sinister cheap hotels surrounding it were dark; up in the Rue Blanche there was more light and a local, colloquial French crowd. The Poet's Cave had disappeared, but the two great mouths of the Café of Heaven and the Café of Hell still yawned – even devoured, as he watched, the meagre contents of a tourist bus – a German, a Japanese and an American couple who glanced at him with frightened eyes.

So much for the effort and ingenuity of Montmartre. All the catering to vice and waste was on an utterly childish scale, and he suddenly realized the meaning of the word "dissipate" – to dissipate into thin air; to make nothing out of something. In the little hours of the night every move from place to place was an enormous human jump, an increase of paying for the privilege of slower and slower motion.

He remembered thousand-franc notes given to an orchestra for playing a single number, hundred-franc notes tossed to a doorman for calling a cab.

But it hadn't been given for nothing.

It had been given, even the most wildly squandered sum, as an offering to destiny that he might not remember the things most worth remembering, the things that now he would always remember – his child taken from his control, his wife escaped to a grave in Vermont.

In the glare of a *brasserie* a woman spoke to him. He bought her some eggs and coffee, and then, eluding her encouraging stare, gave her a twenty-franc note and took a taxi to his hotel.

2

H E WOKE UPON A FINE FALL DAY – football weather. The depression of yesterday was gone, and he liked the people on the streets. At noon he sat opposite Honoria at Le Grand Vatel, the only restaurant he could think of not reminiscent of champagne dinners and long luncheons that began at two and ended in a blurred and vague twilight.

"Now, how about vegetables? Oughtn't you to have some vegetables?"

"Well, yes."

"Here's *épinards* and *chou-fleur* and carrots and *haricots*."*

"*I'd like chou-fleur.*"

"Wouldn't you like to have two vegetables?"

"I usually only have one at lunch."

The waiter was pretending to be inordinately fond of children. "*Qu'elle est mignonne la petite! Elle parle exactement comme une française.*"*

"How about dessert? Shall we wait and see?"

The waiter disappeared. Honoria looked at her father expectantly.

"What are we going to do?"

"First we're going to that toy store in the Rue Saint-Honoré and buy you anything you like. And then we're going to the vaudeville at the Empire."

She hesitated. "I like it about the vaudeville, but not the toy store."

"Why not?"

"Well, you brought me this doll." She had it with her. "And I've got lots of things. And we're not rich any more, are we?"

"We never were. But today you are to have anything you want."

"All right," she agreed resignedly.

9

When there had been her mother and a French nurse, he had been inclined to be strict; now he extended himself, reached out for a new tolerance; he must be both parents to her and not shut any of her out of communication.

"I want to get to know you," he said gravely. "First let me introduce myself. My name is Charles J. Wales, of Prague."

"Oh, Daddy!" her voice cracked with laughter.

"And who are you, please?" he persisted, and she accepted a role immediately: "Honoria Wales, Rue Palatine, Paris."

"Married or single?"

"No, not married. Single."

He indicated the doll. "But I see you have a child, Madame."

Unwilling to disinherit it, she took it to her heart and thought quickly: "Yes, I've been married, but I'm not married now. My husband is dead."

He went on quickly, "And the child's name?"

"Simone. That's after my best friend at school."

"I'm very pleased that you're doing so well at school."

"I'm third this month," she boasted. "Elsie" – that was her cousin – "is only about eighteenth, and Richard is about at the bottom."

"You like Richard and Elsie, don't you?"

"Oh, yes. I like Richard quite well and I like her all right."

Cautiously and casually he asked: "And Aunt Marion and Uncle Lincoln – which do you like best?"

"Oh, Uncle Lincoln, I guess."

He was increasingly aware of her presence. As they came in, a murmur of "…adorable" followed them, and now the people at the next table bent all their silences upon her, staring as if she were something no more conscious than a flower.

"Why don't I live with you?" she asked suddenly. "Because Mamma's dead?"

"You must stay here and learn more French. It would have been hard for Daddy to take care of you so well."

"I don't really need much taking care of any more. I do everything for myself."

Going out of the restaurant, a man and a woman unexpectedly hailed him.

"Well, the old Wales!"

"Hello there, Lorraine… Dunc."

Sudden ghosts out of the past: Duncan Schaeffer, a friend from college. Lorraine Quarries, a lovely, pale blonde of thirty – one of a crowd who had helped them make months into days in the lavish times of three years ago.

"My husband couldn't come this year," she said, in answer to his question. "We're poor as hell. So he gave me two hundred a month and told me I could do my worst on that… This your little girl?"

"What about coming back and sitting down?" Duncan asked.

"Can't do it." He was glad for an excuse. As always, he felt Lorraine's passionate, provocative attraction, but his own rhythm was different now.

"Well, how about dinner?" she asked.

"I'm not free. Give me your address and let me call you."

"Charlie, I believe you're sober," she said judicially. "I honestly believe he's sober, Dunc. Pinch him and see if he's sober."

Charlie indicated Honoria with his head. They both laughed.

"What's your address?" said Duncan sceptically.

He hesitated, unwilling to give the name of his hotel.

"I'm not settled yet. I'd better call you. We're going to see the vaudeville at the Empire."

"There! That's what I want to do," Lorraine said. "I want to see some clowns and acrobats and jugglers. That's just what we'll do, Dunc."

"We've got to do an errand first," said Charlie. "Perhaps we'll see you there."

"All right, you snob… Goodbye, beautiful little girl."

"Goodbye."

Honoria bobbed politely.

Somehow, an unwelcome encounter. They liked him because he was functioning, because he was serious; they wanted to see him because he was stronger than they were now, because they wanted to draw a certain sustenance from his strength.

At the Empire, Honoria proudly refused to sit upon her father's folded coat. She was already an individual with a code of her own, and Charlie was more and more absorbed by the desire of putting a little of himself into her before she crystallized utterly. It was hopeless to try to know her in so short a time.

Between the acts they came upon Duncan and Lorraine in the lobby where the band was playing.

"Have a drink?"

"All right, but not up at the bar. We'll take a table."

"The perfect father."

Listening abstractedly to Lorraine, Charlie watched Honoria's eyes leave their table, and he followed them wistfully about the room, wondering what they saw. He met her glance and she smiled.

"I like that lemonade," she said.

What had she said? What had he expected? Going home in a taxi afterwards, he pulled her over until her head rested against his chest.

"Darling, do you ever think about your mother?"

"Yes, sometimes," she answered vaguely.

"I don't want you to forget her. Have you got a picture of her?"

"Yes, I think so. Anyhow, Aunt Marion has. Why don't you want me to forget her?"

"She loved you very much."

"I loved her too."

They were silent for a moment.

"Daddy, I want to come and live with you," she said suddenly.

His heart leapt; he had wanted it to come like this.

"Aren't you perfectly happy?"

"Yes, but I love you better than anybody. And you love me better than anybody, don't you, now that Mummy's dead?"

"Of course I do. But you won't always like me best, honey. You'll grow up and meet somebody your own age and go marry him and forget you ever had a daddy."

"Yes, that's true," she agreed tranquilly.

He didn't go in. He was coming back at nine o'clock and he wanted to keep himself fresh and new for the thing he must say then.

"When you're safe inside, just show yourself in that window."

"All right. Goodbye, Dads, Dads, Dads, Dads."

He waited in the dark street until she appeared, all warm and glowing, in the window above and kissed her fingers out into the night.

3

THEY WERE WAITING. Marion sat behind the coffee service in a dignified black dinner dress that just faintly suggested mourning. Lincoln was walking up and down with the animation of one who had already been talking. They were as anxious as he was to get into the question. He opened it almost immediately:

"I suppose you know what I want to see you about – why I really came to Paris."

Marion played with the black stars on her necklace and frowned.

"I'm awfully anxious to have a home," he continued. "And I'm awfully anxious to have Honoria in it. I appreciate your taking in Honoria for her mother's sake, but things have changed now" – he hesitated and then continued more forcibly – "changed radically with me, and I want to ask you to reconsider the matter. It would be silly for me to deny that about three years ago I was acting badly—"

Marion looked up at him with hard eyes.

"—but all that's over. As I told you, I haven't had more than a drink a day for over a year, and I take that drink deliberately, so that the idea of alcohol won't get too big in my imagination. You see the idea?"

"No," said Marion succinctly.

"It's a sort of stunt I set myself. It keeps the matter in proportion."

"I get you," said Lincoln. "You don't want to admit it's got any attraction for you."

"Something like that. Sometimes I forget and don't take it. But I try to take it. Anyhow, I couldn't afford to drink in my position. The people I represent are more than satisfied with what I've done, and I'm bringing my sister over from Burlington to keep house for me, and I want awfully to have Honoria too. You know that even when her mother and I weren't getting along well we never let anything that happened touch Honoria. I know she's fond of me and I know I'm able to take care of her and – well, there you are. How do you feel about it?"

He knew that now he would have to take a beating. It would last an hour or two hours, and it would be difficult, but if he modulated his inevitable resentment to the chastened attitude of the reformed sinner, he might win his point in the end.

Keep your temper, he told himself. You don't want to be justified. You want Honoria.

Lincoln spoke first: "We've been talking it over ever since we got your letter last month. We're happy to have Honoria here. She's a dear little thing, and we're glad to be able to help her, but of course that isn't the question—"

Marion interrupted suddenly. "How long are you going to stay sober, Charlie?" she asked.

"Permanently, I hope."

"How can anybody count on that?"

"You know I never did drink heavily until I gave up business and came over here with nothing to do. Then Helen and I began to run around with—"

"Please leave Helen out of it. I can't bear to hear you talk about her like that."

He stared at her grimly; he had never been certain how fond of each other the sisters were in life.

"My drinking only lasted about a year and a half – from the time we came over until I... collapsed."

"It was time enough."

"It was time enough," he agreed.

"My duty is entirely to Helen," she said. "I try to think what she would have wanted me to do. Frankly, from the night you did that terrible thing you haven't really existed for me. I can't help that. She was my sister."

"Yes."

"When she was dying she asked me to look out for Honoria. If you hadn't been in a sanitarium then, it might have helped matters."

He had no answer.

"I'll never in my life be able to forget the morning when Helen knocked at my door, soaked to the skin and shivering, and said you'd locked her out."

Charlie gripped the sides of the chair. This was more difficult than he expected; he wanted to launch out into a long expostulation and explanation, but he only said: "The night I locked her out—" and she interrupted: "I don't feel up to going over that again."

After a moment's silence, Lincoln said: "We're getting off the subject. You want Marion to set aside her legal guardianship and give you Honoria. I think the main point for her is whether she has confidence in you or not."

"I don't blame Marion," Charlie said slowly, "but I think she can have entire confidence in me. I had a good record up to three years ago. Of course, it's within human possibilities I might go wrong any time. But if we wait much longer I'll lose Honoria's childhood and my chance for a home." He shook his head. "I'll simply lose her, don't you see?"

"Yes, I see," said Lincoln.

"Why didn't you think of all this before?" Marion asked.

"I suppose I did, from time to time, but Helen and I were getting along badly. When I consented to the guardianship, I was flat on my back in a sanitarium and the market had cleaned me out. I knew I'd acted badly, and I thought if it would bring any peace to Helen, I'd agree to anything. But now it's different. I'm functioning, I'm behaving damn well, so far as—"

"Please don't swear at me," Marion said.

He looked at her, startled. With each remark the force of her dislike became more and more apparent. She had built up all her fear of life into one wall and faced it towards him. This trivial reproof was possibly the result of some trouble with the cook several hours before. Charlie became increasingly alarmed at leaving Honoria in this atmosphere of hostility against himself; sooner or later it would come out, in a word here, a shake of the head there, and some of that distrust would be irrevocably implanted in Honoria. But he pulled his temper down out of his face and shut it up inside him; he had won a point, for Lincoln realized the absurdity of Marion's remark and asked her lightly since when she had objected to the word "damn".

"Another thing," Charlie said: "I'm able to give her certain advantages now. I'm going to take a French governess to Prague with me. I've got a lease on a new apartment..."

He stopped, realizing that he was blundering. They couldn't be expected to accept with equanimity the fact that his income was again twice as large as their own.

"I suppose you can give her more luxuries than we can," said Marion. "When you were throwing away money we were living along watching every ten francs... I suppose you'll start doing it again."

"Oh, no," he said. "I've learnt. I worked hard for ten years, you know – until I got lucky in the market, like so many people. Terribly lucky. It didn't seem any use working any more, so I quit. It won't happen again."

There was a long silence. All of them felt their nerves straining, and for the first time in a year Charlie wanted a drink. He was sure now that Lincoln Peters wanted him to have his child.

Marion shuddered suddenly; part of her saw that Charlie's feet were planted on the earth now, and her own maternal feeling recognized the naturalness of his desire; but she had lived for a long time with a prejudice – a prejudice founded on a curious disbelief in her sister's happiness, and which, in the shock of one terrible night, had turned to hatred for him. It had all happened at a point in her life where the discouragement of ill health and adverse circumstances made it necessary for her to believe in tangible villainy and a tangible villain.

"I can't help what I think!" she cried out suddenly. "How much you were responsible for Helen's death, I don't know. It's something you'll have to square with your own conscience."

An electric current of agony surged through him; for a moment he was almost on his feet, an unuttered sound echoing in his throat. He hung on to himself for a moment, another moment.

"Hold on there," said Lincoln uncomfortably. "I never thought you were responsible for that."

"Helen died of heart trouble," Charlie said dully.

"Yes, heart trouble." Marion spoke as if the phrase had another meaning for her.

Then, in the flatness that followed her outburst, she saw him plainly and she knew he had somehow arrived at control over the situation. Glancing at her husband, she found no help from him, and as abruptly as if it were a matter of no importance, she threw up the sponge.

"Do what you like!" she cried, springing up from her chair. "She's your child. I'm not the person to stand in your way. I think if it were my child I'd rather see her…" She managed to check herself. "You two decide it. I can't stand this. I'm sick. I'm going to bed."

She hurried from the room; after a moment Lincoln said:

"This has been a hard day for her. You know how strongly she feels…" His voice was almost apologetic: "When a woman gets an idea in her head."

"Of course."

"It's going to be all right. I think she sees now that you… can provide for the child, and so we can't very well stand in your way or Honoria's way."

"Thank you, Lincoln."

"I'd better go along and see how she is."

"I'm going."

He was still trembling when he reached the street, but a walk down the Rue Bonaparte to the *quais* set him up, and as he crossed the Seine, fresh and new by the *quai* lamps, he felt exultant. But back in his room he couldn't sleep. The image of Helen haunted him. Helen whom he had loved so until they had senselessly begun to abuse each other's love, tear it into shreds. On that terrible February night that Marion remembered so vividly, a slow quarrel had gone on for hours. There was a scene at the Florida, and then he attempted to take her home, and then she kissed young Webb at a table; after that there was what she had hysterically said. When he arrived home alone he turned the key in the lock in wild anger. How could he know she would arrive an hour later alone, that there would be a snowstorm in which she wandered about in slippers, too confused to find a taxi? Then the aftermath, her escaping pneumonia by a miracle, and all the attendant horror. They were "reconciled", but that was the beginning of the end, and Marion, who had seen with her own eyes and who imagined it to be one of many scenes from her sister's martyrdom, never forgot.

Going over it again brought Helen nearer, and in the white, soft light that steals upon half-sleep near morning he found himself talking to her again. She said that he was perfectly right about Honoria and that she wanted Honoria to be with him. She said she was glad he was being good and doing better. She said a lot of other things – very friendly things – but she was in a swing in a white dress, and swinging faster and faster all the time, so that at the end he could not hear clearly all that she said.

4

H E WOKE UP FEELING HAPPY. The door of the world was open again. He made plans, vistas, futures for Honoria and himself, but suddenly he grew sad, remembering all the plans he and Helen had made. She had not planned to die. The present was the thing – work to do and someone to love. But not to love too much, for he knew the injury that a father can do to a daughter or a mother to a son by attaching them too closely; afterwards, out in the world, the child would seek in the marriage partner the same blind tenderness and, failing probably to find it, turn against love and life.

It was another bright, crisp day. He called Lincoln Peters at the bank where he worked and asked if he could count on taking Honoria when he left for Prague. Lincoln agreed that there was no reason for delay. One thing – the legal guardianship. Marion wanted to retain that a while longer. She was upset by the whole matter, and it would oil things if she felt that the situation was still in her control for another year. Charlie agreed, wanted only the tangible, visible child.

Then the question of a governess. Charlie sat in a gloomy agency and talked to a cross Béarnaise and to a buxom Breton peasant, neither of whom he could have endured. There were others whom he would see tomorrow.

He lunched with Lincoln Peters at Griffon's, trying to keep down his exultation.

"There's nothing quite like your own child," Lincoln said. "But you understand how Marion feels too."

"She's forgotten how hard I worked for seven years there," Charlie said. "She just remembers one night."

"There's another thing." Lincoln hesitated. "While you and Helen were tearing around Europe throwing money away, we were just getting along. I didn't touch any of the prosperity because I never got ahead enough to carry anything but my insurance. I think Marion felt there was some kind of injustice in it – you not even working towards the end, and getting richer and richer."

"It went just as quick as it came," said Charlie.

"Yes, a lot of it stayed in the hands of *chasseurs* and saxophone players and maîtres d'hôtel – well, the big party's over now. I just said that to explain Marion's feeling about those crazy years. If you drop in about six o'clock tonight before Marion's too tired, we'll settle the details on the spot."

Back at his hotel, Charlie found a *pneumatique** that had been redirected from the Ritz bar where Charlie had left his address for the purpose of finding a certain man.

Dear Charlie: You were so strange when we saw you the other day that I wondered if I did something to offend you. If so, I'm not conscious of it. In fact, I have thought about you too much for the last year, and it's always been in the back of my mind that I might see you if I came over here. We did have such good times that crazy spring, like the night you and I stole the butcher's tricycle, and the time we tried to call on the President and you had the old derby rim and the wire cane. Everybody seems so old lately, but I don't feel old a bit. Couldn't we get together some time today for old time's sake? I've got a vile hangover for the moment, but will be feeling better this afternoon and will look for you about five in the sweatshop at the Ritz.

Always devotedly,

Lorraine

His first feeling was one of awe that he had actually, in his mature years, stolen a tricycle and pedalled Lorraine all over the Étoile between the small hours and dawn. In retrospect it was a nightmare. Locking out Helen didn't fit in with any other act of his life, but the tricycle incident did – it was one of many. How many weeks or months of dissipation to arrive at that condition of utter irresponsibility?

He tried to picture how Lorraine had appeared to him then – very attractive; Helen was unhappy about it, though she said nothing. Yesterday, in the restaurant, Lorraine had seemed trite, blurred, worn away. He emphatically did not want to see her, and he was glad Alix had not given away his hotel address. It was a relief to think, instead, of Honoria, to think of Sundays spent with her and of saying good morning to her and of knowing she was there in his house at night, drawing her breath in the darkness.

At five he took a taxi and bought presents for all the Peters – a piquant cloth doll, a box of Roman soldiers, flowers for Marion, big linen handkerchiefs for Lincoln.

He saw, when he arrived in the apartment, that Marion had accepted the inevitable. She greeted him now as though he were a recalcitrant member of the family, rather than a menacing outsider. Honoria had been told she was going; Charlie was glad to see that her tact made her conceal her excessive happiness. Only on his lap did she whisper her delight and the question "When?" before she slipped away with the other children.

He and Marion were alone for a minute in the room, and on an impulse he spoke out boldly:

"Family quarrels are bitter things. They don't go according to any rules. They're not like aches or wounds; they're more like splits in the skin that won't heal because there's not enough material. I wish you and I could be on better terms."

"Some things are hard to forget," she answered. "It's a question of confidence." There was no answer to this and presently she asked, "When do you propose to take her?"

"As soon as I can get a governess. I hoped the day after tomorrow."

"That's impossible. I've got to get her things in shape. Not before Saturday."

He yielded. Coming back into the room, Lincoln offered him a drink. "I'll take my daily whisky," he said.

It was warm here, it was a home, people together by a fire. The children felt very safe and important; the mother and father were serious, watchful. They had things to do for the children more important than his visit here. A spoonful of medicine was, after all, more important than the strained relations between Marion and himself. They were not dull people, but they were very much in the grip of life and circumstances. He wondered if he couldn't do something to get Lincoln out of his rut at the bank.

A long peal at the doorbell; the *bonne à tout faire** passed through and went down the corridor. The door opened upon another long ring, and then voices, and the three in the salon looked up expectantly; Richard moved to bring the corridor within his range of vision, and Marion rose. Then the maid came back along the corridor, closely followed by the voices, which developed under the light into Duncan Schaeffer and Lorraine Quarries.

They were gay, they were hilarious, they were roaring with laughter. For a moment Charlie was astounded; unable to understand how they ferreted out the Peters' address.

"Ah-h-h!" Duncan wagged his finger roguishly at Charlie. "Ah-h-h!"

They both slid down another cascade of laughter. Anxious and at a loss, Charlie shook hands with them quickly and presented them to Lincoln and Marion. Marion nodded, scarcely speaking. She had drawn back a step towards the fire; her little girl stood beside her, and Marion put an arm about her shoulder.

With growing annoyance at the intrusion, Charlie waited for them to explain themselves. After some concentration Duncan said:

"We came to invite you out to dinner. Lorraine and I insist that all this chichi, cagey business 'bout your address got to stop."

Charlie came closer to them, as if to force them backwards down the corridor.

"Sorry, but I can't. Tell me where you'll be and I'll phone you in half an hour."

This made no impression. Lorraine sat down suddenly on the side of a chair and, focusing her eyes on Richard, cried, "Oh, what a nice little boy! Come here, little boy." Richard glanced at his mother, but did not move. With a perceptible shrug of her shoulders, Lorraine turned back to Charlie:

"Come and dine. Sure your cousins won' mine. See you so sel'om. Or solemn."

"I can't," said Charlie sharply. "You two have dinner and I'll phone you."

Her voice became suddenly unpleasant. "All right, we'll go. But I remember once when you hammered on my door at four a.m. I was enough of a good sport to give you a drink. Come on, Dunc."

Still in slow motion, with blurred, angry faces, with uncertain feet, they retired along the corridor.

"Goodnight," Charlie said.

"Goodnight!" responded Lorraine emphatically.

When he went back into the salon, Marion had not moved, only now her son was standing in the circle of her other arm. Lincoln was still swinging Honoria back and forth like a pendulum from side to side.

"What an outrage!" Charlie broke out. "What an absolute outrage!"

Neither of them answered. Charlie dropped into an armchair, picked up his drink, set it down again and said:

"People I haven't seen for two years having the colossal nerve—"

He broke off. Marion had made the sound "Oh!" in one swift, furious breath, turned her body from him with a jerk and left the room.

Lincoln set down Honoria carefully.

"You children go in and start your soup," he said, and when they obeyed, he said to Charlie:

"Marion's not well, and she can't stand shocks. That kind of people make her really physically sick."

"I didn't tell them to come here. They wormed your name out of somebody. They deliberately—"

"Well, it's too bad. It doesn't help matters. Excuse me a minute."

Left alone, Charlie sat tense in his chair. In the next room he could hear the children eating, talking in monosyllables, already oblivious to the scene between their elders. He heard a murmur of conversation from a farther room and then the ticking bell of a telephone receiver picked up, and in a panic he moved to the other side of the room and out of earshot.

In a minute Lincoln came back. "Look here, Charlie. I think we'd better call off dinner for tonight. Marion's in bad shape."

"Is she angry with me?"

"Sort of," he said, almost roughly. "She's not strong and—"

"You mean she's changed her mind about Honoria?"

"She's pretty bitter right now. I don't know. You phone me at the bank tomorrow."

"I wish you'd explain to her I never dreamt these people would come here. I'm just as sore as you are."

"I couldn't explain anything to her now."

Charlie got up. He took his coat and hat and started down the corridor. Then he opened the door of the dining room and said in a strange voice, "Goodnight, children."

Honoria rose and ran around the table to hug him.

"Goodnight, sweetheart," he said vaguely, and then, trying to make his voice more tender, trying to conciliate something, "Goodnight, dear children."

5

CHARLIE WENT DIRECTLY to the Ritz bar with the furious idea of finding Lorraine and Duncan, but they were not there, and he realized that in any case there was nothing he could do. He had not touched his drink at the Peters', and now he ordered a whisky-and-soda. Paul came over to say hello.

"It's a great change," he said sadly. "We do about half the business we did. So many fellows I hear about back in the States lost everything, maybe not in the first crash, but then in the second. Your friend George Hardt lost every cent, I hear. Are you back in the States?"

"No, I'm in business in Prague."

"I heard that you lost a lot in the crash."

"I did," and he added grimly, "but I lost everything I wanted in the boom."

"Selling short."

"Something like that."

Again the memory of those days swept over him like a nightmare – the people they had met travelling; then people who couldn't add a row of figures or speak a coherent sentence. The little man Helen had consented to dance with at the ship's party, who had insulted her ten feet from the table; the women and girls carried screaming with drink or drugs out of public places...

...The men who locked their wives out in the snow, because the snow of Twenty-nine wasn't real snow. If you didn't want it to be snow, you just paid some money.

He went to the phone and called the Peters' apartment; Lincoln answered.

"I called up because this thing is on my mind. Has Marion said anything definite?"

"Marion's sick," Lincoln answered shortly. "I know this thing isn't altogether your fault, but I can't have her go to pieces about it. I'm afraid we'll have to let it slide for six months; I can't take the chance of working her up to this state again."

"I see."

"I'm sorry, Charlie."

He went back to his table. His whisky glass was empty, but he shook his head when Alix looked at it questionably. There wasn't much he could do now except send Honoria some things; he would send her a lot of things tomorrow. He thought rather angrily that this was just money – he had given so many people money...

"No, no more," he said to another waiter. "What do I owe you?"

He would come back some day; they couldn't make him pay for ever. But he wanted his child, and nothing was much good now, beside that fact. He wasn't young any more, with a lot of nice thoughts and dreams to have by himself. He was absolutely sure Helen wouldn't have wanted him to be so alone.

A New Leaf

1

I T WAS THE FIRST DAY warm enough to eat outdoors in the Bois de Boulogne, while chestnut blossoms slanted down across the tables and dropped impudently into the butter and the wine. Julia Ross ate a few with her bread and listened to the big goldfish rippling in the pool and the sparrows whirring about an abandoned table. You could see everybody again – the waiters with their professional faces, the watchful Frenchwomen all heels and eyes, Phil Hoffman opposite her with his heart balanced on his fork, and the extraordinarily handsome man just coming out on the terrace.

> …The purple noon's transparent might.
> The breath of the moist air is light
> Around each unexpanded bud…*

Julia trembled discreetly; she controlled herself; she didn't spring up and call, "Yi-yi-yi-yi! Isn't this grand?" and push the maître d'hôtel into the lily pond. She sat there, a well-behaved woman of twenty-one, and discreetly trembled.

Phil was rising, napkin in hand. "Hi there, Dick!"

"Hi, Phil!"

It was the handsome man; Phil took a few steps forward and they talked apart from the table.

"…seen Carter and Kitty in Spain…"

27

"...poured onto the Bremen..."

"...so I was going to..."

The man went on, following the head waiter, and Phil sat down.

"Who is that?" she demanded.

"A friend of mine – Dick Ragland."

"He's without doubt the handsomest man I ever saw in my life."

"Yes, he's handsome," he agreed without enthusiasm.

"Handsome! He's an archangel, he's a mountain lion, he's something to eat. Just why didn't you introduce him?"

"Because he's got the worst reputation of any American in Paris."

"Nonsense; he must be maligned. It's all a dirty frame-up – a lot of jealous husbands whose wives got one look at him. Why, that man's never done anything in his life except lead cavalry charges and save children from drowning."

"The fact remains he's not received anywhere – not for one reason but for a thousand."

"What reasons?"

"Everything. Drink, women, jails, scandals, killed somebody with an automobile, lazy, worthless—"

"I don't believe a word of it," said Julia firmly. "I bet he's tremendously attractive. And you spoke to him as if you thought so too."

"Yes," he said reluctantly, "like so many alcoholics, he has a certain charm. If he'd only make his messes off by himself somewhere – except right in people's laps. Just when somebody's taken him up and is making a big fuss over him, he pours the soup down his hostess's back, kisses the serving maid and passes out in the dog kennel. But he's done it too often. He's run through about everybody, until there's no one left."

"There's me," said Julia.

There was Julia, who was a little too good for anybody and sometimes regretted that she had been quite so well endowed. Anything added to beauty has to be paid for – that is to say, the qualities that pass as substitutes can be liabilities when added to beauty itself. Julia's brilliant hazel glance was enough, without the questioning light of intelligence that flickered in it; her irrepressible sense of the ridiculous detracted from the gentle relief of her mouth, and the loveliness of her figure might have been more obvious if she had slouched and postured rather than sat and stood very straight, after the discipline of a strict father.

Equally perfect young men had several times appeared bearing gifts, but generally with the air of being already complete, of having no space for development. On the other hand, she found that men of larger scale had sharp corners and edges in youth, and she was a little too young herself to like that. There was, for instance, this scornful young egotist, Phil Hoffman, opposite her, who was obviously going to be a brilliant lawyer and who had practically followed her to Paris. She liked him as well as anyone she knew, but he had at present all the overbearance of the son of a chief of police.

"Tonight I'm going to London, and Wednesday I sail," he said. "And you'll be in Europe all summer, with somebody new chewing on your ear every few weeks."

"When you've been called for a lot of remarks like that you'll begin to edge into the picture," Julia remarked. "Just to square yourself, I want you to introduce that man Ragland."

"My last few hours!" he complained.

"But I've given you three whole days on the chance you'd work out a better approach. Be a little civilized and ask him to have some coffee."

As Mr Dick Ragland joined them, Julia drew a little breath of pleasure. He was a fine figure of a man, in colouring both tan and blond, with a peculiar luminosity to his face. His voice was quietly intense; it seemed always to tremble a little with a sort of gay despair; the way he looked at Julia made her feel attractive. For half an hour, as their sentences floated pleasantly among the scent of violets and snowdrops, forget-me-nots and pansies, her interest in him grew. She was even glad when Phil said:

"I've just thought about my English visa. I'll have to leave you two incipient love birds together against my better judgement. Will you meet me at the Gare Saint-Lazare at five and see me off?"

He looked at Julia, hoping she'd say, "I'll go along with you now." She knew very well she had no business being alone with this man, but he made her laugh, and she hadn't laughed much lately, so she said: "I'll stay a few minutes; it's so nice and springy here."

When Phil was gone, Dick Ragland suggested a *fine* champagne.

"I hear you have a terrible reputation?" she said impulsively.

"Awful. I'm not even invited out any more. Do you want me to slip on my false moustache?"

"It's so odd," she pursued. "Don't you cut yourself off from all nourishment? Do you know that Phil felt he had to warn me about you before he introduced you? And I might very well have told him not to."

"Why didn't you?"

"I thought you seemed so attractive and it was such a pity."

His face grew bland; Julia saw that the remark had been made so often that it no longer reached him.

"It's none of my business," she said quickly. She did not realize that his being a sort of outcast added to his attraction for her – not the dissipation itself, for never having seen it, it was merely an abstraction – but its result in making him so alone. Something atavistic in her went out to the stranger to the tribe, a being from a world with different habits from hers, who promised the unexpected – promised adventure.

"I'll tell you something else," he said suddenly. "I'm going permanently on the wagon on June fifth, my twenty-eighth birthday. I don't have fun drinking any more. Evidently I'm not one of the few people who can use liquor."

"You sure you can go on the wagon?"

"I always do what I say I'll do. Also I'm going back to New York and go to work."

"I'm really surprised how glad I am." This was rash, but she let it stand.

"Have another *fine*?" Dick suggested. "Then you'll be gladder still."

"Will you go on this way right up to your birthday?"

"Probably. On my birthday I'll be on the *Olympic* in mid-ocean."

"I'll be on that boat too!" she exclaimed.

"You can watch the quick change; I'll do it for the ship's concert."

The tables were being cleared off. Julia knew she should go now, but she couldn't bear to leave him sitting with that unhappy look under his smile. She felt, maternally, that she ought to say something to help him keep his resolution.

"Tell me why you drink so much. Probably some obscure reason you don't know yourself."

"Oh, I know pretty well how it began."

He told her as another hour waned. He had gone to the war at seventeen and, when he came back, life as a Princeton freshman with a little black cap was somewhat tame. So he went up to Boston Tech and then abroad to the Beaux Arts; it was there that something happened to him.

"About the time I came into some money I found that with a few drinks I got expansive and somehow had the ability to please people, and the idea turned my head. Then I began to take a whole lot of drinks to keep going and have everybody think I was wonderful. Well, I got plastered a lot and quarrelled with most of my friends, and then I met a wild bunch and for a while I was expansive with them. But I was inclined to get superior and suddenly think 'What am I doing with this bunch?' They didn't like that much. And when a taxi that I was in killed a man, I was sued. It was just a graft, but it got in the papers, and after I was released the impression remained that I'd killed him. So all I've got to show for the last five years is a reputation that makes mothers rush their daughters away if I'm at the same hotel."

An impatient waiter was hovering near, and she looked at her watch.

"Gosh, we're to see Phil off at five. We've been here all the afternoon."

As they hurried to the Gare Saint-Lazare, he asked: "Will you let me see you again; or do you think you'd better not?"

She returned his long look. There was no sign of dissipation in his face, in his warm cheeks, in his erect carriage.

"I'm always fine at lunch," he added, like an invalid.

"I'm not worried," she laughed. "Take me to lunch day after tomorrow."

They hurried up the steps of the Gare Saint-Lazare, only to see the last carriage of the Golden Arrow disappearing towards the Channel. Julia was remorseful, because Phil had come so far.

As a sort of atonement, she went to the apartment where she lived with her aunt and tried to write a letter to him, but Dick Ragland intruded himself into her thoughts. By morning the effect of his good looks had faded a little; she was inclined to write him a note that she couldn't see him. Still, he had made her a simple appeal and she had brought it all on herself. She waited for him at half-past twelve on the appointed day.

Julia had said nothing to her aunt, who had company for luncheon and might mention his name – strange to go out with a man whose name you couldn't mention. He was late and she waited in the hall, listening to the echolalia of chatter from the luncheon party in the dining room. At one she answered the bell.

There in the outer hall stood a man whom she thought she had never seen before. His face was dead white and erratically shaven, his soft hat was crushed bun-like on his head, his shirt collar was dirty, and all except the band of his tie was out of sight. But at the moment when she recognized the figure as Dick Ragland she perceived a change which dwarfed the others into nothing; it was in his expression. His whole face was one prolonged sneer – the lids held with difficulty from covering the fixed eyes, the drooping mouth drawn up over the upper teeth, the chin wabbling like a made-over chin in which the paraffin had run – it was a face that both expressed and inspired disgust.

"H'lo," he muttered.

For a minute she drew back from him; then, at a sudden silence from the dining room that gave on the hall, inspired by the silence in the hall itself, she half-pushed him over the threshold, stepped out herself and closed the door behind them.

"Oh-h-h!" she said in a single, shocked breath.

"Haven't been home since yest'day. Got involve' on a party at—"

With repugnance, she turned him around by his arm and stumbled with him down the apartment stairs, passing the concierge's wife, who peered out at them curiously from her glass room. Then they came out into the bright sunshine of the Rue Guynemer.

Against the spring freshness of the Luxembourg Gardens opposite, he was even more grotesque. He frightened her; she looked desperately up and down the street for a taxi, but one turning the corner of the Rue de Vaugirard disregarded her signal.

"Where'll we go lunch?" he asked.

"You're in no shape to go to lunch. Don't you realize? You've got to go home and sleep."

"I'm all right. I get a drink I'll be fine."

A passing cab slowed up at her gesture.

"You go home and go to sleep. You're not fit to go anywhere."

As he focused his eyes on her, realizing her suddenly as something fresh, something new and lovely, something alien to the smoky and turbulent world where he had spent his recent hours, a faint current of reason flowed through him. She saw his mouth twist with vague awe, saw him make a vague attempt to stand up straight. The taxi yawned.

"Maybe you're right. Very sorry."

"What's your address?"

He gave it and then tumbled into a corner, his face still struggling towards reality. Julia closed the door.

When the cab had driven off, she hurried across the street and into the Luxembourg Gardens as if someone were after her.

2

QUITE BY ACCIDENT, she answered when he telephoned at seven that night. His voice was strained and shaking:

"I suppose there's not much use apologizing for this morning. I didn't know what I was doing, but that's no excuse. But if you could let me see you for a while somewhere tomorrow – just for a minute – I'd like the chance of telling you in person how terribly sorry—"

"I'm busy tomorrow."

"Well, Friday then, or any day."

"I'm sorry, I'm very busy this week."

"You mean you don't ever want to see me again?"

"Mr Ragland, I hardly see the use of going any further with this. Really, that thing this morning was a little too much. I'm very sorry. I hope you feel better. Goodbye."

She put him entirely out of her mind. She had not even associated his reputation with such a spectacle – a heavy drinker was someone who sat up late and drank champagne and maybe in the small hours rode home singing. This spectacle at high noon was something else again. Julia was through.

Meanwhile, there were other men with whom she lunched at Ciro's and danced in the Bois. There was a reproachful letter from Phil Hoffman in America. She liked Phil better for having been so right about this. A fortnight passed and she would have forgotten Dick Ragland, had she not heard his name mentioned with scorn in several conversations. Evidently he had done such things before.

Then, a week before she was due to sail, she ran into him in the booking department of the White Star Line. He was as handsome – she could hardly believe her eyes. He leant with an elbow on the desk, his fine figure erect, his yellow gloves as stainless as his clear, shining eyes. His strong, gay personality had affected the clerk, who served him with

34

fascinated deference; the stenographers behind looked up for a minute and exchanged a glance. Then he saw Julia; she nodded, and with a quick, wincing change of expression he raised his hat.

They were together by the desk a long time, and the silence was oppressive.

"Isn't this a nuisance?" she said.

"Yes," he said jerkily, and then: "You going by the *Olympic*?"

"Oh, yes."

"I thought you might have changed."

"Of course not," she said coldly.

"I thought of changing; in fact, I was here to ask about it."

"That's absurd."

"You don't hate the sight of me? So it'll make you seasick when we pass each other on the deck?"

She smiled. He seized his advantage:

"I've improved somewhat since we last met."

"Don't talk about that."

"Well then, you have improved. You've got the loveliest costume on I ever saw."

This was presumptuous, but she felt herself shimmering a little at the compliment.

"You wouldn't consider a cup of coffee with me at the café next door, just to recover from this ordeal?"

How weak of her to talk to him like this, to let him make advances. It was like being under the fascination of a snake.

"I'm afraid I can't." Something terribly timid and vulnerable came into his face, twisting a little sinew in her heart. "Well, all right," she shocked herself by saying.

Sitting at the sidewalk table in the sunlight, there was nothing to remind her of that awful day two weeks ago. Jekyll and Hyde. He was courteous, he was charming, he was amusing. He made her feel oh so attractive! He presumed on nothing.

"Have you stopped drinking?" she asked.

"Not till the fifth."

"Oh!"

"Not until I said I'd stop. Then I'll stop."

When Julia rose to go, she shook her head at his suggestion of a further meeting.

"I'll see you on the boat. After your twenty-eighth birthday."

"All right; one more thing: it fits in with the high price of crime that I did something inexcusable to the one girl I've ever been in love with in my life."

She saw him the first day on board, and then her heart sank into her shoes as she realized at last how much she wanted him. No matter what his past was, no matter what he had done. Which was not to say that she would ever let him know, but only that he moved her chemically more than anyone she had ever met, that all other men seemed pale beside him.

He was popular on the boat; she heard that he was giving a party on the night of his twenty-eighth birthday. Julia was not invited; when they met they spoke pleasantly, nothing more.

It was the day after the fifth that she found him stretched in his deck-chair looking wan and white. There were wrinkles on his fine brow and around his eyes, and his hand, as he reached out for a cup of bouillon, was trembling. He was still there in the late afternoon, visibly suffering, visibly miserable. After three times around, Julia was irresistibly impelled to speak to him:

"Has the new era begun?"

He made a feeble effort to rise, but she motioned him not to and sat on the next chair.

"You look tired."

"I'm just a little nervous. This is the first day in five years that I haven't had a drink."

"It'll be better soon."

"I know," he said grimly.

"Don't weaken."

"I won't."

"Can't I help you in any way? Would you like a bromide?"

"I can't stand bromides," he said almost crossly. "No, thanks, I mean."

Julia stood up: "I know you feel better alone. Things will be brighter tomorrow."

"Don't go, if you can stand me."

Julia sat down again.

"Sing me a song – can you sing?"

"What kind of a song?"

"Something sad – some sort of blues."

She sang him Libby Holman's 'This Is How the Story Ends'* in a low, soft voice.

"That's good. Now sing another. Or sing that again."

"All right. If you like, I'll sing to you all afternoon."

3

THE SECOND DAY IN NEW YORK, he called her on the phone. "I've missed you so," he said. "Have you missed me?"

"I'm afraid I have," she said reluctantly.

"Much?"

"I've missed you a lot. Are you better?"

"I'm all right now. I'm still just a little nervous, but I'm starting work tomorrow. When can I see you?"

"When you want."

"This evening then. And look – say that again."

"What?"

"That you're afraid you have missed me."

"I'm afraid that I have," Julia said obediently.

"Missed me," he added.

"I'm afraid I have missed you."

"All right. It sounds like a song when you say it."

"Goodbye, Dick."

"Goodbye, Julia dear."

She stayed in New York two months instead of the fortnight she had intended, because he would not let her go. Work took the place of drink in the daytime, but afterwards he must see Julia.

Sometimes she was jealous of his work when he telephoned that he was too tired to go out after the theatre. Lacking drink, night life was less than nothing to him – something quite spoilt and well lost. For Julia, who never drank, it was a stimulus in itself – the music and the parade of dresses and the handsome couple they made dancing together. At first they saw Phil Hoffman once in a while; Julia considered that he took the matter rather badly; then they didn't see him any more.

A few unpleasant incidents occurred. An old schoolmate, Esther Cary, came to her to ask if she knew of Dick Ragland's reputation. Instead of growing angry, Julia invited her to meet Dick and was delighted with the ease with which Esther's convictions were changed. There were other, small, annoying episodes, but Dick's misdemeanours had, fortunately, been confined to Paris and assumed here a faraway unreality. They loved each other deeply now – the memory of that morning slowly being effaced from Julia's imagination – but she wanted to be sure.

"After six months, if everything goes along like this, we'll announce our engagement. After another six months we'll be married."

"Such a long time," he mourned.

"But there were five years before that," Julia answered. "I trust you with my heart and with my mind, but something else says, 'Wait.' Remember, I'm also deciding for my children."

Those five years – oh so lost and gone.

In August, Julia went to California for two months to see her family. She wanted to know how Dick would get along alone. They wrote every day; his letters were by turns cheerful, depressed, weary and hopeful. His work was going better. As things came back to him, his uncle had begun really to believe in him, but all the time he missed his Julia so. It was when an occasional note of despair began to appear that she cut her visit short by a week and came east to New York.

"Oh, thank God you're here!" he cried as they linked arms and walked out of the Grand Central station. "It's been so hard. Half a dozen times lately I've wanted to go on a bust and I had to think of you, and you were so far away."

"Darling – darling, you're so tired and pale. You're working too hard."

"No, only that life is so bleak alone. When I go to bed my mind churns on and on. Can't we get married sooner?"

"I don't know; we'll see. You've got your Julia near you now, and nothing matters."

After a week, Dick's depression lifted. When he was sad, Julia made him her baby, holding his handsome head against her breast, but she liked it best when he was confident and could cheer her up, making her laugh and feel taken care of and secure. She had rented an apartment with another girl and she took courses in biology and domestic science in Columbia. When deep fall came, they went to football games and the new shows together, and walked through the first snow in Central Park, and several times a week spent long evenings together in front of her fire. But time was going by and they were both impatient. Just before Christmas, an unfamiliar visitor – Phil Hoffman – presented himself at her door. It was the first time in many months. New York, with its quality of many independent ladders set side by side, is unkind to even the meetings of close friends; so, in the case of strained relations, meetings are easy to avoid.

And they were strange to each other. Since his expressed scepticism of Dick, he was automatically her enemy; on another count, she saw that he had improved, some of the hard angles were worn off; he was now an assistant district attorney, moving around with increasing confidence through his profession.

"So you're going to marry Dick?" he said. "When?"

"Soon now. When Mother comes East."

He shook his head emphatically. "Julia, don't marry Dick. This isn't jealousy – I know when I am licked – but it seems awful for a lovely girl like you to take a blind dive into a lake full of rocks. What makes you think that people change their courses? Sometimes they dry up or even flow into a parallel channel, but I've never known anybody to change."

"Dick's changed."

"Maybe so. But isn't that an enormous 'maybe'? If he was unattractive and you liked him, I'd say go ahead with it. Maybe I'm all wrong, but it's so darn obvious that what fascinates you is that handsome pan of his and those attractive manners."

"You don't know him," Julia answered loyally. "He's different with me. You don't know how gentle he is, and responsive. Aren't you being rather small and mean?"

"Hm." Phil thought for a moment. "I want to see you again in a few days. Or perhaps I'll speak to Dick."

"You let Dick alone," she cried. "He has enough to worry him without your nagging him. If you were his friend you'd try to help him instead of coming to me behind his back."

"I'm your friend first."

"Dick and I are one person now."

But three days later Dick came to see her at an hour when he would usually have been at the office.

"I'm here under compulsion," he said lightly, "under threat of exposure by Phil Hoffman."

Her heart dropping like a plummet, "Has he given up?" she thought. "Is he drinking again?"

"It's about a girl. You introduced me to her last summer and told me to be very nice to her – Esther Cary."

Now her heart was beating slowly.

"After you went to California I was lonesome and I ran into her. She'd liked me that day, and for a while we saw quite a bit of each other. Then you came back and I broke it off. It was a little difficult; I hadn't realized that she was so interested."

"I see." Her voice was starved and aghast.

"Try and understand. Those terribly lonely evenings. I think if it hadn't been for Esther, I'd have fallen off the wagon. I never loved her – I never loved anybody but you – but I had to see somebody who liked me."

He put his arm around her, but she felt cold all over and he drew away.

"Then any woman would have done," Julia said slowly. "It didn't matter who."

"No!" he cried.

"I stayed away so long to let you stand on your own feet and get back your self-respect by yourself."

"I only love you, Julia."

"But any woman can help you. So you don't really need me, do you?"

His face wore that vulnerable look that Julia had seen several times before; she sat on the arm of his chair and ran her hand over his cheek.

"Then what do you bring me?" she demanded. "I thought that there'd be the accumulated strength of having beaten your weakness. What do you bring me now?"

"Everything I have."

She shook her head. "Nothing. Just your good looks – and the head waiter at dinner last night had that."

They talked for two days and decided nothing. Sometimes she would pull him close and reach up to his lips that she loved so well, but her arms seemed to close around straw.

41

"I'll go away and give you a chance to think it over," he said despairingly. "I can't see any way of living without you, but I suppose you can't marry a man you don't trust or believe in. My uncle wanted me to go to London on some business…"

The night he left, it was sad on the dim pier. All that kept her from breaking was that it was not an image of strength that was leaving her; she would be just as strong without him. Yet, as the murky lights fell on the fine structure of his brow and chin, as she saw the faces turn towards him, the eyes that followed him, an awful emptiness seized her and she wanted to say: "Never mind, dear; we'll try it together."

But try what? It was human to risk the toss between failure and success, but to risk the desperate gamble between adequacy and disaster…

"Oh, Dick, be good and be strong and come back to me. Change, change, Dick – change!"

"Goodbye, Julia – goodbye."

She last saw him on the deck, his profile cut sharp as a cameo against a match as he lit a cigarette.

4

I T WAS PHIL HOFFMAN who was to be with her at the beginning and the end. It was he who broke the news as gently as it could be broken. He reached her apartment at half-past eight and carefully threw away the morning paper outside. Dick Ragland had disappeared at sea.

After her first wild burst of grief, he became purposely a little cruel.

"He knew himself. His will had given out; he didn't want life any more. And, Julia, just to show you how little you can possibly blame yourself, I'll tell you this: he'd hardly gone to his office for four months – since you went to California. He wasn't fired, because of his uncle; the business he went to London on was of no importance at all. After his first enthusiasm was gone he'd given up."

She looked at him sharply. "He didn't drink, did he? He wasn't drinking?"

For a fraction of a second Phil hesitated. "No, he didn't drink; he kept his promise – he held on to that."

"That was it," she said. "He kept his promise and he killed himself doing it."

Phil waited uncomfortably.

"He did what he said he would and broke his heart doing it," she went on chokingly. "Oh, isn't life cruel sometimes – so cruel, never to let anybody off. He was so brave – he died doing what he said he'd do."

Phil was glad he had thrown away the newspaper that hinted of Dick's gay evening in the bar – one of many gay evenings that Phil had known of in the past few months. He was relieved that was over, because Dick's weakness had threatened the happiness of the girl he loved; but he was terribly sorry for him – even understanding how it was necessary for him to turn his maladjustment to life towards one mischief or another – but he was wise enough to leave Julia with the dream that she had saved out of wreckage.

There was a bad moment a year later, just before their marriage, when she said:

"You'll understand the feeling I have and always will have about Dick, won't you, Phil? It wasn't just his good looks. I believed in him – and I was right in a way. He broke rather than bent; he was a ruined man, but not a bad man. In my heart I knew when I first looked at him."

Phil winced, but he said nothing. Perhaps there was more behind it than they knew. Better let it all alone in the depths of her heart and the depths of the sea.

A Freeze-out

1

H ERE AND THERE in a sunless corner skulked a little snow under a veil of coal specks, but the men taking down storm windows were labouring in shirt sleeves and the turf was becoming firm underfoot.

In the streets, dresses dyed after fruit, leaf and flower emerged from beneath the shed sombre skins of animals; now only a few old men wore mousy caps pulled down over their ears. That was the day Forrest Winslow forgot the long fret of the past winter as one forgets inevitable afflictions, sickness and war, and turned with blind confidence towards the summer, thinking he already recognized in it all the summers of the past – the golfing, sailing, swimming summers.

For eight years Forrest had gone East to school and then to college; now he worked for his father in a large Minnesota city. He was handsome, popular and rather spoilt in a conservative way, and so the past year had been a comedown. The discrimination that had picked Scroll and Key* at New Haven was applied to sorting furs; the hand that had signed the Junior Prom expense cheques had since rocked in a sling for two months with mild *dermatitis venenata*. After work, Forrest found no surcease in the girls with whom he had grown up. On the contrary, the news of a stranger within the tribe stimulated him, and during the transit of a popular visitor he displayed a convulsive activity. So far, nothing had happened; but here was summer.

On the day spring broke through and summer broke through – it is much the same thing in Minnesota – Forrest stopped his coupé in front

44

of a music store and took his pleasant vanity inside. As he said to the clerk "I want some records", a little bomb of excitement exploded in his larynx, causing an unfamiliar and almost painful vacuum in his upper diaphragm. The unexpected detonation was caused by the sight of a corn-coloured girl who was being waited on across the counter.

She was a stalk of ripe corn, but bound not as cereals are but as a rare first edition, with all the binder's art. She was lovely and expensive, and about nineteen, and he had never seen her before. She looked at him for just an unnecessary moment too long, with so much self-confidence that he felt his own rush out and away to join hers – "…from him that hath not shall be taken away even that which he hath".* Then her head swayed forward and she resumed her inspection of a catalogue.

Forrest looked at the list a friend had sent him from New York. Unfortunately, the first title was: 'When Voo-do-o-do Meets Boop-boop-a-doop, There'll Soon Be a Hot-Cha-Cha'. Forrest read it with horror. He could scarcely believe a title could be so repulsive.

Meanwhile the girl was asking: "Isn't there a record of Prokofiev's *Fils prodigue*?"

"I'll see, madam." The saleswoman turned to Forrest.

"'When Voo…'" Forrest began, and then repeated, "'When Voo…'"

There was no use; he couldn't say it in front of that nymph of the harvest across the table.

"Never mind that one," he said quickly. "Give me 'Huggable…'"

Again he broke off.

"'Huggable, Kissable You'?" suggested the clerk helpfully, and her assurance that it was very nice suggested a humiliating community of taste.

"I want Stravinsky's *Fire Bird*," said the other customer, "and this album of Chopin waltzes."

Forrest ran his eye hastily down the rest of his list: 'Digga Diggity', 'Ever So Goosy', 'Bunkey Doodle I Do'.

"Anybody would take me for a moron," he thought. He crumpled up the list and fought for air – his own kind of air, the air of casual superiority.

"I'd like," he said coldly, "Beethoven's *Moonlight Sonata*."

There was a record of it at home, but it didn't matter. It gave him the right to glance at the girl again and again. Life became interesting; she was the loveliest concoction; it would be easy to trace her. With the *Moonlight Sonata* wrapped face to face with 'Huggable, Kissable You', Forrest quitted the shop.

There was a new bookstore down the street, and here also he entered, as if books and records could fill the vacuum that spring was making in his heart. As he looked among the lifeless words of many titles together, he was wondering how soon he could find her, and what then.

"I'd like a hard-boiled detective story," he said.

A weary young man shook his head with patient reproof; simultaneously, a spring draft from the door blew in with it the familiar glow of cereal hair.

"We don't carry detective stories or stuff like that," said the young man in an unnecessarily loud voice. "I imagine you'll find it at a department store."

"I thought you carried books," said Forrest feebly.

"Books, yes, but not that kind." The young man turned to wait on his other customer.

As Forrest stalked out, passing within the radius of the girl's perfume, he heard her ask:

"Have you got anything of Louis Aragon's,* either in French or in translation?"

"She's just showing off," he thought angrily. "They skip right from Peter Rabbit to Marcel Proust these days."

Outside, parked just behind his own adequate coupé, he found an enormous silver-coloured roadster of English make and custom design. Disturbed, even upset, he drove homeward through the moist, golden afternoon.

The Winslows lived in an old, wide-verandaed house on Crest Avenue – Forrest's father and mother, his great-grandmother and his sister Eleanor. They were solid people as that phrase goes since the war. Old Mrs Forrest was entirely solid; with convictions based on a way of life that had worked for eighty-four years. She was a character in the city; she remembered the Sioux war and she had been in Stillwater the day the James brothers shot up the main street.*

Her own children were dead, and she looked on these remoter descendants from a distance, oblivious of the forces that had formed them. She understood that the Civil War and the opening up of the West were forces, while the Free Silver Movement* and the World War had reached her only as news. But she knew that her father, killed at Cold Harbor,* and her husband, the merchant, were larger in scale than her son or her grandson. People who tried to explain contemporary phenomena to her seemed, to her, to be talking against the evidence of their own senses. Yet she was not atrophied: last summer she had travelled over half of Europe with only a maid.

Forrest's father and mother were something else again. They had been in the susceptible middle thirties when the cocktail party and its concomitants arrived in 1921. They were divided people, leaning forward and backward. Issues that presented no difficulty to Mrs Forrest caused them painful heat and agitation. Such an issue arose before they had been five minutes at table that night.

"Do you know the Rikkers are coming back?" said Mrs Winslow. "They've taken the Warner house." She was a woman with many uncertainties, which she concealed from herself by expressing her opinions very slowly and thoughtfully, to convince her own ears. "It's a wonder Dan Warner would rent them his house. I suppose Cathy thinks everybody will fall all over themselves."

"What Cathy?" asked old Mrs Forrest.

"She was Cathy Chase. Her father was Reynold Chase. She and her husband are coming back here."

"Oh, yes."

"I scarcely knew her," continued Mrs Winslow, "but I know that when they were in Washington they were pointedly rude to everyone from Minnesota – went out of their way. Mary Cowan was spending a winter there, and she invited Cathy to lunch or tea at least half a dozen times. Cathy never appeared."

"I could beat that record," said Pierce Winslow. "Mary Cowan could invite me a hundred times and I wouldn't go."

"Anyhow," pursued his wife slowly, "in view of all the scandal, it's just asking for the cold shoulder to come out here."

"They're asking for it all right," said Winslow. He was a Southerner, well liked in the city, where he had lived for thirty years. "Walter Hannan came in my office this morning and wanted me to second Rikker for the Kennemore Club. I said: 'Walter, I'd rather second Al Capone.' What's more, Rikker'll get into the Kennemore Club over my dead body."

"Walter had his nerve. What's Chauncey Rikker to you? It'll be hard to get anyone to second him."

"Who are they?" Eleanor asked. "Somebody awful?"

She was eighteen and a debutante. Her current appearances at home were so rare and brief that she viewed such table topics with as much detachment as her great-grandmother.

"Cathy was a girl here; she was younger then I was, but I remember that she was always considered fast. Her husband, Chauncey Rikker, came from some little town upstate."

"What did they do that was so awful?"

"Rikker went bankrupt and left town," said her father. "There were a lot of ugly stories. Then he went to Washington and got mixed up in the alien-property scandal;* and then he got in trouble in New York – he was in the bucket-shop business – but he skipped out to Europe. After a few

48

years the chief government witness died and he came back to America. They got him for a few months for contempt of court." He expanded into eloquent irony: "And now, with true patriotism, he comes back to his beautiful Minnesota, a product of its lovely woods, its rolling wheat fields—"

Forrest called him impatiently: "Where do you get that, Father? When did two Kentuckians ever win Nobel prizes in the same year? And how about an upstate boy named Lind—"

"Have the Rikkers any children?" Eleanor asked.

"I think Cathy has a daughter about your age, and a boy about sixteen."

Forrest uttered a small, unnoticed exclamation. Was it possible? French books and Russian music – that girl this afternoon had lived abroad. And with the probability his resentment deepened – the daughter of a crook putting on all that dog! He sympathized passionately with his father's refusal to second Rikker for the Kennemore Club.

"Are they rich?" old Mrs Forrest suddenly demanded.

"They must be well off if they took Dan Warner's house."

"Then they'll get in all right."

"They won't get into the Kennemore Club," said Pierce Winslow. "I happen to come from a state with certain traditions."

"I've seen the bottom rail get to be the top rail many times in this town," said the old lady blandly.

"But this man's a criminal, Grandma," explained Forrest. "Can't you see the difference? It isn't a social question. We used to argue at New Haven whether we'd shake hands with Al Capone if we met him—"

"Who is Al Capone?" asked Mrs Forrest.

"He's another criminal, in Chicago."

"Does he want to join the Kennemore Club too?"

They laughed, but Forrest had decided that if Rikker came up for the Kennemore Club, his father's would not be the only black ball in the box.

Abruptly it became full summer. After the last April storm someone came along the street one night, blew up the trees like balloons, scattered bulbs and shrubs like confetti, opened a cage full of robins and, after a quick look around, signalled up the curtain upon a new backdrop of summer sky.

Tossing back a strayed baseball to some kids in a vacant lot, Forrest's fingers, on the stitched seams of the stained leather cover, sent a wave of ecstatic memories to his brain. One must hurry and get there – "there" was now the fairway of the golf course, but his feeling was the same. Only when he teed off at the eighteenth that afternoon did he realize that it wasn't the same, that it would never be enough any more. The evening stretched large and empty before him, save for the set pieces of a dinner party and bed.

While he waited with his partner for a match to play off, Forrest glanced at the tenth tee, exactly opposite and two hundred yards away.

One of the two figures on the ladies' tee was addressing her ball; as he watched, she swung up confidently and cracked a long drive down the fairway.

"Must be Mrs Horrick," said his friend. "No other woman can drive like that."

At that moment the sun glittered on the girl's hair and Forrest knew who it was; simultaneously, he remembered what he must do this afternoon. That night Chauncey Rikker's name was to come up before the membership committee on which his father sat, and before going home, Forrest was going to pass the clubhouse and leave a certain black slip in a little box. He had carefully considered all that; he loved the city where his people had lived honourable lives for five generations. His grandfather had been a founder of this club in the '90s, when it went in for sailboat racing instead of golf, and when it took a fast horse three hours to trot out here from town. He agreed with his father that certain people were without the pale. Tightening his face, he drove his ball two hundred yards down the fairway, where it curved gently into the rough.

The eighteenth and tenth holes were parallel and faced in opposite directions. Between tees they were separated by a belt of trees forty feet wide. Though Forrest did not know it, Miss Rikker's hostess, Helen

Hannan, had dubbed into this same obscurity, and as he went in search of his ball he heard female voices twenty feet away.

"You'll be a member after tonight," he heard Helen Hannan say, "and then you can get some real competition from Stella Horrick."

"Maybe I won't be a member," said a quick, clear voice. "Then you'll have to come and play with me on the public links."

"Alida, don't be absurd."

"Why? I played on the public links in Buffalo all last spring. For the moment there wasn't anywhere else. It's like playing on some courses in Scotland."

"But I'd feel so silly... Oh, gosh, let's let the ball go."

"There's nobody behind us. As to feeling silly – if I cared about public opinion any more, I'd spend my time in my bedroom." She laughed scornfully. "A tabloid published a picture of me going to see Father in prison. And I've seen people change their tables away from us on steamers, and once I was cut by all the American girls in a French school... Here's your ball."

"Thanks... Oh, Alida, it seems terrible."

"All the terrible part is over. I just said that so you wouldn't be too sorry for us if people didn't want us in this club. I wouldn't care; I've got a life of my own and my own standard of what trouble is. It wouldn't touch me at all."

They passed out of the clearing, and their voices disappeared into the open sky on the other side. Forrest abandoned the search for his lost ball and walked towards the caddie house.

"What a hell of a note," he thought. "To take it out on a girl that had nothing to do with it" – which was what he was doing this minute as he went up towards the club. "No," he said to himself abruptly, "I can't do it. Whatever her father may have done, she happens to be a lady. Father can do what he feels he has to do, but I'm out."

After lunch the next day, his father said rather diffidently: "I see you didn't do anything about the Rikkers and the Kennemore Club."

"No."

"It's just as well," said his father. "As a matter of fact, they got by. The club has got rather mixed anyhow in the last five years – a good many queer people in it. And, after all, in a club you don't have to know anybody you don't want to. The other people on the committee felt the same way."

"I see," said Forrest drily. "Then you didn't argue against the Rikkers?"

"Well, no. The thing is I do a lot of business with Walter Hannan, and it happened yesterday I was obliged to ask him rather a difficult favour."

"So you traded with him." To both father and son, the word "traded" sounded like traitor.

"Not exactly. The matter wasn't mentioned."

"I understand," Forrest said. But he did not understand, and some old childhood faith in his father died at that moment.

2

To snub anyone effectively one must have him within range. The admission of Chauncey Rikker to the Kennemore Club and, later, to the Downtown Club was followed by angry talk and threats of resignation that simulated the sound of conflict, but there was no indication of a will underneath. On the other hand, unpleasantness in crowds is easy, and Chauncey Rikker was a facile object for personal dislike; moreover, a recurrent echo of the bucket-shop scandal sounded from New York, and the matter was reviewed in the local newspapers, in case anyone had missed it. Only the liberal Hannan family stood by the Rikkers, and their attitude aroused considerable resentment, and their attempt to launch them with a series of small parties proved a failure. Had the Rikkers attempted to "bring Alida out", it would have been for the inspection of a motley crowd indeed, but they didn't.

When, occasionally, during the summer, Forrest encountered Alida Rikker, they crossed eyes in the curious way of children who don't know each other. For a while he was haunted by her curly yellow head, by the golden-brown defiance of her eyes; then he became interested in another girl. He wasn't in love with Jane Drake, though he thought he might marry her. She was "the girl across the street"; he knew her qualities, good and bad, so that they didn't matter. She had an essential reality underneath, like a relative. It would please their families. Once, after several highballs and some casual necking, he almost answered seriously when she provoked him with "But you don't really care about me"; but he sat tight and next morning was relieved that he had. Perhaps in the dull days after Christmas... Meanwhile, at the Christmas dances among the Christmas girls he might find the ecstasy and misery, the infatuation that he wanted. By autumn he felt that his predestined girl was already packing her trunk in some Eastern or Southern city.

It was in his more restless mood that one November Sunday he went to a small tea. Even as he spoke to his hostess he felt Alida Rikker across the firelit room; her glowing beauty and her unexplored novelty pressed up against him, and there was a relief in being presented to her at last. He bowed and passed on, but there had been some sort of communication. Her look said that she knew the stand that his family had taken, that she didn't mind, and was even sorry to see him in such a silly position, for she knew that he admired her. His look said: "Naturally, I'm sensitive to your beauty, but you see how it is; we've had to draw the line at the fact that your father is a dirty dog, and I can't withdraw from my present position."

Suddenly in a silence, she was talking, and his ears swayed away from his own conversation.

"...Helen had this odd pain for over a year and, of course, they suspected cancer. She went to have an X-ray; she undressed behind a screen, and the doctor looked at her through the machine, and then he said, 'But I told you to take off all your clothes,' and Helen said, 'I have.' The doctor looked again, and said, 'Listen, my dear, I brought you into the world, so there's no use being modest with me. Take off everything.' So Helen said, 'I've got every stitch off; I swear.' But the doctor said, 'You have not. The X-ray shows me a safety pin in your brassiere.' Well, they finally found out that she'd been suspected of swallowing a safety pin when she was two years old."

The story, floating in her clear, crisp voice upon the intimate air, disarmed Forrest. It had nothing to do with what had taken place in Washington or New York ten years before. Suddenly he wanted to go and sit near her, because she was the tongue of flame that made the firelight vivid. Leaving, he walked for an hour through feathery snow, wondering again why he couldn't know her, why it was his business to represent a standard.

"Well, maybe I'll have a lot of fun some day doing what I ought to do," he thought ironically – "when I'm fifty."

The first Christmas dance was the charity ball at the armoury. It was a large, public affair; the rich sat in boxes. Everyone came who felt he belonged, and many out of curiosity, so the atmosphere was tense with a strange haughtiness and aloofness.

The Rikkers had a box. Forrest, coming in with Jane Drake, glanced at the man of evil reputation and at the beaten woman frozen with jewels who sat beside him. They were the city's villains, gaped at by the people of reserved and timid lives. Oblivious of the staring eyes, Alida and Helen Hannan held court for several young men from out of town. Without question, Alida was incomparably the most beautiful girl in the room.

Several people told Forrest the news – the Rikkers were giving a big dance after New Year's. There were written invitations, but these were being supplemented by oral ones. Rumour had it that one had merely to be presented to any Rikker in order to be bidden to the dance.

As Forrest passed through the hall, two friends stopped him and with a certain hilarity introduced him to a youth of seventeen, Mr Teddy Rikker.

"We're giving a dance," said the young man immediately. "January third. Be very happy if you could come."

Forrest was afraid he had an engagement.

"Well, come if you change your mind."

"Horrible kid, but shrewd," said one of his friends later. "We were feeding him people, and when we brought up a couple of saps, he looked at them and didn't say a word. Some refuse and a few accept and most of them stall, but he goes right on; he's got his father's crust."

Into the highways and byways. Why didn't the girl stop it? He was sorry for her when he found Jane in a group of young women revelling in the story.

"I hear they asked Bodman, the undertaker, by mistake, and then took it back."

"Mrs Carleton pretended she was deaf."

"There's going to be a carload of champagne from Canada."

"Of course I won't go, but I'd love to, just to see what happens. There'll be a hundred men to every girl – and that'll be meat for her. "

The accumulated malice repelled him, and he was angry at Jane for being part of it. Turning away, his eyes fell on Alida's proud form swaying along a wall, watched the devotion of her partners with an unpleasant resentment. He did not know that he had been a little in love with her for many months. Just as two children can fall in love during a physical struggle over a ball, so their awareness of each other had grown to surprising proportions.

"She's pretty," said Jane. "She's not exactly overdressed, but considering everything, she dresses too elaborately."

"I suppose she ought to wear sackcloth and ashes or half-mourning."

"I was honoured with a written invitation, but of course I'm not going."

"Why not?"

Jane looked at him in surprise. "You're not going."

"That's different. I would if I were you. You see, you don't care what her father did."

"Of course I care."

"No, you don't. And all this small meanness just debases the whole thing. Why don't they let her alone? She's young and pretty and she's done nothing wrong. "

Later in the week he saw Alida at the Hannans' dance and noticed that many men danced with her. He saw her lips moving, heard her laughter, caught a word or so of what she said; irresistibly he found himself guiding partners around in her wake. He envied visitors to the city who didn't know who she was.

The night of the Rikkers' dance he went to a small dinner; before they sat down at table he realized that the others were all going on to the Rikkers'. They talked of it as a sort of comic adventure; insisted that he come too.

"Even if you weren't invited, it's all right," they assured him. "We were told we could bring anyone. It's just a free-for-all; it doesn't put you under any obligations. Norma Nash is going, and she didn't invite Alida Rikker to her party. Besides, she's really very nice. My brother's quite crazy about her. Mother is worried sick, because he says he wants to marry her."

Clasping his hand about a new highball, Forrest knew that if he drank it he would probably go. All his reasons for not going seemed old and tired, and, fatally, he had begun to seem absurd to himself. In vain he tried to remember the purpose he was serving, and found none. His father had weakened on the matter of the Kennemore Club. And now suddenly he found reasons for going – men could go where their women could not.

"All right," he said.

The Rikkers' dance was in the ballroom of the Minnekada Hotel. The Rikkers' gold, ill-gotten, tainted, had taken the form of a forest of palms, vines and flowers. The two orchestras moaned in pergolas lit with fireflies, and many-coloured spotlights swept the floor, touching a buffet where dark bottles gleamed. The receiving line was still in action when Forrest's party came in, and Forrest grinned ironically at the prospect of taking Chauncey Rikker by the hand. But at the sight of Alida, her look that at last fell frankly on him, he forgot everything else.

"Your brother was kind enough to invite me," he said.

"Oh, yes." She was polite, but vague; not at all overwhelmed by his presence. As he waited to speak to her parents, he started, seeing his sister in a group of dancers. Then, one after another, he identified people he knew: it might have been any one of the Christmas dances; all the younger crowd were there. He discovered abruptly that he and Alida were alone; the receiving line had broken up. Alida glanced at him questioningly and with a certain amusement.

So he danced out on the floor with her, his head high, but slightly spinning. Of all things in the world, he had least expected to lead off the Chauncey Rikkers' ball.

3

NEXT MORNING HIS FIRST REALIZATION was that he had kissed her; his second was a feeling of profound shame for his conduct of the evening. Lord help him, he had been the life of the party; he had helped to run the cotillion. From the moment when he danced out on the floor, coolly meeting the surprised and interested glances of his friends, a mood of desperation had come over him. He rushed Alida Rikker, until a friend asked him what Jane was going to say. "What business is it of Jane's?" he demanded impatiently. "We're not engaged." But he was impelled to approach his sister and ask her if he looked all right.

"Apparently," Eleanor answered, "but when in doubt, don't take any more."

So he hadn't. Exteriorly he remained correct, but his libido was in a state of wild extroversion. He sat with Alida Rikker and told her he had loved her for months.

"Every night I thought of you just before you went to sleep." His voice trembled with insincerity. "I was afraid to meet you or speak to you. Sometimes I'd see you in the distance moving along like a golden chariot, and the world would be good to live in."

After twenty minutes of this eloquence, Alida began to feel exceedingly attractive. She was tired and rather happy, and eventually she said:

"All right, you can kiss me if you want to, but it won't mean anything. I'm just not in that mood."

But Forrest had moods enough for both; he kissed her as if they stood together at the altar. A little later he had thanked Mrs Rikker with deep emotion for the best time he had ever had in his life.

It was noon, and as he groped his way upright in bed, Eleanor came in in her dressing gown.

"How are you?" she asked.

"Awful."

"How about what you told me coming back in the car? Do you actually want to marry Alida Rikker?"

"Not this morning."

"That's all right then. Now, look: the family are furious."

"Why?" he asked with some redundancy.

"Both you and I being there. Father heard that you led the cotillion. My explanation was that my dinner party went, and so I had to go; but then you went too!"

Forrest dressed and went down to Sunday dinner. Over the table hovered an atmosphere of patient, puzzled, unworldly disappointment. Finally Forrest launched into it:

"Well, we went to Al Capone's party and had a fine time."

"So I've heard," said Pierce Winslow drily. Mrs Winslow said nothing.

"Everybody was there – the Kayes, the Schwanes, the Martins and the Blacks. From now on, the Rikkers are pillars of society. Every house is open to them."

"Not this house," said his mother. "They won't come into this house." And after a moment: "Aren't you going to eat anything, Forrest?"

"No, thanks. I mean, yes, I am eating." He looked cautiously at his plate. "The girl is very nice. There isn't a girl in town with better manners or more stuff. If things were like they were before the war, I'd say..."

He couldn't think exactly what it was he would have said; all he knew was that he was now on an entirely different road from his parents'.

"This city was scarcely more than a village before the war," said old Mrs Forrest.

"Forrest means the World War, granny," said Eleanor.

"Some things don't change," said Pierce Winslow. Both he and Forrest thought of the Kennemore Club matter and, feeling guilty, the older man lost his temper:

"When people start going to parties given by a convicted criminal, there's something serious the matter with them."

"We won't discuss it any more at table," said Mrs Winslow hastily.

About four, Forrest called a number on the telephone in his room. He had known for some time that he was going to call a number.

"Is Miss Rikker at home?... Oh, hello. This is Forrest Winslow."

"How are you?"

"Terrible. It was a good party."

"Wasn't it?"

"Too good. What are you doing?"

"Entertaining two awful hangovers."

"Will you entertain me too?"

"I certainly will. Come on over."

The two young men could only groan and play sentimental music on the phonograph, but presently they departed; the fire leapt up, day went out behind the windows, and Forrest had rum in his tea.

"So we met at last," he said.

"The delay was all yours."

"Damn prejudice," he said. "This is a conservative city, and your father being in this trouble—"

"I can't discuss my father with you."

"Excuse me. I only wanted to say that I've felt like a fool lately for not knowing you. For cheating myself out of the pleasure of knowing you for a silly prejudice," he blundered on. "So I decided to follow my own instincts."

She stood up suddenly. "Goodbye, Mr Winslow."

"What? Why?"

"Because it's absurd for you to come here as if you were doing me a favour. And after accepting our hospitality, to remind me of my father's troubles is simply bad manners."

He was on his feet, terribly upset. "That isn't what I meant. I said I had felt that way, and I despised myself for it. Please don't be sore."

"Then don't be condescending." She sat back in her chair. Her mother came in, stayed only a moment, and threw Forrest a glance of resentment and suspicion as she left. But her passage through had brought them together, and they talked frankly for a long time.

"I ought to be upstairs dressing."

"I ought to have gone an hour ago, and I can't."

"Neither can I."

With the admission they had travelled far. At the door he kissed her unreluctant lips and walked home, throwing futile buckets of reason on the wildfire.

Less than two weeks later it happened. In a car parked in a blizzard he poured out his worship, and she lay on his chest, sighing, "Oh, me too – me too."

Already Forrest's family knew where he went in the evenings; there was a frightened coolness, and one morning his mother said:

"Son, you don't want to throw yourself away on some girl that isn't up to you. I thought you were interested in Jane Drake."

"Don't bring that up. I'm not going to talk about it."

But it was only a postponement. Meanwhile the days of this February were white and magical, the nights were starry and crystalline. The town lay under a cold glory; the smell of her furs was incense, her bright cheeks were flames upon a northern altar. An ecstatic pantheism for his land

and its weather welled up in him. She had brought him finally back to it; he would live here always.

"I want you so much that nothing can stand in the way of that," he said to Alida. "But I owe my parents a debt that I can't explain to you. They did more than spend money on me; they tried to give me something more intangible – something that their parents had given them and that they thought was worth handing on. Evidently it didn't take with me, but I've got to make this as easy as possible for them." He saw by her face that he had hurt her. "Darling—"

"Oh, it frightens me when you talk like that," she said. "Are you going to reproach me later? It would be awful. You'll have to get it out of your head that you're doing anything wrong. My standards are as high as yours, and I can't start out with my father's sins on my shoulders." She thought for a moment. "You'll never be able to reconcile it all like a children's story. You've got to choose. Probably you'll have to hurt either your family or hurt me."

A fortnight later the storm broke at the Winslow house. Pierce Winslow came home in a quiet rage and had a session behind closed doors with his wife. Afterwards she knocked at Forrest's door.

"Your father had a very embarrassing experience today. Chauncey Rikker came up to him in the Downtown Club and began talking about you as if you were on terms of some understanding with his daughter. Your father walked away, but we've got to know. Are you serious about Miss Rikker?"

"I want to marry her," he said.

"Oh, Forrest!"

She talked for a long time, recapitulating, as if it were a matter of centuries, the eighty years that his family had been identified with the city; when she passed from this to the story of his father's health, Forrest interrupted:

"That's all so irrelevant, Mother. If there was anything against Alida personally, what you say would have some weight, but there isn't."

"She's overdressed; she runs around with everybody—"

"She isn't a bit different from Eleanor. She's absolutely a lady in every sense. I feel like a fool even discussing her like this. You're just afraid it'll connect you in some way with the Rikkers."

"I'm not afraid of that," said her mother, annoyed. "Nothing would ever do that. But I'm afraid that it'll separate you from everything worthwhile, everybody that loves you. It isn't fair for you to upset our lives, let us in for disgraceful gossip—"

"I'm to give up the girl I love because you're afraid of a little gossip."

The controversy was resumed next day, with Pierce Winslow debating. His argument was that he was born in old Kentucky, that he had always felt uneasy at having begotten a son upon a pioneer Minnesota family, and that this was what he might have expected. Forrest felt that his parents' attitude was trivial and disingenuous. Only when he was out of the house, acting against their wishes, did he feel any compunction. But always he felt that something precious was being frayed away – his youthful companionship with his father and his love and trust for his mother. Hour by hour he saw the past being irreparably spoilt and, save when he was with Alida, he was deeply unhappy.

One spring day when the situation had become unendurable, with half the family meals taken in silence, Forrest's great-grandmother stopped him on the stair landing and put her hand on his arm.

"Has this girl really a good character?" she asked, her fine, clear, old eyes resting on his.

"Of course she has, Gramma."

"Then marry her."

"Why do you say that?" Forrest asked curiously.

"It would stop all this nonsense and we could have some peace. And I've been thinking I'd like to be a great-great-grandmother before I die."

Her frank selfishness appealed to him more than the righteousness of the others. That night he and Alida decided to be married the first of June, and telephoned the announcement to the papers.

Now the storm broke in earnest. Crest Avenue rang with gossip – how Mrs Rikker had called on Mrs Winslow, who was not at home. How Forrest had gone to live in the University Club. How Chauncey Rikker and Pierce Winslow had had words in the Downtown Club.

It was true that Forrest had gone to the University Club. On a May night, with summer sounds already gathered on the window screens, he packed his trunk and his suitcases in the room where he had lived as a boy. His throat contracted and he smeared his face with his dusty hand as he took a row of golf cups off the mantelpiece, and he choked to himself: "If they won't take Alida, then they're not my family any more."

As he finished packing, his mother came in.

"You're not really leaving." Her voice was stricken.

"I'm moving to the University Club."

"That's so unnecessary. No one bothers you here. You do what you want."

"I can't bring Alida here."

"Father—"

"Hell with Father!" he said wildly.

She sat down on the bed beside him. "Stay here, Forrest. I promise not to argue with you any more. But stay here."

"I can't."

"I can't have you go!" she wailed. "It seems as if we're driving you out, and we're not!"

"You mean it looks as though you were driving me out."

"I don't mean that."

"Yes, you do. And I want to say that I don't think you and Father really care a hang about Chauncey Rikker's moral character."

"That's not true, Forrest. I hate people that behave badly and break the laws. My own father would never have let Chauncey Rikker—"

"I'm not talking about your father. But neither you nor my father care a bit what Chauncey Rikker did. I bet you don't even know what it was."

"Of course I know. He stole some money and went abroad, and when he came back they put him in prison."

"They put him in prison for contempt of court."

"Now you're defending him, Forrest."

"I'm not! I hate his guts; undoubtedly he's a crook. But I tell you it was a shock to me to find that Father didn't have any principles. He and his friends sit around the Downtown Club and pan Chauncey Rikker, but when it comes to keeping him out of a club, they develop weak spines."

"That was a small thing."

"No, it wasn't. None of the men of Father's age have any principles. I don't know why. I'm willing to make an allowance for an honest conviction, but I'm not going to be booed by somebody that hasn't got any principles and simply pretends to have."

His mother sat helplessly, knowing that what he said was true. She and her husband and all their friends had no principles. They were good or bad according to their natures; often they struck attitudes remembered from the past, but they were never sure as her father or her grandfather had been sure. Confusedly she supposed it was something about religion. But how could you get principles just by wishing for them?

The maid announced the arrival of a taxi.

"Send up Olsen for my baggage," said Forrest; then to his mother, "I'm not taking the coupé; I left the keys. I'm just taking my clothes. I suppose Father will let me keep my job downtown."

"Forrest, don't talk that way. Do you think your father would take your living away from you, no matter what you did?"

"Such things have happened."

"You're hard and difficult," she wept. "Please stay here a little longer, and perhaps things will be better and Father will get a little more reconciled. Oh, stay, stay! I'll talk to Father again. I'll do my best to fix things."

"Will you let me bring Alida here?"

"Not now. Don't ask me that. I couldn't bear—"

"All right," he said grimly.

Olsen came in for the bags. Crying and holding on to his coat sleeve, his mother went with him to the front door.

"Won't you say goodbye to Father?"

"Why? I'll see him tomorrow in the office."

"Forrest, I was thinking, why don't you go to a hotel instead of the University Club?"

"Why, I thought I'd be more comfortable…" Suddenly he realized that his presence would be less conspicuous at a hotel. Shutting up his bitterness inside him, he kissed his mother roughly and went to the cab.

Unexpectedly, it stopped by the corner lamp-post at a hail from the sidewalk, and the May twilight yielded up Alida, miserable and pale.

"What is it?" he demanded.

"I had to come," she said. "Stop the car. I've been thinking of you leaving your house on account of me, and how you loved your family – the way I'd like to love mine – and I thought how terrible it was to spoil all that. Listen, Forrest! Wait! I want you to go back. Yes, I do. We can wait. We haven't any right to cause all this pain. We're young. I'll go away for a while, and then we'll see."

He pulled her towards him by her shoulders.

"You've got more principles than the whole bunch of them," he said. "Oh, my girl, you love me and, gosh, it's good that you do!"

4

IT WAS TO BE A HOUSE WEDDING, Forrest and Alida having vetoed the Rikkers' idea that it was to be a sort of public revenge. Only a few intimate friends were invited.

During the week before the wedding, Forrest deduced from a series of irresolute and ambiguous telephone calls that his mother wanted to attend the ceremony, if possible. Sometimes he hoped passionately she would; at others it seemed unimportant.

The wedding was to be at seven. At five o'clock Pierce Winslow was walking up and down the two interconnecting sitting rooms of his house.

"This evening," he murmured, "my only son is being married to the daughter of a swindler."

He spoke aloud so that he could listen to the words, but they had been evoked so often in the past few months that their strength was gone and they died thinly upon the air.

He went to the foot of the stairs and called: "Charlotte!" No answer. He called again, and then went into the dining room, where the maid was setting the table.

"Is Mrs Winslow out?"

"I haven't seen her come in, Mr Winslow."

Back in the sitting room he resumed his walking; unconsciously he was walking like his father, the judge, dead thirty years ago; he was parading his dead father up and down the room.

"You can't bring that woman into this house to meet your mother. Bad blood is bad blood."

The house seemed unusually quiet. He went upstairs and looked into his wife's room, but she was not there; old Mrs Forrest was slightly indisposed; Eleanor, he knew, was at the wedding.

He felt genuinely sorry for himself as he went downstairs again. He knew his role – the usual evening routine carried out in complete obliviousness of the wedding – but he needed support, people begging him to relent, or else deferring to his wounded sensibilities. This isolation was different: it was almost the first isolation he had ever felt, and like all men who are fundamentally of the group, of the herd, he was incapable of taking a strong stand with the inevitable loneliness that it implied. He could only gravitate towards those who did.

"What have I done to deserve this?" he demanded of the standing ashtray. "What have I failed to do for my son that lay within my power?"

The maid came in. "Mrs Winslow told Hilda she wouldn't be here for dinner, and Hilda didn't tell me."

The shameful business was complete. His wife had weakened, leaving him absolutely alone. For a moment he expected to be furiously angry with her, but he wasn't; he had used up his anger exhibiting it to others. Nor did it make him feel more obstinate, more determined; it merely made him feel silly.

"That's it. I'll be the goat. Forrest will always hold it against me, and Chauncey Rikker will be laughing up his sleeve."

He walked up and down furiously.

"So I'm left holding the bag. They'll say I'm an old grouch and drop me out of the picture entirely. They've licked me. I suppose I might as well be graceful about it." He looked down in horror at the hat he held in his hand. "I can't... I can't bring myself to do it, but I must. After all, he's my only son. I couldn't bear that he should hate me. He's determined to marry her, so I might as well put a good face on the matter."

In sudden alarm he looked at his watch, but there was still time. After all, it was a large gesture he was making, sacrificing his principles in this manner. People would never know what it cost him.

An hour later, old Mrs Forrest woke up from her doze and rang for her maid.

"Where's Mrs Winslow?"

"She's not in for dinner. Everybody's out. "

The old lady remembered.

"Oh, yes, they've gone over to get married. Give me my glasses and the telephone book... Now, I wonder how you spell Capone."

"Rikker, Mrs Forrest."

In a few minutes she had the number. "This is Mrs Hugh Forrest," she said firmly. "I want to speak to young Mrs Forrest Winslow... No, not to Miss Rikker; to Mrs Forrest Winslow." As there was as yet no such person, this was impossible. "Then I will call after the ceremony," said the old lady.

When she called again, in an hour, the bride came to the phone.

"This is Forrest's great-grandmother. I called up to wish you every happiness and to ask you to come and see me when you get back from your trip if I'm still alive."

"You're very sweet to call, Mrs Forrest."

"Take good care of Forrest, and don't let him get to be a ninny like his father and mother. God bless you."

"Thank you."

"All right. Goodbye, Miss Capo... Goodbye, my dear."

Having done her whole duty, Mrs Forrest hung up the receiver.

Six of One...

B ARNES STOOD ON THE WIDE STAIRS looking down through a wide hall into the living room of the country place and at the group of youths. His friend Schofield was addressing some benevolent remarks to them, and Barnes did not want to interrupt; as he stood there, immobile, he seemed to be drawn suddenly into rhythm with the group below; he perceived them as statuesque beings, set apart, chiselled out of the Minnesota twilight that was setting on the big room.

In the first place all five, the two young Schofields and their friends, were fine-looking boys, very American, dressed in a careless but not casual way over well-set-up bodies, and with responsive faces open to all four winds. Then he saw that they made a design, the faces profile upon profile, the heads blond and dark, turning towards Mr Schofield, the erect yet vaguely lounging bodies, never tense but ever ready under the flannels and the soft angora-wool sweaters, the hands placed on other shoulders, as if to bring each one into the solid freemasonry of the group. Then suddenly, as though a group of models posing for a sculptor were being dismissed, the composition broke and they all moved towards the door. They left Barnes with a sense of having seen something more than five young men between sixteen and eighteen going out to sail or play tennis or golf, but having gained a sharp impression of a whole style, a whole mode of youth, something different from his own less assured, less graceful generation, something unified by standards that he didn't know. He wondered vaguely what the standards of 1920 were, and whether they were worth anything – had a sense of waste, of much effort for a purely aesthetic achievement. Then Schofield saw him and called him down into the living room.

"Aren't they a fine bunch of boys?" Schofield demanded. "Tell me, did you ever see a finer bunch?"

"A fine lot," agreed Barnes, with a certain lack of enthusiasm. He felt a sudden premonition that his generation in its years of effort had made possible a Periclean age, but had evolved no prospective Pericles. They had set the scene: was the cast adequate?

"It isn't just because two of them happen to be mine," went on Schofield. "It's self-evident. You couldn't match that crowd in any city in the country. First place, they're such a husky lot. Those two little Kavenaughs aren't going to be big men – more like their father – but the oldest one could make any college hockey team in the country right now."

"How old are they?" asked Barnes.

"Well, Howard Kavenaugh, the oldest, is nineteen – going to Yale next year. Then comes my Wister – he's eighteen, also going to Yale next year. You liked Wister, didn't you? I don't know anybody who doesn't. He'd make a great politician, that kid. Then there's a boy named Larry Patt who wasn't here today – he's eighteen too, and he's State golf champion. Fine voice too; he's trying to get in Princeton."

"Who's the blond-haired one who looks like a Greek god?"

"That's Beau Lebaume. He's going to Yale, too, if the girls will let him leave town. Then there's the other Kavenaugh, the stocky one – he's going to be an even better athlete than his brother. And finally there's my youngest, Charley; he's sixteen." Schofield sighed reluctantly. "But I guess you've heard all the boasting you can stand."

"No, tell me more about them – I'm interested. Are they anything more than athletes?"

"Why, there's not a dumb one in the lot, except maybe Beau Lebaume; but you can't help liking him anyhow. And every one of them's a natural leader. I remember a few years ago a tough gang tried to start something with them, calling them 'candies' – well, that gang must be running yet. They sort of remind me of young knights. And what's the matter with their

70

being athletes? I seem to remember you stroking the boat at New London, and that didn't keep you from consolidating railroad systems and—"

"I took up rowing because I had a sick stomach," said Barnes. "By the way, are these boys all rich?"

"Well, the Kavenaughs are, of course; and my boys will have something." Barnes's eyes twinkled.

"So I suppose since they won't have to worry about money, they're brought up to serve the State," he suggested. "You spoke of one of your sons having a political talent and their all being like young knights, so I suppose they'll go out for public life and the army and navy."

"I don't know about that," Schofield's voice sounded somewhat alarmed. "I think their fathers would be pretty disappointed if they didn't go into business. That's natural, isn't it?"

"It's natural, but it isn't very romantic," said Barnes good-humouredly.

"You're trying to get my goat," said Schofield. "Well, if you can match that—"

"They're certainly an ornamental bunch," admitted Barnes. "They've got what you call glamour. They certainly look like the cigarette ads in the magazine; but—"

"But you're an old sour-belly," interrupted Schofield. "I've explained that these boys are all well rounded. My son Wister led his class at school this year, but I was a darn sight prouder that he got the medal for best all-around boy."

The two men faced each other with the uncut cards of the future on the table before them. They had been in college together, and were friends of many years' standing. Barnes was childless, and Schofield was inclined to attribute his lack of enthusiasm to that.

"I somehow can't see them setting the world on fire, doing better than their fathers," broke out Barnes suddenly. "The more charming they are, the harder it's going to be for them. In the East people are beginning to realize what wealthy boys are up against. Match them? Maybe not now." He leant forward, his eyes lighting up. "But I could pick six boys from any high school in Cleveland, give them an education, and I believe that ten years from this time your young fellows here would be utterly outclassed. There's so little demanded of them, so little expected of them – what could be softer than just to have to go on being charming and athletic?"

"I know your idea," objected Schofield scoffingly. "You'd go to a big municipal high school and pick out the six most brilliant scholars—"

"I'll tell you what I'll do…" Barnes noticed that he had unconsciously substituted "I will" for "I would", but he didn't correct himself. "I'll go to the little town in Ohio, where I was born – there probably aren't fifty or sixty boys in the high school there, and I wouldn't be likely to find six geniuses out of that number."

"And what?"

"I'll give them a chance. If they fail, the chance is lost. That is a serious responsibility, and they've got to take it seriously. That's what these boys haven't got – they're only asked to be serious about trivial things." He thought for a moment. "I'm going to do it."

"Do what?"

"I'm going to see."

A fortnight later he was back in the small town in Ohio where he had been born – where, he felt, the driving emotions of his own youth still haunted the quiet streets. He interviewed the principal of the high school, who made suggestions; then by the – for Barnes – difficult means of making an address and afterwards attending a reception, he got in touch with teachers and pupils. He made a donation to the school, and under cover of this found opportunities of watching the boys at work and at play.

It was fun – he felt his youth again. There were some boys that he liked immediately, and he began a weeding-out process, inviting them in groups of five or six to his mother's house, rather like a fraternity-rushing freshman. When a boy interested him, he looked up his record and that of his family – and at the end of a fortnight he had chosen five boys.

In the order in which he chose them, there was first Otto Schlach, a farmer's son who had already displayed extraordinary mechanical aptitude and a gift for mathematics. Schlach was highly recommended by his teachers, and he welcomed the opportunity offered him of entering the Massachusetts Institute of Technology.

A drunken father left James Matsko as his only legacy to the town of Barnes's youth. From the age of twelve, James had supported himself by keeping a newspaper-and-candy store with a three-foot frontage; and now at seventeen he was reputed to have saved five hundred dollars. Barnes found it difficult to persuade him to study money and banking at Columbia, for Matsko was already assured of his ability to make money. But Barnes had prestige as the town's most successful son, and he convinced Matsko that otherwise he would lack frontage, like his own place of business.

Then there was Jack Stubbs, who had lost an arm hunting, but in spite of this handicap played on the high-school football team. He was not among the leaders in studies; he had developed no particular bent; but the fact that he had overcome that enormous handicap enough to play football – to tackle and to catch punts – convinced Barnes that no obstacles would stand in Jack Stubbs's way.

The fourth selection was George Winfield, who was almost twenty. Because of the death of his father, he had left school at fourteen, helped to support his family for four years, and then, things being better, he had come back to finish high school. Barnes felt, therefore, that Winfield would place a serious value on an education.

Next came a boy whom Barnes found personally antipathetic. Louis Ireland was at once the most brilliant scholar and most difficult boy at school. Untidy, insubordinate and eccentric, Louis drew scurrilous caricatures behind his Latin book, but when called upon inevitably produced a perfect recitation. There was a big talent nascent somewhere in him – it was impossible to leave him out.

The last choice was the most difficult. The remaining boys were mediocrities, or at any rate they had so far displayed no qualities that set them apart. For a time Barnes, thinking patriotically of his old university, considered the football captain, a virtuosic halfback who would have been welcome on any Eastern squad; but that would have destroyed the integrity of the idea.

He finally chose a younger boy, Gordon Vandervere, of a rather higher standing than the others. Vandervere was the handsomest and one of the most popular boys in school. He had been intended for college, but his father, a harassed minister, was glad to see the way made easy.

Barnes was content with himself; he felt godlike in being able to step in to mould these various destinies. He felt as if they were his own sons, and he telegraphed Schofield in Minneapolis:

HAVE CHOSEN HALF A DOZEN OF THE OTHER, AND AM BACKING THEM AGAINST THE WORLD.

And now, after all this biography, the story begins…

The continuity of the frieze is broken. Young Charley Schofield had been expelled from Hotchkiss. It was a small but painful tragedy – he and four other boys, nice boys, popular boys, broke the honour system as to smoking. Charley's father felt the matter deeply, varying between disappointment about Charley and anger at the school. Charley came home to Minneapolis in a desperate humour and went to the country day school while it was decided what he was to do.

It was still undecided in midsummer. When school was over, he spent his time playing golf, or dancing at the Minnekada Club – he was a handsome boy of eighteen, older than his age, with charming manners, with no serious vices, but with a tendency to be easily influenced by his admirations.

His principal admiration at the time was Gladys Irving, a young married woman scarcely two years older than himself. He rushed her at the club dances and felt sentimentally about her, though Gladys on her part was in love with her husband and asked from Charley only the confirmation of her own youth and charm that a belle often needs after her first baby.

Sitting out with her one night on the veranda of the Lafayette Club, Charley felt a necessity to boast to her, to pretend to be more experienced, and so more potentially protective.

"I've seen a lot of life for my age," he said. "I've done things I couldn't even tell you about."

Gladys didn't answer.

"In fact last week..." he began, and thought better of it. "In any case I don't think I'll go to Yale next year – I'd have to go East right away, and tutor all summer. If I don't go, there's a job open in Father's office; and after Wister goes back to college in the fall, I'll have the roadster to myself."

"I thought you were going to college," Gladys said coldly.

"I was. But I've thought things over, and now I don't know. I've usually gone with older boys, and I feel older than boys my age. I like older girls, for instance." When Charley looked at her then, suddenly he seemed unusually attractive to her – it would be very pleasant to have him here, to cut in on her at dances all summer. But Gladys said:

"You'd be a fool to stay here."

"Why?"

"You started something – you ought to go through with it. A few years running around town, and you won't be good for anything."

"You think so," he said indulgently.

Gladys didn't want to hurt him or to drive him away from her; yet she wanted to say something stronger.

"Do you think I'm thrilled when you tell me you've had a lot of dissipated experience? I don't see how anybody could claim to be your friend and encourage you in that. If I were you, I'd at least pass your examinations for college. Then they can't say you just lay down after you were expelled from school."

"You think so?" Charley said, unruffled and in his grave, precocious manner, as though he were talking to a child. But she had convinced him, because he was in love with her and the moon was around her. 'Oh me, oh my, oh you' was the last music they had danced to on the Wednesday before, and so it was one of those times.

Had Gladys let him brag to her, concealing her curiosity under a mask of companionship, if she had accepted his own estimate of himself as a man formed, no urging of his father's would have mattered. As it was, Charley passed into college that fall, thanks to a girl's tender reminiscences and her own memories of the sweetness of youth's success in young fields.

And it was well for his father that he did. If he had not, the catastrophe of his older brother Wister that autumn would have broken Schofield's heart. The morning after the Harvard game the New York papers carried a headline:

YALE BOYS AND FOLLIES GIRLS IN

MOTOR CRASH NEAR RYE

IRENE DALEY IN GREENWICH HOSPITAL

THREATENS BEAUTY SUIT

MILLIONAIRE'S SON INVOLVED

The four boys came up before the dean a fortnight later. Wister Schofield, who had driven the car, was called first.

"It was not your car, Mr Schofield," the dean said. "It was Mr Kavenaugh's car, wasn't it?"

"Yes sir."

"How did you happen to be driving?"

"The girls wanted me to. They didn't feel safe."

"But you'd been drinking too, hadn't you?"

"Yes, but not so much."

"Tell me this," asked the dean. "Haven't you ever driven a car when you'd been drinking – perhaps drinking even more than you were that night?"

"Why – perhaps once or twice, but I never had any accidents. And this was so clearly unavoidable—"

"Possibly," the dean agreed, "but we'll have to look at it this way: up to this time you had no accidents even when you deserved to have them. Now you've had one when you didn't deserve it. I don't want you to go out of here feeling that life or the University or I myself haven't given you a square deal, Mr Schofield. But the newspapers have given this a great deal of prominence, and I'm afraid that the University will have to dispense with your presence."

Moving along the frieze to Howard Kavenaugh, the dean's remarks to him were substantially the same.

"I am particularly sorry in your case, Mr Kavenaugh. Your father has made substantial gifts to the University, and I took pleasure in watching you play hockey with your usual brilliance last winter."

Howard Kavenaugh left the office with uncontrollable tears running down his cheeks.

Since Irene Daley's suit for her ruined livelihood, her ruined beauty, was directed against the owner and the driver of the automobile, there were lighter sentences for the other two occupants of the car. Beau Lebaume came into the dean's office with his arm in a sling and his handsome head swathed in bandages and was suspended for the remainder of the current year. He took it jauntily and said goodbye to the dean with as cheerful a smile as could show through the bandages. The last case, however, was the most difficult. George Winfield, who had entered high school late because work in the world had taught him the value of an education, came in looking at the floor.

"I can't understand your participation in this affair," said the dean. "I know your benefactor, Mr Barnes, personally. He told me how you left school to go to work, and how you came back to it four years later to continue your education, and he felt that your attitude towards life was essentially serious. Up to this point you have a good record here at New Haven, but it struck me several months ago that you were running with a rather gay crowd, boys with a great deal of money to spend. You are old enough to realize that they couldn't possibly give you as much in material ways as they took away from you in others. I've got to give you a year's suspension. If you come back, I have every hope you'll justify the confidence that Mr Barnes reposed in you."

"I won't come back," said Winfield. "I couldn't face Mr Barnes after this. I'm not going home."

At the suit brought by Irene Daley, all four of them lied loyally for Wister Schofield. They said that before they hit the gasoline pump they had seen Miss Daley grab the wheel. But Miss Daley was in court, with her face, familiar to the tabloids, permanently scarred; and her counsel exhibited a letter cancelling her recent moving-picture contract. The students' case looked bad, so in the intermission, on their lawyer's advice, they settled for forty thousand dollars. Wister Schofield and Howard Kavenaugh were snapped by a dozen photographers leaving the courtroom, and served up in flaming notoriety next day.

That night, Wister, the three Minneapolis boys, Howard and Beau Lebaume started for home. George Winfield said goodbye to them in the Pennsylvania station and, having no home to go to, walked out into New York to start life over.

Of all Barnes's protégés, Jack Stubbs with his one arm was the favourite. He was the first to achieve fame – when he played on the tennis team at Princeton, the rotogravure section carried pictures showing how he threw the ball from his racket in serving. When he was graduated, Barnes took him into his own office – he was often spoken of as an adopted son. Stubbs, together with Schlach, now a prominent consulting engineer, were the most satisfactory of his experiments, although James Matsko at twenty-seven had just been made a partner in a Wall Street broker-age house. Financially he was the most successful of the six, yet Barnes found himself somewhat repelled by his hard egoism. He wondered, too, if he, Barnes, had really played any part in Matsko's career – did it after all matter whether Matsko was a figure in metropolitan finance or a big merchant in the Middle West, as he would have undoubtedly become without any assistance at all?

One morning in 1930 he handed Jack Stubbs a letter that led to a balancing-up of the book of boys.

"What do you think of this?"

The letter was from Louis Ireland in Paris. About Louis they did not agree, and as Jack read, he prepared once more to intercede in his behalf.

My dear Sir:

After your last communication, made through your bank here and enclosing a cheque which I hereby acknowledge, I do not feel that I am under any obligation to write you at all. But because the concrete fact of an object's commercial worth may be able to move you, while you remain utterly insensitive to the value of an abstract idea – because of this I write to tell you that my exhibition was an unqualified success. To bring the matter even nearer to your intellectual level, I may tell you that I sold two pieces – a head of Lallette, the actress, and a bronze animal group – for a total of seven thousand francs ($280.00). Moreover I have commissions which will take me all summer – I enclose a piece about me cut from Cahiers d'Art, *which will show you that whatever your estimate of my abilities and my career, it is by no means unanimous.*

This is not to say that I am ungrateful for your well-intentioned attempt to "educate" me. I suppose that Harvard was no worse than any other polite finishing school – the years that I wasted there gave me a sharp and well-documented attitude on American life and institutions. But your suggestions that I come to America and make standardized nymphs for profiteers' fountains was a little too much...

Stubbs looked up with a smile.

"Well," Barnes said, "what do you think? Is he crazy – or now that he has sold some statues, does it prove that I'm crazy?"

"Neither one," laughed Stubbs. "What you objected to in Louis wasn't his talent. But you never got over that year he tried to enter a monastery and then got arrested in the Sacco-Vanzetti demonstrations,* and then ran away with the professor's wife."

"He was just forming himself," said Barnes drily, "just trying his little wings. God knows what he's been up to abroad."

"Well, perhaps he's formed now," Stubbs said lightly. He had always liked Louis Ireland – privately he resolved to write and see if he needed money.

"Anyhow, he's graduated from me," announced Barnes. "I can't do any more to help him or hurt him. Suppose we call him a success, though that's pretty doubtful – let's see how we stand. I'm going to see Schofield out in Minneapolis next week, and I'd like to balance accounts. To my mind, the successes are you, Otto Schlach, James Matsko – whatever you and I may think of him as a man – and let's assume that Louis Ireland is going to be a great sculptor. That's four. Winfield's disappeared. I've never had a line from him."

"Perhaps he's doing well somewhere."

"If he were doing well, I think he'd let me know. We'll have to count him as a failure so far as my experiment goes. Then there's Gordon Vandervere."

Both were silent for a moment.

"I can't make it out about Gordon," Barnes said. "He's such a nice fellow, but since he left college, he doesn't seem to come through. He was younger than the rest of you, and he had the advantage of two years at Andover before he went to college, and at Princeton he knocked them cold, as you say. But he seems to have worn his wings out – for four years now he's done nothing at all; he can't hold a job; he can't get his mind on his work, and he doesn't seem to care. I'm about through with Gordon."

At this moment Gordon was announced over the phone.

"He asked for an appointment," explained Barnes. "I suppose he wants to try something new."

A personable young man with an easy and attractive manner strolled into the office.

"Good afternoon, Uncle Ed. Hi there, Jack!" Gordon sat down. "I'm full of news."

"About what?" asked Barnes.

"About myself."

"I know. You've just been appointed to arrange a merger between J.P. Morgan and the Queensboro Bridge."

"It's a merger," agreed Vandervere, "but those are not the parties to it. I'm engaged to be married."

Barnes glowered.

"Her name," continued Vandervere, "is Esther Crosby."

"Let me congratulate you," said Barnes ironically. "A relation of H.B. Crosby, I presume."

"Exactly," said Vandervere unruffled. "In fact, his only daughter."

For a moment there was silence in the office. Then Barnes exploded.

"*You're* going to marry H.B. Crosby's daughter? Does he know that last month you retired by request from one of his banks?"

"I'm afraid he knows everything about me. He's been looking me over for four years. You see, Uncle Ed," he continued cheerfully, "Esther and I got engaged during my last year at Princeton – my room-mate brought her down to a house party, but she switched over to me. Well, quite naturally Mr Crosby wouldn't hear of it until I'd proved myself."

"Proved yourself!" repeated Barnes. "Do you consider that you've proved yourself?"

"Well – yes."

"How?"

"By waiting four years. You see, either Esther or I might have married anybody else in that time, but we didn't. Instead we sort of wore him away. That's really why I haven't been able to get down to anything. Mr Crosby is a strong personality, and it took a lot of time and energy wearing him away. Sometimes Esther and I didn't see each other for months, so she couldn't eat; so then thinking of that I couldn't eat, so then I couldn't work—"

"And you mean he's really given his consent?"

"He gave it last night."

"Is he going to let you loaf?"

"No. Esther and I are going into the diplomatic service. She feels that the family has passed through the banking phase." He winked at Stubbs. "I'll look up Louis Ireland when I get to Paris, and send Uncle Ed a report."

Suddenly Barnes roared with laughter.

"Well, it's all in the lottery box," he said. "When I picked out you six, I was a long way from guessing..." He turned to Stubbs and demanded: "Shall we put him under *failure* or under *success*?"

"A howling success," said Stubbs. "Top of the list."

A fortnight later Barnes was with his old friend Schofield in Minneapolis. He thought of the house with the six boys as he had last seen it – now it seemed to bear scars of them, like the traces that pictures leave on a wall that they have long protected from the mark of time. Since he did not know what had become of Schofield's sons, he refrained from referring to their conversation of ten years before until he knew whether it was dangerous ground. He was glad of his reticence later in the evening when Schofield spoke of his elder son, Wister.

"Wister never seems to have found himself – and he was such a high-spirited kid! He was the leader of every group he went into; he could always make things go. When he was young, our houses in town and at the lake were always packed with young people. But after he left Yale, he lost interest in things – got sort of scornful about everything. I thought for a while that it was because he drank too much, but he married a nice girl and she took that in hand. Still, he hasn't any ambition – he talked about country life, so I bought him a silver-fox farm, but that didn't go; and I sent him to Florida during the boom, but that wasn't any better. Now he has an interest in a dude ranch in Montana; but since the Depression—"

Barnes saw his opportunity and asked:

"What became of those friends of your sons' that I met one day?"

"Let's see – I wonder who you mean. There was Kavenaugh – you know, the flour people – he was here a lot. Let's see – he eloped with an Eastern girl, and for a few years he and his wife were the leaders of the gay crowd here – they did a lot of drinking and not much else. It seems to me I heard the other day that Howard's getting a divorce. Then there was the younger brother – he never could get into college. Finally he married a manicurist, and they live here rather quietly. We don't hear much about them."

They had had a glamour about them, Barnes remembered; they had been so sure of themselves, individually, as a group; so high-spirited, a frieze of Greek youths, graceful of body, ready for life.

"Then Larry Patt, you might have met him here. A great golfer. He couldn't stay in college – there didn't seem to be enough fresh air there for Larry." And he added defensively: "But he capitalized what he could do – he opened a sporting-goods store and made a good thing of it, I understand. He has a string of three or four."

"I seem to remember an exceptionally handsome one."

"Oh – Beau Lebaume. He was in that mess at New Haven too. After that he went to pieces – drink and what not. His father's tried everything, and now he won't have anything more to do with him." Schofield's face warmed suddenly; his eyes glowed. "But let me tell you, I've got a boy – my Charley! I wouldn't trade him for the lot of them – he's coming over presently, and you'll see. He had a bad start, got into trouble at

Hotchkiss – but did he quit? Never. He went back and made a fine record at New Haven, senior society and all that. Then he and some other boys took a trip around the world, and then he came back here and said: 'All right, Father, I'm ready – when do I start?' I don't know what I'd do without Charley. He got married a few months back, a young widow he'd always been in love with; and his mother and I are still missing him, though they come over often…"

Barnes was glad about this, and suddenly he was reconciled at not having any sons in the flesh – one out of two made good, and sometimes better, and sometimes nothing; but just going along getting old by yourself when you'd counted on so much from sons…

"Charley runs the business," continued Schofield. "That is, he and a young man named Winfield that Wister got me to take on five or six years ago. Wister felt responsible about him, felt he'd got him into this trouble at New Haven – and this boy had no family. He's done well here."

Another one of Barnes's six accounted for! He felt a surge of triumph, but he saw he must keep it to himself; a little later, when Schofield asked him if he'd carried out his intention of putting some boys through college, he avoided answering. After all, any given moment has its value; it can be questioned in the light of after-events, but the moment remains. The young princes in velvet gathered in lovely domesticity around the queen amid the hush of rich draperies may presently grow up to be Pedro the Cruel or Charles the Mad,* but the moment of beauty was there. Back there ten years, Schofield had seen his sons and their friends as samurai, as something shining and glorious and young, perhaps as something he had missed from his own youth. There was later a price to be paid by those boys, all too fulfilled, with the whole balance of their life pulled forward into their youth so that everything afterward would inevitably be anticlimax; these boys brought up as princes with none of the responsibilities of princes! Barnes didn't know how much their mothers might have had to do with it, what their mothers may have lacked.

But he was glad that his friend Schofield had one true son.

His own experiment – he didn't regret it, but he wouldn't have done it again. Probably it proved something, but he wasn't quite sure what. Perhaps that life is constantly renewed, and glamour and beauty make way for it; and he was glad that he was able to feel that the republic could survive the mistakes of a whole generation, pushing the waste aside, sending ahead the vital and the strong. Only it was too bad and very American that there should be all that waste at the top; and he felt that he would not live long enough to see it end, to see great seriousness in the same skin with great opportunity – to see the race achieve itself at last.

Family in the Wind

1

T HE TWO MEN DROVE UP THE HILL towards the blood-red sun. The cotton fields bordering the road were thin and withered, and no breeze stirred in the pines.

"When I am totally sober," the doctor was saying, "I mean when I am totally sober – I don't see the same world that you do. I'm like a friend of mine who had one good eye and got glasses made to correct his bad eye; the result was that he kept seeing elliptical suns and falling off tilted kerbs, until he had to throw the glasses away. Granted that I am thoroughly anaesthetized the greater part of the day – well, I only undertake work that I know I can do when I am in that condition."

"Yeah," agreed his brother Gene uncomfortably. The doctor was a little tight at the moment and Gene could find no opening for what he had to say. Like so many Southerners of the humbler classes, he had a deep-seated courtesy, characteristic of all violent and passionate lands – he could not change the subject until there was a moment's silence, and Forrest would not shut up.

"I'm very happy," he continued, "or very miserable. I chuckle or I weep alcoholically and, as I continue to slow up, life accommodatingly goes faster, so that the less there is of myself inside, the more diverting becomes the moving picture without. I have cut myself off from the respect of my fellow man, but I am aware of a compensatory cirrhosis of the emotions. And because my sensitivity, my pity, no longer has direction, but fixes itself on whatever is at hand, I have become an exceptionally good fellow – much more so than when I was a good doctor."

As the road straightened after the next bend and Gene saw his house in the distance, he remembered his wife's face as she had made him promise, and he could wait no longer: "Forrest, I got a thing…"

But at that moment the doctor brought his car to a sudden stop in front of a small house just beyond a grove of pines. On the front steps a girl of eight was playing with a grey cat.

"This is the sweetest little kid I ever saw," the doctor said to Gene, and then to the child, in a grave voice: "Helen, do you need any pills for kitty?"

The little girl laughed.

"Well, I don't know," she said doubtfully. She was playing another game with the cat now, and this came as rather an interruption.

"Because kitty telephoned me this morning," the doctor continued, "and said her mother was neglecting her and couldn't I get her a trained nurse from Montgomery."

"She did not." The little girl grabbed the cat close indignantly; the doctor took a nickel from his pocket and tossed it to the steps.

"I recommend a good dose of milk," he said as he put the car into gear. "Goodnight, Helen."

"Goodnight, doctor."

As they drove off, Gene tried again: "Listen: stop," he said. "Stop here a little way down… Here."

The doctor stopped the car and the brothers faced each other. They were alike as to robustness of figure and a certain asceticism of feature, and they were both in their middle forties; they were unlike in that the doctor's glasses failed to conceal the veined, weeping eyes of a soak, and that he wore corrugated city wrinkles; Gene's wrinkles bounded fields, followed the lines of rooftrees, of poles propping up sheds. His eyes were a fine, furry blue. But the sharpest contrast lay in the fact that Gene Janney was a country man while Doctor Forrest Janney was obviously a man of education.

"Well?" the doctor asked.

"You know Pinky's at home," Gene said, looking down the road.

"So I hear," the doctor answered non-committally.

"He got in a row in Birmingham and somebody shot him in the head." Gene hesitated. "We got Doc Behrer because we thought maybe you wouldn't... maybe you wouldn't..."

"I wouldn't," agreed Doctor Janney blandly.

"But look, Forrest: here's the thing," Gene insisted. "You know how it is – you often say Doc – Behrer doesn't know nothing. Shucks, I never thought he was much either. He says the bullet's pressing on the... pressing on the brain, and he can't take it out without causin' a hemmering, and he says he doesn't know whether we could get him to Birmingham or Montgomery, or not, he's so low. Doc wasn't no help. What we want—"

"No," said his brother, shaking his head. "No."

"I just want you to look at him and tell us what to do," Gene begged. "He's unconscious, Forrest. He wouldn't know you; you'd hardly know him. Thing is, his mother's about crazy."

"She's in the grip of a purely animal instinct." The doctor took from his hip a flask containing half water and half Alabama corn, and drank. "You and I know that boy ought to been drowned the day he was born."

Gene flinched. "He's bad," he admitted, "but I don't know... You see him lying there..."

As the liquor spread over the doctor's insides, he felt an instinct to do something, not to violate his prejudices but simply to make some gesture, to assert his own moribund but still struggling will to power.

"All right, I'll see him," he said. "I'll do nothing myself to help him, because he ought to be dead. And even his death wouldn't make up for what he did to Mary Decker."

Gene Janney pursed his lips. "Forrest, you sure about that?"

"Sure about it!" exclaimed the doctor. "Of course I'm sure. She died of starvation; she hadn't had more than a couple cups of coffee in a week. And if you looked at her shoes, you could see she'd walked for miles."

"Doc Behrer says—"

"What does he know? I performed the autopsy the day they found her on the Birmingham Highway. There was nothing the matter with her but starvation. That… that" – his voice shook with feeling – "that Pinky got tired of her and turned her out, and she was trying to get home. It suits me fine that he was invalided home himself a couple of weeks later."

As he talked, the doctor had plunged the car savagely into gear and let the clutch out with a jump; in a moment they drew up before Gene Janney's home.

It was a square frame house with a brick foundation and a well-kept lawn blocked off from the farm, a house rather superior to the buildings that composed the town of Bending and the surrounding agricultural area, yet not essentially different in type or in its interior economy. The last of the plantation houses in this section of Alabama had long disappeared, the proud pillars yielding to poverty, rot and rain.

Gene's wife, Rose, got up from her rocking chair on the porch.

"Hello, doc." She greeted him a little nervously and without meeting his eyes. "You been a stranger here lately."

The doctor met her eyes for several seconds. "How do you do, Rose?" he said. "Hi, Edith… Hi, Eugene" – this to the little boy and girl who stood beside their mother; and then: "Hi, Butch!" to the stocky youth of nineteen who came around the corner of the house hugging a round stone.

"Goin' to have a sort of low wall along the front here – kind of neater," Gene explained.

All of them had a lingering respect for the doctor. They felt reproachful towards him because they could no longer refer to him as their celebrated relative – "one of the bess surgeons up in Montgomery, yes, suh" – but there was his learning and the position he had once occupied in the larger world, before he had committed professional suicide by taking to cynicism and drink. He had come home to Bending and bought a half-interest in the local drugstore two years ago, keeping up his licence, but practising only when sorely needed.

"Rose," said Gene, "doc says he'll take a look at Pinky."

Pinky Janney, his lips curved mean and white under a new beard, lay in bed in a darkened room. When the doctor removed the bandage from his head, his breath blew into a low groan, but his paunchy body did not move. After a few minutes, the doctor replaced the bandage and, with Gene and Rose, returned to the porch.

"Behrer wouldn't operate?" he asked.

"No."

"Why didn't they operate in Birmingham?"

"I don't know."

"H'm." The doctor put on his hat. "That bullet ought to come out, and soon. It's pressing against the carotid sheath. That's the… anyhow, you can't get him to Montgomery with that pulse."

"What'll we do?" Gene's question carried a little tail of silence as he sucked his breath back.

"Get Behrer to think it over. Or else get somebody in Montgomery. There's about a twenty-five-per-cent chance that the operation would save him; without the operation he hasn't any chance at all."

"Who'll we get in Montgomery?" asked Gene.

"Any good surgeon would do it. Even Behrer could do it if he had any nerve."

Suddenly Rose Janney came close to him, her eyes straining and burning with an animal maternalism. She seized his coat where it hung open.

"Doc, you do it! You can do it. You know you were as good a surgeon as any of 'em once. Please, doc, you go on do it."

He stepped back a little so that her hands fell from his coat, and held out his own hands in front of him.

"See how they tremble?" he said with elaborate irony. "Look close and you'll see. I wouldn't dare operate."

"You could do it all right," said Gene hastily, "with a drink to stiffen you up."

The doctor shook his head and said, looking at Rose: "No. You see, my decisions are not reliable, and if anything went wrong, it would seem to be my fault." He was acting a little now – he chose his words carefully. "I hear that when I found that Mary Decker died of starvation, my opinion was questioned on the ground that I was a drunkard."

"I didn't say that," lied Rose breathlessly.

"Certainly not. I just mention it to show how careful I've got to be." He moved down the steps. "Well, my advice is to see Behrer again or, failing that, get somebody from the city. Goodnight."

But before he had reached the gate, Rose came tearing after him, her eyes white with fury.

"I did say you were a drunkard!" she cried. "When you said Mary Decker died of starvation, you made it out as if it was Pinky's fault – you, swilling yourself full of corn all day! How can anybody tell whether you know what you're doing or not? Why did you think so much about Mary Decker, anyhow – a girl half your age? Everybody saw how she used to come in your drugstore and talk to you—"

Gene, who had followed, seized her arms. "Shut up now, Rose... Drive along, Forrest."

Forrest drove along, stopping at the next bend to drink from his flask. Across the fallow cotton fields he could see the house where Mary Decker had lived, and had it been six months before, he might have detoured to ask her why she hadn't come into the store that day for her free soda, or to delight her with a sample cosmetic left by a salesman that morning. He had not told Mary Decker how he felt about her; never intended to – she was seventeen, he was forty-five, and he no longer dealt in futures

– but only after she ran away to Birmingham with Pinky Janney did he realize how much his love for her had counted in his lonely life.

His thoughts went back to his brother's house.

"Now, if I were a gentleman," he thought, "I wouldn't have done like that. And another person might have been sacrificed to that dirty dog, because if he died afterwards Rose would say I killed him."

Yet he felt pretty bad as he put his car away; not that he could have acted differently, but just that it was all so ugly.

He had been home scarcely ten minutes when a car creaked to rest outside and Butch Janney came in. His mouth was set tight and his eyes were narrowed as though to permit of no escape to the temper that possessed him until it should be unleashed upon its proper objective.

"Hi, Butch."

"I want to tell you, Uncle Forrest, you can't talk to my mother thataway. I'll kill you, you talk to my mother like that!"

"Now shut up, Butch, and sit down," said the doctor sharply.

"She's already 'bout sick on account of Pinky, and you come over and talk to her like that."

"Your mother did all the insulting that was done, Butch. I just took it."

"She doesn't know what she's saying and you ought to understand that."

The doctor thought a minute. "Butch, what do you think of Pinky?"

Butch hesitated uncomfortably. "Well, I can't say I ever thought so much of him" – his tone changed defiantly – "but after all, he's my own brother—"

"Wait a minute, Butch. What do you think of the way he treated Mary Decker?"

But Butch had shaken himself free, and now he let go the artillery of his rage:

"That an't the point; the point is anybody that doesn't do right to my mother has me to answer to. It's only fair when you got all the education—"

"I got my education myself, Butch."

"I don't care. We're going to try again to get Doc Behrer to operate or get us some fellow from the city. But if we can't, I'm coming and get you, and you're going to take that bullet out if I have to hold a gun to you while you do it." He nodded, panting a little; then he turned and went out and drove away.

"Something tells me," said the doctor to himself, "that there's no more peace for me in Chilton County." He called to his coloured boy to put supper on the table. Then he rolled himself a cigarette and went out on the back stoop.

The weather had changed. The sky was now overcast and the grass stirred restlessly, and there was a sudden flurry of drops without a sequel. A minute ago it had been warm, but now the moisture on his forehead was suddenly cool, and he wiped it away with his handkerchief. There was a buzzing in his ears and he swallowed and shook his head. For a moment he thought he must be sick; then suddenly the buzzing detached itself from him, grew into a swelling sound, louder and ever nearer, that might have been the roar of an approaching train.

2

BUTCH JANNEY WAS HALFWAY HOME when he saw it – a huge, black, approaching cloud whose lower edge bumped the ground. Even as he stared at it vaguely, it seemed to spread until it included the whole southern sky, and he saw pale electric fire in it and* heard an increasing roar. He was in a strong wind now; blown debris, bits of broken branches, splinters, larger objects unidentifiable in the growing darkness, flew by him. Instinctively he got out of his car and, by now hardly able to stand against the wind, ran for a bank, or rather found himself thrown and pinned against a bank. Then for a minute, two minutes, he was in the black centre of pandemonium.

First there was the sound, and he was part of the sound, so engulfed in it and possessed by it that he had no existence apart from it. It was not a collection of sounds, it was just Sound itself: a great screeching bow drawn across the chords of the universe. The sound and force were inseparable. The sound as well as the force held him to what he felt was the bank like a man crucified. Somewhere in this first moment his face, pinned sideways, saw his automobile make a little jump, spin halfway around and then go bobbing off over a field in a series of great helpless leaps. Then began the bombardment, the sound dividing its sustained cannon note into the cracks of a gigantic machine gun. He was only half-conscious as he felt himself become part of one of those cracks, felt himself lifted away from the bank to tear through space, through a blinding, lacerating mass of twigs and branches, and then, for an incalculable time, he knew nothing at all.

His body hurt him. He was lying between two branches in the top of a tree; the air was full of dust and rain, and he could hear nothing; it was a long time before he realized that the tree he was in had been blown down and that his involuntary perch among the pine needles was only five feet from the ground.

"Say, man!" he cried aloud, outraged. "Say, man! Say, what a wind! Say, man!"

Made acute by pain and fear, he guessed that he had been standing on the tree's root and had been catapulted by the terrific wrench as the big pine was torn from the earth. Feeling over himself, he found that his left ear was caked full of dirt, as if someone had wanted to take an impression of the inside. His clothes were in rags, his coat had torn on the back seam, and he could feel where, as some stray gust tried to undress him, it had cut into him under the arms.

Reaching the ground, he set off in the direction of his father's house, but it was a new and unfamiliar landscape he traversed. The Thing – he did not know it was a tornado – had cut a path a quarter of a mile wide, and he was confused, as the dust slowly settled, by vistas he had never seen before. It was unreal that Bending church tower should be visible from here; there had been groves of trees between.

But where was here? For he should be close to the Baldwin house; only as he tripped over great piles of boards, like a carelessly kept lumberyard, did Butch realize that there was no more Baldwin house, and then, looking around wildly, that there was no Necrawney house on the hill, no Peltzer house below it. There was not a light, not a sound, save the rain falling on the fallen trees.

He broke into a run. When he saw the bulk of his father's house in the distance, he gave a "Hey!" of relief, but coming closer, he realized that something was missing. There were no outhouses, and the built-on wing that held Pinky's room had been sheared completely away.

"Mother!" he called. "Dad!" There was no answer; a dog bounded out of the yard and licked his hand...

...It was full dark twenty minutes later when Doc Janney stopped his car in front of his own drugstore in Bending. The electric lights had gone out, but there were men with lanterns in the street, and in a minute a small crowd had collected around him. He unlocked the door hurriedly.

"Somebody break open the old Wiggins Hospital." He pointed across the street. "I've got six badly injured in my car. I want some fellows to carry 'em in. Is Doc Behrer here?"

"Here he is," offered eager voices out of the darkness as the doctor, case in hand, came through the crowd. The two men stood face to face by lantern light, forgetting that they disliked each other.

"God knows how many more there's going to be," said Doc Janney. "I'm getting dressing and disinfectant. There'll be a lot of fractures..." He raised his voice, "Somebody bring me a barrel!"

"I'll get started over there," said Doc Behrer. "There's about half a dozen more crawled in."

"What's been done?" demanded Doc Janney of the men who followed him into the drugstore. "Have they called Birmingham and Montgomery?"

"The telephone wires are down, but the telegraph got through."

"Well, somebody get Doctor Cohen from Wettala, and tell any people who have automobiles to go up the Willard Pike and cut across towards Corsica and all through those roads there. There's not a house left at the crossroads by the nigger store. I passed a lot of folks walking in, all of them hurt, but I didn't have room for anybody else." As he talked he was throwing bandages, disinfectant and drugs into a blanket. "I thought I had a lot more stuff than this in stock! And wait!" he called. "Somebody drive out and look down in that hollow where the Wooleys live. Drive right across the fields – the road's blocked… Now, you with the cap – Ed Jenks, ain't it?"

"Yes, doc."

"You see what I got here? You collect everything in the store that looks like this and bring it across the way, understand?"

"Yes, doc."

As the doctor went out into the street, the victims were streaming into town – a woman on foot with a badly injured child, a buckboard full of groaning Negroes, frantic men gasping terrible stories. Everywhere confusion and hysteria mounted in the dimly illumined darkness. A mud-covered reporter from Birmingham drove up in a sidecar, the wheels crossing the fallen wires and brushwood that clogged the street, and there was the siren of a police car from Cooper, thirty miles away.

Already a crowd pressed around the doors of the hospital, closed these three months for lack of patients. The doctor squeezed past the mêlée of white faces and established himself in the nearest ward, grateful for the waiting row of old iron beds. Doctor Behrer was already at work across the hall.

"Get me half a dozen lanterns," he ordered.

"Doctors Behrer wants iodine and adhesive."

"All right, there it is… Here, you, Shinkey, stand by the door and keep everybody out except cases that can't walk. Somebody run over and see if there ain't some candles in the grocery store."

The street outside was full of sound now – the cries of women, the contrary directions of volunteer gangs trying to clear the highway, the tense staccato of people rising to an emergency. A little before midnight arrived the first unit of the Red Cross. But the three doctors, presently joined by two others from nearby villages, had lost track of time long before that. The dead began to be brought in by ten o'clock; there were twenty, twenty-five, thirty, forty – the list grew. Having no more needs, these waited, as became simple husbandmen, in a garage behind, while the stream of injured – hundreds of them – flowed through the old hospital built to house only a score. The storm had dealt out fractures of the leg, collarbone, ribs and hip, lacerations of the back, elbows, ears, eyelids, nose; there were wounds from flying planks, and odd splinters in odd places, and a scalped man, who would recover to grow a new head of hair. Living or dead, Doc Janney knew every face, almost every name.

"Don't you fret now. Billy's all right. Hold still and let me tie this. People are drifting in every minute, but it's so consarned dark they can't find 'em… All right, Mrs Oakey. That's nothing. Ev here'll touch it with iodine… Now let's see this man."

Two o'clock. The old doctor from Wettala gave out, but now there were fresh men from Montgomery to take his place. Upon the air of the room, heavy with disinfectant, floated the ceaseless babble of human speech reaching the doctor dimly through layer after layer of increasing fatigue:

"…Over and over – just rolled me over and over. Got hold of a bush and the bush came along too."

"*Jeff! Where's Jeff?*"

"…I bet that pig sailed a hundred yards…"

"…just stopped the train in time. All the passengers got out and helped pull the poles…"

"Where's Jeff?"

"He says, 'Let's get down cellar,' and I says, 'We ain't got no cellar'…"

"…If there's no more stretchers, find some light doors."

"…Five seconds? Say, it was more like five minutes!"

At some time he heard that Gene and Rose had been seen with their two youngest children. He had passed their house on the way in and, seeing it standing, hurried on. The Janney family had been lucky; the doctor's own house was outside the sweep of the storm.

Only as he saw the electric lights go on suddenly in the streets and glimpsed the crowd waiting for hot coffee in front of the Red Cross did the doctor realize how tired he was.

"You better go rest," a young man was saying. "I'll take this side of the room. I've got two nurses with me."

"All right – all right. I'll finish this row."

The injured were being evacuated to the cities by train as fast as their wounds were dressed, and their places taken by others. He had only two beds to go – in the first one he found Pinky Janney.

He put his stethoscope to the heart. It was beating feebly. That he, so weak, so nearly gone, had survived this storm at all was remarkable. How he had got there, who had found him and carried him, was a mystery in itself. The doctor went over the body; there were small contusions and lacerations, two broken fingers, the dirt-filled ears that marked every case – nothing else. For a moment the doctor hesitated, but even when he closed his eyes, the image of Mary Decker seemed to have receded, eluding him. Something purely professional that had nothing to do with human sensibilities had been set in motion inside him, and he was powerless to head it off. He held out his hands before him; they were trembling slightly.

"Hell's bells!" he muttered.

He went out of the room and around the corner of the hall, where he drew from his pocket the flask containing the last of the corn and water he had had in the afternoon. He emptied it. Returning to the ward, he disinfected two instruments and applied a local anaesthetic to a square section at the base of Pinky's skull where the wound had healed over the bullet. He called a nurse to his side and then, scalpel in hand, knelt on one knee beside his nephew's bed.

3

TWO DAYS LATER, the doctor drove slowly around the mournful countryside. He had withdrawn from the emergency work after the first desperate night, feeling that his status as a pharmacist might embarrass his collaborators. But there was much to be done in bringing the damage to outlying sections under the aegis of the Red Cross, and he devoted himself to that.

The path of the demon was easy to follow. It had pursued an irregular course on its seven-league boots, cutting cross country, through woods, or even urbanely keeping to roads until they curved, when it went off on its own again. Sometimes the trail could be traced by cotton fields, apparently in full bloom, but this cotton came from the insides of hundreds of quilts and mattresses redistributed in the fields by the storm.

At a lumber pile that had lately been a Negro cabin, he stopped a moment to listen to a dialogue between two reporters and two shy piccaninnies. The old grandmother, her head bandaged, sat among the ruins, gnawing some vague meat and moving her rocker ceaselessly.

"But where is the river you were blown across?" one of the reporters demanded.

"There."

"Where?"

The piccaninnies looked to their grandmother for aid.

"Right there behind you all," spoke up the old woman.

The newspapermen looked disgustedly at a muddy stream four yards wide.

"That's no river."

"That's a Menada River, we always calls it ever since I was a gull. Yes, suh, that's a Menada River. An' them two boys was blowed right across it an' set down on the othah side just as pretty, 'thout any hurt at all. Chimney fell on me," she concluded, feeling her head.

"Do you mean to say that's all it was?" demanded the younger reporter indignantly. "That's the river they were blown across! And one hundred and twenty million people have been led to believe—"

"That's all right, boys," interrupted Doc Janney. "That's a right good river for these parts. And it'll get bigger as those little fellas get older."

He tossed a quarter to the old woman and drove on.

Passing a country church, he stopped and counted the new brown mounds that marred the graveyard. He was nearing the centre of the holocaust now. There was the Howden house where three had been killed; there remained a gaunt chimney, a rubbish heap and a scarecrow surviving ironically in the kitchen garden. In the ruins of the house across the way a rooster strutted on top of a piano, reigning vociferously over an estate of trunks, boots, cans, books, calendars, rugs, chairs and window frames, a twisted radio and a legless sewing machine. Everywhere there was bedding – blankets, mattresses, bent springs, shredded padding – he had not realized how much of people's lives was spent in bed. Here and there, cows and horses, often stained with disinfectant, were grazing again in the fields. At intervals there were Red Cross tents and, sitting by one of these, with the grey cat in her arms, the doctor came upon little Helen Kilrain. The usual lumber pile, like a child's building game knocked down in a fit of temper, told the story.

"Hello, dear," he greeted her, his heart sinking. "How did kitty like the tornado?"

"She didn't."

"What did she do?"

"She meowed."

"Oh."

"She wanted to get away, but I hanged on to her and she scratched me – see?"

He glanced at the Red Cross tent.

"Who's taking care of you?"

"The lady from the Red Cross and Mrs Wells," she answered. "My father got hurt. He stood over me so it wouldn't fall on me, and I stood over kitty. He's in the hospital in Birmingham. When he comes back, I guess he'll build our house again."

The doctor winced. He knew that her father would build no more houses; he had died that morning. She was alone, and she did not know she was alone. Around her stretched the dark universe, impersonal, inconscient. Her lovely little face looked up at him confidently as he asked: "You got any kin anywhere, Helen?"

"I don't know."

"You've got kitty, anyhow, haven't you?"

"It's just a cat," she admitted calmly, but, anguished by her own betrayal of her love, she hugged it closer.

"Taking care of a cat must be pretty hard."

"Oh, no," she said hurriedly. "It isn't any trouble at all. It doesn't eat hardly anything."

He put his hand in his pocket, and then changed his mind suddenly.

"Dear, I'm coming back and see you later – later today. You take good care of kitty now, won't you?"

"Oh, yes," she answered lightly.

The doctor drove on. He stopped next at a house that had escaped damage. Walt Cupps, the owner, was cleaning a shotgun on his front porch.

"What's that, Walt? Going to shoot up the next tornado?"

"Ain't going to be a next tornado."

"You can't tell. Just take a look at that sky now. It's getting mighty dark."

Walt laughed and slapped his gun. "Not for a hundred years, anyhow. This here is for looters. There's a lot of 'em around, and not all black either. Wish when you go to town that you'd tell 'em to scatter some militia out here."

"I'll tell 'em now. You come out all right?"

"I did, thank God. With six of us in the house. It took off one hen, and probably it's still carrying it around somewhere."

The doctor drove on towards town, overcome by a feeling of uneasiness he could not define.

"It's the weather," he thought. "It's the same kind of feel in the air there was last Saturday."

For a month the doctor had felt an urge to go away permanently. Once this countryside had seemed to promise peace. When the impetus that had lifted him temporarily out of tired old stock was exhausted, he had come back here to rest, to watch the earth put forth and live on simple, pleasant terms with his neighbours. Peace! He knew that the present family quarrel would never heal, nothing would ever be the same; it would all be bitter for ever. And he had seen the placid countryside turned into a land of mourning. There was no peace here. Move on!

On the road he overtook Butch Janney walking to town.

"I was coming to see you," said Butch, frowning. "You operated on Pinky after all, didn't you?"

"Jump in... Yes, I did. How did you know?"

"Doc Behrer told us." He shot a quick look at the doctor, who did not miss the quality of suspicion in it. "They don't think he'll last out the day."

"I'm sorry for your mother."

Butch laughed unpleasantly. "Yes, you are."

"I said I'm sorry for your mother," said the doctor sharply.

"I heard you."

They drove for a moment in silence.

"Did you find your automobile?"

"Did I?" Butch laughed ruefully. "I found something – I don't know whether you'd call it a car any more. And, you know, I could of had tornado insurance for twenty-five cents." His voice trembled indignantly: "Twenty-five cents – but who would ever of thought of getting tornado insurance?"

It was growing darker; there was a thin crackle of thunder far to the southward.

"Well, all I hope," said Butch with narrowed glance, "is that you hadn't been drinking anything when you operated on Pinky."

"You know, Butch," the doctor said slowly, "that was a pretty dirty trick of mine to bring that tornado here."

He had not expected the sarcasm to hit home, but he expected a retort – when suddenly he caught sight of Butch's face. It was fish-white, the mouth was open, the eyes fixed and staring, and from the throat came a mewling sound. Limply he raised one hand before him, and then the doctor saw.

Less than a mile away, an enormous, top-shaped black cloud filled the sky and bore towards them, dipping and swirling, and in front of it sailed already a heavy, singing wind.

"It's come back!" the doctor yelled.

Fifty yards ahead of them was the old iron bridge spanning Bilby Creek. He stepped hard on the accelerator and drove for it. The fields were full of running figures headed in the same direction. Reaching the bridge, he jumped out and yanked Butch's arm.

"Get out, you fool! Get out!"

A nerveless mass stumbled from the car; in a moment they were in a group of half a dozen, huddled in the triangular space that the bridge made with the shore.

"Is it coming here?"

"No, it's turning!"

"We had to leave Grampa!"

"Oh, save me, save me! Jesus save me! Help me!"

"Jesus save my soul!"

There was a quick rush of wind outside, sending little tentacles under the bridge with a curious tension in them that made the doctor's skin crawl. Then immediately there was a vacuum, with no more wind, but a sudden thresh of rain. The doctor crawled to the edge of the bridge and put his head up cautiously.

"It's passed," he said. "We only felt the edge; the centre went way to the right of us."

He could see it plainly; for a second he could even distinguish objects in it – shrubbery and small trees, planks and loose earth. Crawling farther out, he produced his watch and tried to time it, but the thick curtain of rain blotted it from sight.

Soaked to the skin, he crawled back underneath. Butch lay shivering in the farthest corner, and the doctor shook him.

"It went in the direction of your house!" the doctor cried. "Pull yourself together! Who's there?"

"No one," Butch groaned. "They're all down with Pinky."

The rain had changed to hail now; first small pellets, then larger ones, and larger, until the sound of their fall upon the iron bridge was an ear-splitting tattoo.

The spared wretches under the bridge were slowly recovering, and in the relief there were titters of hysterical laughter. After a certain point of strain, the nervous system makes its transitions without dignity or reason. Even the doctor felt the contagion.

"This is worse than a calamity," he said drily. "It's getting to be a nuisance."

4

THERE WERE TO BE no more tornadoes in Alabama that spring. The second one – it was popularly thought to be the first one come back; for to the people of Chilton County it had become a personified force, definite as a pagan god – took a dozen houses, Gene Janney's among them, and injured about thirty people. But this time – perhaps because everyone had developed some scheme of self-protection – there were no fatalities. It made its last dramatic bow by sailing down the main street of Bending, prostrating the telephone poles and crushing in the fronts of three shops, including Doc Janney's drugstore.

At the end of a week, houses were going up again, made of the old boards; and before the end of the long, lush Alabama summer the grass would be green again on all the graves. But it will be years before the people of the country cease to reckon events as happening "before the tornado" or "after the tornado" – and for many families things will never be the same.

Doctor Janney decided that this was as good a time to leave as any. He sold the remains of his drugstore, gutted alike by charity and catastrophe, and turned over his house to his brother until Gene could rebuild his own. He was going up to the city by train, for his car had been rammed against a tree and couldn't be counted on for much more than the trip to the station.

Several times on the way in he stopped by the roadside to say goodbye – once it was to Walter Cupps.

"So it hit you, after all," he said, looking at the melancholy back house which alone marked the site.

"It's pretty bad," Walter answered. "But just think: they was six of us in or about the house and not one was injured. I'm content to give thanks to God for that."

"You were lucky there, Walt," the doctor agreed. "Do you happen to have heard whether the Red Cross took little Helen Kilrain to Montgomery or to Birmingham?"

"To Montgomery. Say, I was there when she came into town with that cat, tryin' to get somebody to bandage up its paw. She must of walked miles through that rain and hail, but all that mattered to her was her kitty. Bad as I felt, I couldn't help laughin' at how spunky she was."

The doctor was silent for a moment. "Do you happen to recollect if she has any people left?"

"I don't, suh," Walter replied, "but I think as not."

At his brother's place, the doctor made his last stop. They were all there, even the youngest, working among the ruins; already Butch had a shed erected to house the salvage of their goods. Save for this, the most orderly thing surviving was the pattern of round white stone which was to have enclosed the garden.

The doctor took a hundred dollars in bills from his pocket and handed it to Gene.

"You can pay it back sometime, but don't strain yourself," he said. "It's money I got from the store." He cut off Gene's thanks: "Pack up my books carefully when I send for 'em."

"You reckon to practise medicine up there, Forrest?"

"I'll maybe try it."

The brothers held on to each other's hands for a moment; the two youngest children came up to say goodbye. Rose stood in the background in an old blue dress – she had no money to wear black for her eldest son.

"Goodbye, Rose," said the doctor.

"Goodbye," she responded, and then added in a dead voice, "Good luck to you, Forrest."

For a moment he was tempted to say something conciliatory, but he saw it was no use. He was up against the maternal instinct, the same force that had sent little Helen through the storm with her injured cat.

At the station he bought a one-way ticket to Montgomery. The village was drab under the sky of a retarded spring, and as the train pulled out, it was odd to think that six months ago it had seemed to him as good a place as any other.

He was alone in the white section of the day coach; presently he felt for a bottle on his hip and drew it forth. "After all, a man of forty-five is entitled to more artificial courage when he starts over again." He began thinking of Helen. "She hasn't got any kin. I guess she's my little girl now."

He patted the bottle, then looked down at it as if in surprise.

"Well, we'll have to put you aside for a while, old friend. Any cat that's worth all that trouble and care is going to need a lot of grade-B milk."

He settled down in his seat, looking out the window. In his memory of that terrible week the winds still sailed about him, came in as draughts through the corridor of the car – winds of the world – cyclones, hurricane, tornadoes – grey and black, expected or unforeseen, some from the sky, some from the caves of hell.

But he would not let them touch Helen again – if he could help it. He dozed momentarily, but a haunting dream woke him: "*Daddy stood over me and I stood over Kitty.*"

"All right, Helen," he said aloud, for he often talked to himself, "I guess the old brig can keep afloat a little longer – in any wind."

What a Handsome Pair!

1

A T FOUR O'CLOCK on a November afternoon in 1902, Teddy Van Beck got out of a hansom cab in front of a brownstone house on Murray Hill. He was a tall, round-shouldered young man with a beaked nose and soft brown eyes in a sensitive face. In his veins quarrelled the blood of colonial governors and celebrated robber barons; in him the synthesis had produced, for that time and place, something different and something new.

His cousin, Helen Van Beck, waited in the drawing room. Her eyes were red from weeping, but she was young enough for it not to detract from her glossy beauty – a beauty that had reached the point where it seemed to contain in itself the secret of its own growth, as if it would go on increasing for ever. She was nineteen and, contrary to the evidence, she was extremely happy.

Teddy put his arm around her and kissed her cheek, and found it changing into her ear as she turned her face away. He held her for a moment, his own enthusiasm chilling; then he said:

"You don't seem very glad to see me."

Helen had a premonition that this was going to be one of the memorable scenes of her life, and with unconscious cruelty she set about extracting from it its full dramatic value. She sat in a corner of the couch, facing an easy chair.

"Sit there," she commanded, in what was then admired as a "regal manner", and then, as Teddy straddled the piano stool: "No, don't sit there. I can't talk to you if you're going to revolve around."

"Sit on my lap," he suggested.

"No."

Playing a one-handed flourish on the piano, he said, "I can listen better here."

Helen gave up hopes of beginning on the sad and quiet note.

"This is a serious matter, Teddy. Don't think I've decided it without a lot of consideration. I've got to ask you... to ask you to release me from our understanding."

"What?" Teddy's face paled with shock and dismay.

"I'll have to tell you from the beginning. I've realized for a long time that we have nothing in common. You're interested in your music, and I can't even play chopsticks." Her voice was weary as if with suffering; her small teeth tugged at her lower lip.

"What of it?" he demanded, relieved. "I'm musician enough for both. You wouldn't have to understand banking to marry a banker, would you?"

"This is different," Helen answered. "What would we do together? One important thing is that you don't like riding; you told me you were afraid of horses."

"Of course I'm afraid of horses," he said, and added reminiscently: "They try to bite me."

"It makes it so—"

"I've never met a horse – socially, that is – who didn't try to bite me. They used to do it when I put the bridle on; then, when I gave up putting the bridle on, they began reaching their heads around trying to get at my calves."

The eyes of her father, who had given her a Shetland at three, glistened, cold and hard, from her own.

"You don't even like the people I like, let alone the horses," she said.

"I can stand them. I've stood them all my life."

"Well, it would be a silly way to start a marriage. I don't see any grounds for mutual... mutual..."

"Riding?"

"Oh, not that." Helen hesitated, and then said in an unconvinced tone, "Probably I'm not clever enough for you."

"Don't talk such stuff!" He demanded some truth: "Who's the man?"

It took her a moment to collect herself. She had always resented Teddy's tendency to treat women with less ceremony than was the custom of the day. Often he was an unfamiliar, almost frightening young man.

"There is someone," she admitted. "It's someone I've always known slightly, but about a month ago, when I went to Southampton, I was... thrown with him."

"Thrown from a horse?"

"Please, Teddy," she protested gravely. "I'd been getting more unhappy about you and me, and whenever I was with him everything seemed all right." A note of exaltation that she would not conceal came into Helen's voice. She rose and crossed the room, her straight, slim legs outlined by the shadows of her dress. "We rode and swam and played tennis together – did the things we both liked to do."

He stared into the vacant space she had created for him. "Is that all that drew you to this fellow?"

"No, it was more than that. He was thrilling to me like nobody ever has been." She laughed. "I think what really started me thinking about it was one day we came in from riding and everybody said aloud what a nice pair we made."

"Did you kiss him?"

She hesitated. "Yes, once."

He got up from the piano stool. "I feel as if I had a cannon ball in my stomach," he exclaimed.

The butler announced Mr Stuart Oldhorne.

"Is he the man?" Teddy demanded tensely.

She was suddenly upset and confused. "He should have come later. Would you rather go without meeting him?"

But Stuart Oldhorne, made confident by his new sense of proprietor-ship, had followed the butler.

The two men regarded each other with a curious impotence of expres-sion; there can be no communication between men in that position, for their relation is indirect and consists in how much each of them has pos-sessed or will possess of the woman in question, so that their emotions pass through her divided self as through a bad telephone connection.

Stuart Oldhorne sat beside Helen, his polite eyes never leaving Teddy. He had the same glowing physical power as she. He had been a star athlete at Yale and a Rough Rider in Cuba, and was the best young horseman on Long Island. Women loved him not only for his points but for a real sweetness of temper.

"You've lived so much in Europe that I don't often see you," he said to Teddy. Teddy didn't answer, and Stuart Oldhorne turned to Helen: "I'm early; I didn't realize—"

"You came at the right time," said Teddy rather harshly. "I stayed to play you my congratulations."

To Helen's alarm, he turned and ran his fingers over the keyboard. Then he began.

What he was playing, neither Helen nor Stuart knew, but Teddy always remembered. He put his mind in order with a short résumé of the history of music, beginning with some chords from *The Messiah* and ending with Debussy's 'La plus que lente', which had an evocative quality for him, because he had first heard it the day his brother died. Then, pausing for an instant, he began to play more thoughtfully, and the lovers on the sofa could feel that they were alone – that he had left them and had no more traffic with them – and Helen's discomfort lessened. But the flight, the elusiveness of the music, piqued her, gave her a feeling of annoyance. If Teddy had played the current sentimental song from *Erminie*,* and had played it with feeling, she would have understood and been moved, but he was plunging her suddenly into a world of mature emotions, whither her nature neither could nor wished to follow.

She shook herself slightly and said to Stuart: "Did you buy the horse?"

"Yes, and at a bargain... Do you know I love you?"

"I'm glad," she whispered.

The piano stopped suddenly. Teddy closed it and swung slowly around: "Did you like my congratulations?"

"Very much," they said together.

"It was pretty good," he admitted. "That last was only based on a little counterpoint. You see, the idea of it was that you make such a handsome pair."

He laughed unnaturally; Helen followed him out into the hall.

"Goodbye, Teddy," she said. "We're going to be good friends, aren't we?"

"Aren't we?" he repeated. He winked without smiling, and with a clicking, despairing sound of his mouth, went out quickly.

For a moment Helen tried vainly to apply a measure to the situation, wondering how she had come off with him, realizing reluctantly that she had never for an instant held the situation in her hands. She had a dim realization that Teddy was larger in scale; then the very largeness frightened her and, with relief and a warm tide of emotion, she hurried into the drawing room and the shelter of her lover's arms.

Their engagement ran through a halcyon summer. Stuart visited Helen's family at Tuxedo, and Helen visited his family in Wheatley Hills. Before breakfast, their horses' hoofs sedately scattered the dew in sentimental glades, or curtained them with dust as they raced on dirt roads. They bought a tandem bicycle and pedalled all over Long Island – which Mrs Cassius Ruthven, a contemporary Cato, considered "rather fast" for a couple not yet married. They were seldom at rest, but when they were, they reminded people of *His Move* on a Gibson pillow.*

Helen's taste for sport was advanced for her generation. She rode nearly as well as Stuart and gave him a decent game in tennis. He taught her some polo, and they were golf-crazy when it was still considered a comic game. They liked to feel fit and cool together. They thought of themselves as a team, and it was often remarked how well mated they were. A chorus of pleasant envy followed in the wake of their effortless glamour.

They talked.

"It seems a pity you've got to go to the office," she would say. "I wish you did something we could do together, like taming lions."

"I've always thought that in a pinch I could make a living breeding and racing horses," said Stuart.

"I know you could, you darling."

In August he brought a Thomas automobile and toured all the way to Chicago with three other men. It was an event of national interest and their pictures were in all the papers. Helen wanted to go, but it wouldn't have been proper, so they compromised by driving down Fifth Avenue on a sunny September morning, one with the fine day and the fashionable crowd, but distinguished by their unity, which made them each as strong as two.

"What do you suppose?" Helen demanded. "Teddy sent me the oddest present – a cup rack."

Stuart laughed. "Obviously he means that all we'll ever do is win cups."

"I thought it was rather a slam," Helen ruminated. "I saw that he was invited to everything, but he didn't answer a single invitation. Would you mind very much stopping by his apartment now? I haven't seen him for months and I don't like to leave anything unpleasant in the past."

He wouldn't go in with her. "I'll sit and answer questions about the auto from passers-by."

The door was opened by a woman in a cleaning cap, and Helen heard the sound of Teddy's piano from the room beyond. The woman seemed reluctant to admit her.

"He said don't interrupt him, but I suppose if you're his cousin…"

Teddy welcomed her, obviously startled and somewhat upset, but in a minute he was himself again.

"I won't marry you," he assured her. "You've had your chance."

"All right," she laughed.

"How are you?" He threw a pillow at her. "You're beautiful! Are you happy with this... this centaur? Does he beat you with his riding crop?" He peered at her closely. "You look a little duller than when I knew you. I used to whip you up to a nervous excitement that bore a resemblance to intelligence."

"I'm happy, Teddy. I hope you are."

"Sure, I'm happy; I'm working. I've got MacDowell on the run and I'm going to have a shebang at Carnegie Hall next September." His eyes became malicious. "What did you think of my girl?"

"Your girl?"

"The girl who opened the door for you."

"Oh, I thought it was a maid." She flushed and was silent.

He laughed. "Hey, Betty!" he called. "You were mistaken for the maid!"

"And that's the fault of my cleaning on Sunday," answered a voice from the next room.

Teddy lowered his voice. "Do you like her?" he demanded.

"Teddy!" She teetered on the arm of the sofa, wondering whether she should leave at once.

"What would you think if I married her?" he asked confidentially.

"Teddy!" She was outraged; it had needed but a glance to place the woman as common. "You're joking. She's older than you... You wouldn't be such a fool as to throw away your future that way."

He didn't answer.

"Is she musical?" Helen demanded. "Does she help you with your work?"

"She doesn't know a note. Neither did you, but I've got enough music in me for twenty wives."

Visualizing herself as one of them, Helen rose stiffly.

"All I can ask you is to think how your mother would have felt – and those who care for you... Goodbye, Teddy."

He walked out the door with her and down the stairs.

"As a matter of fact, we've been married for two months," he said casually. "She was a waitress in a place where I used to eat."

Helen felt that she should be angry and aloof, but tears of hurt vanity were springing to her eyes.

"And do you love her?"

"I like her; she's a good person and good for me. Love is something else. I loved you, Helen, and that's all dead in me for the present. Maybe it's coming out in my music. Some day I'll probably love other women – or maybe there'll never be anything but you. Goodbye, Helen."

The declaration touched her. "I hope you'll be happy, Teddy. Bring your wife to the wedding."

He bowed non-committally. When she had gone, he returned thoughtfully to his apartment.

"That was the cousin that I was in love with," he said.

"And was it?" Betty's face, Irish and placid, brightened with interest. "She's a pretty thing."

"She wouldn't have been as good for me as a nice peasant like you."

"Always thinking of yourself, Teddy Van Beck."

He laughed. "Sure I am, but you love me, anyhow?"

"That's a big wur-red."

"All right. I'll remember that when you come begging around for a kiss. If my grandfather knew I married a bog-trotter, he'd turn over in his grave. Now get out and let me finish my work."

He sat at the piano, a pencil behind his ear. Already his face was resolved, composed, but his eyes grew more intense minute by minute, until there was a glaze in them, behind which they seemed to have joined his ears in counting and hearing. Presently there was no more indication in his face that anything had occurred to disturb the tranquillity of his Sunday morning.

2

MRS CASSIUS RUTHVEN AND A FRIEND, veils flung back across their hats, sat in their auto on the edge of the field.

"A young woman playing polo in breeches." Mrs Ruthven sighed. "Amy Van Beck's daughter. I thought when Helen organized the Amazons she'd stop at divided skirts. But her husband apparently has no objections, for there he stands, egging her on. Of course, they always have liked the same things."

"A pair of thoroughbreds, those two," said the other woman complacently, meaning that she admitted them to be her equals. "You'd never look at them and think that anything had gone wrong."

She was referring to Stuart's mistake in the panic of 1907. His father had bequeathed him a precarious situation, and Stuart had made an error of judgement. His honour was not questioned and his crowd stood by him loyally, but his usefulness in Wall Street was over and his small fortune was gone.

He stood in a group of men with whom he would presently play, noting things to tell Helen after the game – she wasn't turning with the play soon enough, and several times she was unnecessarily ridden off at important moments. Her ponies were sluggish – the penalty for playing with borrowed mounts – but she was, nevertheless, the best player on the field, and in the last minute she made a save that brought applause.

"Good girl! Good girl!"

Stuart had been delegated with the unpleasant duty of chasing the women from the field. They had started an hour late and now a team from New Jersey was waiting to play; he sensed trouble as he cut across to join Helen and walked beside her towards the stables. She was splendid, with her flushed cheeks, her shining, triumphant eyes, her short, excited breath. He temporized for a minute.

"That was good – that last," he said.

"Thanks. It almost broke my arm. Wasn't I pretty good all through?"

"You were the best out there."

"I know it."

He waited while she dismounted and handed the pony to a groom.

"Helen, I believe I've got a job."

"What is it?"

"Don't jump on the idea till you think it over. Gus Myers wants me to manage his racing stables. Eight thousand a year."

Helen considered. "It's a nice salary – and I bet you could make yourself up a nice string from his ponies."

"The principal thing is that I need the money; I'd have as much as you and things would be easier."

"You'd have as much as me," Helen repeated. She almost regretted that he would need no more help from her. "But with Gus Myers, isn't there a string attached? Wouldn't he expect a boost-up?"

"He probably would," answered Stuart bluntly, "and if I can help him socially, I will. As a matter of fact, he wants me at a stag dinner tonight."

"All right, then," Helen said absently. Still hesitating to tell her her game was over, Stuart followed her glance towards the field, where a runabout had driven up and parked by the ropes.

"There's your old friend, Teddy," he remarked drily – "or rather, your new friend, Teddy. He's taking a sudden interest in polo. Perhaps he thinks the horses aren't biting this summer."

"You're not in a very good humour," protested Helen. "You know, if you say the word, I'll never see him again. All I want in the world is for you and I to be together."

"I know," he admitted regretfully. "Selling horses and giving up clubs put a crimp in that. I know the women all fall for Teddy now he's getting famous, but if he tries to fool around with you I'll break his piano over his head... Oh, another thing," he began, seeing the men already riding on the field. "About your last chukker..."

As best he could, he put the situation up to her. He was not prepared for the fury that swept over her.

"But it's an outrage! I got up the game and it's been posted on the bulletin board for three days."

"You started an hour late."

"And do you know why?" she demanded. "Because your friend Joe Morgan insisted that Celie ride side-saddle. He tore her habit off her three times, and she only got here by climbing out the kitchen window."

"I can't do anything about it."

"Why can't you? Weren't you once a governor of this club? How can women ever expect to be any good if they have to quit every time the men want the field? All the men want is for the women to come up to them in the evening and tell them what a beautiful game they played!"

Still raging and blaming Stuart, she crossed the field to Teddy's car. He got out and greeted her with concentrated intensity:

"I've reached the point where I can neither sleep nor eat from thinking of you. What point is that?"

There was something thrilling about him that she had never been conscious of in the old days; perhaps the stories of his philanderings had made him more romantic to her.

"Well, don't think of me as I am now," she said. "My face is getting rougher every day and my muscles lean out of an evening dress like a female impersonator. People are beginning to refer to me as handsome instead of pretty. Besides, I'm in a vile humour. It seems to me women are always just edged out of everything. "

Stuart's game was brutal that afternoon. In the first five minutes, he realized that Teddy's runabout was no longer there, and his long slugs began to tally from all angles. Afterwards, he bumped home across country at a gallop; his mood was not assuaged by a note handed him by the children's nurse:

Dear: Since your friends made it possible for us to play, I wasn't going to sit there just dripping; so I had Teddy bring me home. And since you'll be out to dinner, I'm going into New York with him to the theatre. I'll either be out on the theatre train or spend the night at Mother's.
Helen

Stuart went upstairs and changed into his dinner coat. He had no defence against the unfamiliar claws of jealousy that began a slow dissection of his insides. Often Helen had gone to plays or dances with other men, but this was different. He felt towards Teddy the faint contempt of the physical man for the artist, but the last six months had bruised his pride. He perceived the possibility that Helen might be seriously interested in someone else.

He was in a bad humour at Gus Myers's dinner – annoyed with his host for talking so freely about their business arrangement. When at last they rose from the table, he decided that it was no-go and called Myers aside.

"Look here. I'm afraid this isn't a good idea, after all."

"Why not?" His host looked at him in alarm. "Are you going back on me? My dear fellow—"

"I think we'd better call it off."

"And why, may I ask? Certainly I have the right to ask why."

Stuart considered. "All right, I'll tell you. When you made that little speech, you mentioned me as if you had somehow bought me, as if I was a sort of employee in your office. Now, in the sporting world that doesn't go; things are more… more democratic. I grew up with all these men here tonight, and they didn't like it any better than I did."

"I see," Mr Myers reflected carefully – "I see." Suddenly he clapped Stuart on the back. "That is exactly the sort of thing I like to be told; it helps me. From now on I won't mention you as if you were in my… as if we had a business arrangement. Is that all right?"

After all, the salary was eight thousand dollars.

"Very well, then," Stuart agreed. "But you'll have to excuse me tonight. I'm catching a train to the city."

"I'll put an automobile at your disposal."

At ten o'clock he rang the bell of Teddy's apartment on 48th Street.

"I'm looking for Mr Van Beck," he said to the woman who answered the door. "I know he's gone to the theatre, but I wonder if you can tell me…" Suddenly he guessed who the woman was. "I'm Stuart Oldhorne," he explained. "I married Mr Van Beck's cousin."

"Oh, come in," said Betty pleasantly. "I know all about who you are."

She was just this side of forty, stoutish and plain of face, but full of a keen, brisk vitality. In the living room they sat down.

"You want to see Teddy?"

"He's with my wife and I want to join them after the theatre. I wonder if you know where they went?"

"Oh, so Teddy's with your wife." There was a faint, pleasant brogue in her voice. "Well, now, he didn't say exactly where he'd be tonight."

"Then you don't know?"

"I don't – not for the life of me," she admitted cheerfully. "I'm sorry."

He stood up, and Betty saw the thinly hidden anguish in his face. Suddenly she was really sorry.

"I did hear him say something about the theatre," she said ruminatively. "Now sit down and let me think what it was. He goes out so much, and a play once a week is enough for me, so that one night mixes up with the others in my head. Didn't your wife say where to meet them?"

"No. I only decided to come in after they'd started. She said she'd catch the theatre train back to Long Island or go to her mother's."

"That's it," Betty said triumphantly, striking her hands together like cymbals. "That's what he said when he called up – that he was putting a lady on the theatre train for Long Island, and would be home himself right afterward. We've had a child sick and it's driven things from my mind."

"I'm very sorry I bothered you under those conditions."

"It's no bother. Sit down. It's only just after ten."

Feeling easier, Stuart relaxed a little and accepted a cigar.

"No, if I tried to keep up with Teddy, I'd have white hair by now," Betty said. "Of course, I go to his concerts, but often I fall asleep – not that he ever knows it. So long as he doesn't take too much to drink and knows where his home is, I don't bother about where he wanders." As Stuart's face grew serious again, she changed her tone: "All and all, he's a good husband to me and we have a happy life together, without interfering with each other. How would he do working next to the nursery and groaning at every sound? And how would I do going to Mrs Ruthven's with him, and all of them talking about high society and high art?"

A phrase of Helen's came back to Stuart: "Always together – I like for us to do everything together."

"You have children, haven't you, Mr Oldhorne?"

"Yes. My boy's almost big enough to sit a horse."

"Ah, yes; you're both great for horses."

"My wife says that as soon as their legs are long enough to reach stirrups, she'll be interested in them again." This didn't sound right to Stuart and he modified it: "I mean she always has been interested in them, but she never let them monopolize her or come between us. We've always believed that marriage ought to be founded on companionship, on having the same interests. I mean, you're musical and you help your husband."

Betty laughed. "I wish Teddy could hear that. I can't read a note or carry a tune."

"No?" He was confused. "I'd somehow got the impression that you were musical."

"You can't see why else he'd have married me?"

"Not at all. On the contrary."

After a few minutes, he said goodnight, somehow liking her. When he had gone, Betty's expression changed slowly to one of exasperation; she went to the telephone and called her husband's studio:

"There you are, Teddy. Now listen to me carefully. I know your cousin is with you and I want to talk with her... Now, don't lie. You put her on the phone. Her husband has been here, and if you don't let me talk to her it might be a serious matter."

She could hear an unintelligible colloquy, and then Helen's voice: "Hello."

"Good evening, Mrs Oldhorne. Your husband came here, looking for you and Teddy. I told him I didn't know which play you were at, so you'd better be thinking which one. And I told him Teddy was leaving you at the station in time for the theatre train."

"Oh, thank you very much. We—"

"Now, you meet your husband or there's trouble for you, or I'm no judge of men. And... wait a minute. Tell Teddy, if he's going to be up late, that Josie's sleeping light, and he's not to touch the piano when he gets home."

Betty heard Teddy come in at eleven, and she came into the drawing room smelling of camomile vapour. He greeted her absently; there was a look of suffering in his face, and his eyes were bright and faraway.

"You call yourself a great musician, Teddy Van Beck," she said, "but it seems to me you're much more interested in women."

"Let me alone, Betty."

"I do let you alone, but when the husbands start coming here, it's another matter."

"This was different, Betty. This goes way back into the past."

"It sounds like the present to me."

"Don't make any mistake about Helen," he said. "She's a good woman."

"Not through any fault of yours, I know."

He sank his head wearily in his hands. "I've tried to forget her. I've avoided her for six years. And then, when I met her a month ago, it all rushed over me. Try and understand, Bet. You're my best friend; you're the only person that ever loved me. "

"When you're good I love you," she said.

"Don't worry. It's over. She loves her husband; she just came to New York with me because she's got some spite against him. She follows me a certain distance just like she always has, and then... Anyhow, I'm not going to see her any more. Now go to bed, Bet. I want to play for a while."

He was on his feet when she stopped him.

"You're not to touch the piano tonight."

"Oh, I forgot about Josie," he said remorsefully. "Well, I'll drink a bottle of beer and then I'll come to bed."

He came close and put his arm around her.

"Dear Bet, nothing could ever interfere with us."

"You're a bad boy, Teddy," she said. "I wouldn't ever be so bad to you."

"How do you know, Bet? How do you know what you'd do?"

He smoothed down her plain brown hair, knowing for the thousandth time that she had none of the world's dark magic for him, and that he couldn't live without her for six consecutive hours. "Dear Bet," he whispered. "Dear Bet."

3

T HE OLDHORNES WERE VISITING. In the last four years, since Stuart had terminated his bondage to Gus Myers, they had become visiting people. The children visited Grandmother Van Beck during the winter and attended school in New York. Stuart and Helen visited friends in Asheville, Aiken and Palm Beach, and in the summer usually occupied a small cottage on someone's Long Island estate. "My dear, it's just standing there empty. I wouldn't dream of accepting any rent. You'll be doing us a favour by occupying it."

Usually, they were; they gave out a great deal of themselves in that eternal willingness and enthusiasm which makes a successful guest – it became their profession. Moving through a world that was growing rich with the war in Europe, Stuart had somewhere lost his way. Twice playing brilliant golf in the national amateur, he accepted a job as professional at a club which his father had helped to found. He was restless and unhappy.

This weekend they were visiting a pupil of his. As a consequence of a mixed foursome, the Oldhornes went upstairs to dress for dinner surcharged with the unpleasant accumulation of many unsatisfactory months. In the afternoon, Stuart had played with their hostess and Helen with another man – a situation which Stuart always dreaded, because it forced him into competition with Helen. He had actually tried to miss that putt on the eighteenth – to just miss it. But the ball dropped in the cup. Helen went through the superficial motions of a good loser, but she devoted herself pointedly to her partner for the rest of the afternoon.

Their expressions still counterfeited amusement as they entered their room.

When the door closed, Helen's pleasant expression faded and she walked towards the dressing table as though her own reflection was the only decent company with which to foregather. Stuart watched her, frowning.

"I know why you're in a rotten humour," he said, "though I don't believe you know yourself."

"I'm not in a rotten humour," Helen responded in a clipped voice.

"You are; and I know the real reason – the one you don't know. It's because I holed that putt this afternoon."

She turned slowly, incredulously, from the mirror.

"Oh, so I have a new fault! I've suddenly become, of all things, a poor sport!"

"It's not like you to be a poor sport," he admitted, "but otherwise why all this interest in other men, and why do you look at me as if I'm... well, slightly gamy?"

"I'm not aware of it."

"I am." He was aware, too, that there was always some man in their life now – some man of power and money who paid court to Helen and gave her the sense of solidity which he failed to provide. He had no cause to be jealous of any particular man, but the pressure of many was irritating. It annoyed him that, on so slight a grievance, Helen should remind him by her actions that he no longer filled her entire life.

"If Anne can get any satisfaction out of winning, she's welcome to it," said Helen suddenly.

"Isn't that rather petty? She isn't in your class; she won't qualify for the third flight in Boston."

Feeling herself in the wrong, she changed her tone.

"Oh, that isn't it," she broke out. "I just keep wishing you and I could play together like we used to. And now you have to play with dubs, and get their wretched shots out of traps. Especially" – she hesitated – "especially when you're so unnecessarily gallant."

The faint contempt in her voice, the mock jealousy that covered a growing indifference was apparent to him. There had been a time when, if he danced with another woman, Helen's stricken eyes followed him around the room.

"My gallantry is simply a matter of business," he answered. "Lessons have brought in three hundred a month all summer. How could I go to see you play at Boston next week, except that I'm going to coach other women?"

"And you're going to see me win," announced Helen. "Do you know that?"

"Naturally, I want nothing more," Stuart said automatically. But the unnecessary defiance in her voice repelled him, and he suddenly wondered if he really cared whether she won or not.

At the same moment, Helen's mood changed and for a moment she saw the true situation – that she could play in amateur tournaments and Stuart could not, that the new cups in the rack were all hers now, that he had given up the fiercely competitive sportsmanship that had been the breath of life to him in order to provide necessary money.

"Oh, I'm so sorry for you, Stuart!" There were tears in her eyes. "It seems such a shame that you can't do the things you love, and I can. Perhaps I oughtn't to play this summer."

"Nonsense," he said. "You can't sit home and twirl your thumbs."

She caught at this. "You wouldn't want me to. I can't help being good at sports; you taught me nearly all I know. But I wish I could help you."

"Just try to remember I'm your best friend. Sometimes you act as if we were rivals."

She hesitated, annoyed by the truth of his words and unwilling to concede an inch; but a wave of memories rushed over her, and she thought how brave he was in his eked-out, pieced-together life; she came and threw her arms around him.

"Darling, darling, things are going to be better. You'll see."

Helen won the finals in the tournament at Boston the following week. Following around with the crowd, Stuart was very proud of her. He hoped that instead of feeding her egotism, the actual achievement would make things easier between them. He hated the conflict that had grown out of their wanting the same excellences, the same prizes from life.

Afterwards he pursued her progress towards the clubhouse, amused and a little jealous of the pack that fawned around her. He reached the club among the last, and a steward accosted him. "Professionals are served in the lower grill, please," the man said.

"That's all right. My name's Oldhorne."

He started to walk by, but the man barred his way.

"Sorry, sir. I realize that Mrs Oldhorne's playing in the match, but my orders are to direct the professionals to the lower grill, and I understand you are a professional."

"Why, look here…" Stuart began, wildly angry, and stopped. A group of people were listening. "All right; never mind," he said gruffly, and turned away.

The memory of the experience rankled; it was the determining factor that drove him, some weeks later, to a momentous decision. For a long time he had been playing with the idea of joining the Canadian Air Force, for service in France. He knew that his absence would have little practical bearing on the lives of Helen and the children; happening on some friends who were also full of the restlessness of 1915, the matter was suddenly decided. But he had not counted on the effect upon Helen; her reaction was not so much one of grief or alarm, but as if she had been somehow outwitted.

"But you might have told me!" she wailed. "You leave me dangling; you simply take yourself away without any warning."

Once again Helen saw him as the bright and intolerably blinding hero, and her soul winced before him as it had when they first met. He was a warrior: for him, peace was only the interval between wars, and peace was destroying him. Here was the game of games beckoning him… Without throwing over the whole logic of their lives, there was nothing she could say.

"This is my sort of thing," he said confidently, younger with his excitement. "A few more years of this life and I'd go to pieces, take to drink. I've somehow lost your respect, and I've got to have that, even if I'm far away."

She was proud of him again; she talked to everyone of his impending departure. Then, one September afternoon, she came home from the city, full of the old feeling of comradeship and bursting with news, to find him buried in an utter depression.

"Stuart," she cried, "I've got the…" She broke off. "What's the matter, darling? Is something the matter?"

He looked at her dully. "They turned me down," he said.

"What?"

"My left eye." He laughed bitterly. "Where that dub cracked me with the brassie. I'm nearly blind in it."

"Isn't there anything you can do?"

"Nothing."

"Stuart!" She stared at him aghast. "Stuart, and I was going to tell you! I was saving it for a surprise. Elsa Prentice has organized a Red Cross unit to serve with the French, and I joined it because I thought it would be wonderful if we both went. We've been measured for uniforms and bought our outfits, and we're sailing the end of next week."

4

HELEN WAS A BLURRED FIGURE among other blurred figures on a boat deck, dark against the threat of submarines. When the ship had slid out into the obscure future, Stuart walked eastward along 57th Street. His grief at the severance of many ties was a weight he carried in his body, and he walked slowly, as if adjusting himself to it. To balance this there was a curious sensation of lightness in his mind. For the first time in twelve years he was alone, and the feeling came over him that he was alone for good; knowing Helen and knowing war, he could guess at the experiences she would go through, and he could not form any picture of a renewed life together afterwards. He was discarded; she had proved the stronger at last. It seemed very strange and sad that his marriage should have such an ending.

He came to Carnegie Hall, dark after a concert, and his eye caught the name of Theodore Van Beck, large on the posted bills. As he stared at it, a green door opened in the side of the building and a group of people in evening dress came out. Stuart and Teddy were face to face before they recognized each other.

"Hello, there!" Teddy cried cordially. "Did Helen sail?"

"Just now."

"I met her on the street yesterday and she told me. I wanted you both to come to my concert. Well, she's quite a heroine, going off like that… Have you met my wife?"

Stuart and Betty smiled at each other.

"We've met."

"And I didn't know it," protested Teddy. "Women need watching when they get towards their dotage… Look here, Stuart; we're having a few people up to the apartment. No heavy music or anything. Just supper and a few debutantes to tell me I was divine.

It will do you good to come. I imagine you're missing Helen like the devil."

"I don't think I—"

"Come along. They'll tell you you're divine too."

Realizing that the invitation was inspired by kindliness, Stuart accepted. It was the sort of gathering he had seldom attended, and he was surprised to meet so many people he knew. Teddy played the lion in a manner at once assertive and sceptical. Stuart listened as he enlarged to Mrs Cassius Ruthven on one of his favourite themes:

"People tried to make marriages cooperative and they've ended by becoming competitive. Impossible situation. Smart men will get to fight shy of ornamental women. A man ought to marry somebody who'll be grateful, like Betty here."

"Now don't talk so much, Theodore Van Beck," Betty interrupted. "Since you're such a fine musician, you'd do well to express yourself with music instead of rash words."

"I don't agree with your husband," said Mrs Ruthven. "English girls hunt with their men and play politics with them on absolutely equal terms, and it tends to draw them together."

"It does not," insisted Teddy. "That's why English society is the most disorganized in the world. Betty and I are happy because we haven't any qualities in common at all."

His exuberance grated on Stuart, and the success that flowed from him swung his mind back to the failure of his own life. He could not know that his life was not destined to be a failure. He could not read the fine story that three years later would be carved proud above his soldier's grave, or know that his restless body, which never spared itself in sport or danger, was destined to give him one last proud gallop at the end.

"They turned me down," he was saying to Mrs Ruthven. "I'll have to stick to Squadron A, unless we get drawn in."

"So Helen's gone." Mrs Ruthven looked at him, reminiscing. "I'll never forget your wedding. You were both so handsome, so ideally suited to each other. Everybody spoke of it."

Stuart remembered; for the moment it seemed that he had little else that it was fun to remember.

"Yes," he agreed, nodding his head thoughtfully, "I suppose we were a handsome pair."

Crazy Sunday

1

IT WAS SUNDAY – NOT A DAY, but rather a gap between two other days. Behind, for all of them, lay sets and sequences, the long waits under the crane that swung the microphone, the hundred miles a day by automobiles to and fro across a county, the struggles of rival ingenuities in the conference rooms, the ceaseless compromise, the clash and strain of many personalities fighting for their lives. And now Sunday, with individual life starting up again, with a glow kindling in eyes that had been glazed with monotony the afternoon before. Slowly, as the hours waned, they came awake like Puppenfeen* in a toy shop: an intense colloquy in a corner, lovers disappearing to neck in a hall. And the feeling of: "Hurry, it's not too late, but for God's sake hurry before the blessed forty hours of leisure are over."

Joel Coles was writing continuity. He was twenty-eight and not yet broken by Hollywood. He had had what were considered nice assignments since his arrival six months before and he submitted his scenes and sequences with enthusiasm. He referred to himself modestly as a hack, but really did not think of it that way. His mother had been a successful actress; Joel had spent his childhood between London and New York trying to separate the real from the unreal, or at least to keep one guess ahead. He was a handsome man with the pleasant cow-brown eyes that in 1913 had gazed out at Broadway audiences from his mother's face.

When the invitation came it made him sure that he was getting somewhere. Ordinarily he did not go out on Sundays but stayed sober and took work home with him. Recently they had given him a Eugene O'Neill play destined for a very important lady indeed. Everything he had done so far had pleased Miles Calman, and Miles Calman was the only director on the lot who did not work under a supervisor and was responsible to the money men alone. Everything was clicking into place in Joel's career. ("This is Mr Calman's secretary. Will you come to tea from four to six Sunday – he lives in Beverly Hills, number...")

Joel was flattered. It would be a party out of the top drawer. It was a tribute to himself as a young man of promise. The Marion Davies* crowd, the high hats, the big currency numbers, perhaps even Dietrich and Garbo and the Marquise, people who were not seen everywhere, would probably be at Calman's.

"I won't take anything to drink," he assured himself. Calman was audibly tired of rummies, and thought it was a pity the industry could not get along without them.

Joel agreed that writers drank too much – he did himself, but he wouldn't this afternoon. He wished Miles would be within hearing when the cocktails were passed to hear his succinct, unobtrusive "No, thank you".

Miles Calman's house was built for great emotional moments – there was an air of listening, as if the far silences of its vistas hid an audience, but this afternoon it was thronged, as though people had been bidden rather than asked. Joel noted with pride that only two other writers from the studio were in the crowd, an ennobled Limey and, somewhat to his surprise, Nat Keogh, who had evoked Calman's impatient comment on drunks.

Stella Calman (Stella Walker, of course) did not move on to her other guests after she spoke to Joel. She lingered – she looked at him with the sort of beautiful look that demands some sort of acknowledgement, and Joel drew quickly on the dramatic adequacy inherited from his mother:

"Well, you look about sixteen! Where's your kiddy car?"

She was visibly pleased; she lingered. He felt that he should say something more, something confident and easy – he had first met her when she was struggling for bits in New York. At the moment a tray slid up and Stella put a cocktail glass into his hand.

"Everybody's afraid, aren't they?" he said, looking at it absently. "Everybody watches for everybody else's blunders, or tries to make sure they're with people that'll do them credit. Of course that's not true in your house," he covered himself hastily. "I just meant generally in Hollywood."

Stella agreed. She presented several people to Joel as if he were important. Reassuring himself that Miles was at the other side of the room, Joel drank the cocktail.

"So you have a baby?" he said. "That's the time to look out. After a pretty woman has had her first child, she's very vulnerable, because she wants to be reassured about her own charm. She's got to have some new man's unqualified devotion to prove to herself she hasn't lost anything."

"I never get anybody's unqualified devotion," Stella said rather resentfully.

"They're afraid of your husband."

"You think that's it?" She wrinkled her brow over the idea; then the conversation was interrupted at the exact moment Joel would have chosen.

Her attentions had given him confidence. Not for him to join safe groups, to slink to refuge under the wings of such acquaintances as he saw about the room. He walked to the window and looked out towards the Pacific, colourless under its sluggish sunset. It was good here – the American Riviera and all that, if there were ever time to enjoy it. The handsome, well-dressed people in the room, the lovely girls and the... well, the lovely girls. You couldn't have everything.

He saw Stella's fresh boyish face, with the tired eyelid that always drooped a little over one eye, moving about among her guests, and he wanted to sit with her and talk a long time as if she were a girl instead of a name; he followed her to see if she paid anyone as much attention as she had paid him. He took another cocktail – not because he needed confidence, but because she had given him so much of it. Then he sat down beside the director's mother.

"Your son's gotten to be a legend, Mrs Calman – Oracle and a Man of Destiny and all that. Personally, I'm against him, but I'm in a minority. What do you think of him? Are you impressed? Are you surprised how far he's gone?"

"No, I'm not surprised," she said calmly. "We always expected a lot from Miles."

"Well now, that's unusual," remarked Joel. "I always think all mothers are like Napoleon's mother. My mother didn't want me to have anything to do with the entertainment business. She wanted me to go to West Point and be safe."

"We always had every confidence in Miles…"

He stood by the built-in bar of the dining room with the good-humoured, heavy-drinking, highly paid Nat Keogh.

"…I made a hundred grand during the year and lost forty grand gambling, so now I've hired a manager."

"You mean an agent," suggested Joel.

"No, I've got that too. I mean a manager. I make over everything to my wife and then he and my wife get together and hand me out the money. I pay him five thousand a year to hand me out my money."

"You mean your agent."

"No, I mean my manager, and I'm not the only one – a lot of other irresponsible people have him."

"Well, if you're irresponsible why are you responsible enough to hire a manager?"

"I'm just irresponsible about gambling. Look here—"

A singer performed; Joel and Nat went forward with the others to listen.

2

THE SINGING REACHED JOEL VAGUELY; he felt happy and friendly towards all the people gathered there, people of bravery and industry, superior to a bourgeoisie that outdid them in ignorance and loose living, risen to a position of the highest prominence in a nation that for a decade had wanted only to be entertained. He liked them – he loved them. Great waves of good feeling flowed through him.

As the singer finished his number and there was a drift towards the hostess to say goodbye, Joel had an idea. He would give them 'Building It up', his own composition. It was his only parlour trick, it had amused several parties and it might please Stella Walker. Possessed by the hunch, his blood throbbing with the scarlet corpuscles of exhibitionism, he sought her.

"Of course," she cried. "Please! Do you need anything?"

"Someone has to be the secretary that I'm supposed to be dictating to."

"I'll be her."

As the word spread, the guests in the hall, already putting on their coats to leave, drifted back, and Joel faced the eyes of many strangers. He had a dim foreboding, realizing that the man who had just performed was a famous radio entertainer. Then someone said "Sh!" and he was alone with Stella, the centre of a sinister Indian-like half-circle. Stella smiled up at him expectantly – he began.

His burlesque was based upon the cultural limitations of Mr Dave Silverstein, an independent producer; Silverstein was presumed to be dictating a letter outlining a treatment of a story he had bought.

"...a story of divorce, the younger generators and the Foreign Legion," he heard his voice saying, with intonations of Mr Silverstein. "But we got to build it up, see?"

A sharp pang of doubt struck through him. The faces surrounding him in the gently moulded light were intent and curious, but there was no ghost of a smile anywhere; directly in front the Great Lover of the screen glared at him with an eye as keen as the eye of a potato. Only Stella Walker looked up at him with a radiant, never faltering smile.

"If we make him a Menjou type, then we get a sort of Michael Arlen,* only with a Honolulu atmosphere."

Still not a ripple in front, but in the rear a rustling, a perceptible shift towards the left, towards the front door.

"...then she says she feels the sex appil for him and he burns out and says, 'Oh go on destroy yourself'..."

At some point he heard Nat Keogh snicker and here and there were a few encouraging faces, but as he finished he had the sickening realization that he had made a fool of himself in view of an important section of the picture world, upon whose favour depended his career.

For a moment he existed in the midst of a confused silence, broken by a general trek for the door. He felt the undercurrent of derision that rolled through the gossip; then – all this was in the space of ten seconds – the Great Lover, his eye hard and empty as the eye of a needle, shouted "Boo! Boo!", voicing in an overtone what he felt was the mood of the crowd. It was the resentment of the professional towards the amateur, of the community towards the stranger, the thumbs-down of the clan.

Only Stella Walker was still standing near and thanking him as if he had been an unparalleled success, as if it hadn't occurred to her that anyone hadn't liked it. As Nat Keogh helped him into his overcoat, a great wave of self-disgust swept over him and he clung desperately to his rule of never betraying an inferior emotion until he no longer felt it.

"I was a flop," he said lightly, to Stella. "Never mind, it's a good number when appreciated. Thanks for your cooperation."

The smile did not leave her face – he bowed rather drunkenly, and Nat drew him towards the door...

The arrival of his breakfast awakened him into a broken and ruined world. Yesterday he was himself, a point of fire against an industry, today he felt that he was pitted under an enormous disadvantage, against those faces, against individual contempt and collective sneer. Worse than that, to Miles Calman he was become one of those rummies, stripped of dignity, whom Calman regretted he was compelled to use. To Stella Walker, on whom he had forced a martyrdom to preserve the courtesy of her house – her opinion he did not dare to guess. His gastric juices ceased to flow and he set his poached eggs back on the telephone table. He wrote:

Dear Miles: you can imagine my profound self-disgust. I confess to a taint of exhibitionism, but at six o'clock in the afternoon, in broad daylight! Good God! My apologies to your wife.

Yours ever,

Joel Coles

Joel emerged from his office on the lot only to slink like a malefactor to the tobacco store. So suspicious was his manner that one of the studio police asked to see his admission card. He had decided to eat lunch when Nat Keogh, confident and cheerful, overtook him. "What do you mean you're in permanent retirement? What if that Three-Piece Suit did boo you?"

"Why, listen," he continued, drawing Joel into the studio restaurant. "The night of one of his premieres at Grauman's, Joe Squires kicked his tail while he was bowing to the crowd. The ham said Joe'd hear from him later, but when Joe called him up at eight o'clock next day and said, 'I thought I was going to hear from you,' he hung up the phone."

The preposterous story cheered Joel, and he found a gloomy consolation in staring at the group at the next table – the sad, lovely Siamese twins, the mean dwarfs, the proud giant from the circus picture. But looking beyond at the yellow-stained faces of pretty women, their eyes all melancholy and startling with mascara, their ball gowns garish in full day, he saw a group who had been at Calman's and winced.

"Never again," he exclaimed aloud, "absolutely my last social appearance in Hollywood!"

The following morning a telegram was waiting for him at his office:

YOU WERE ONE OF THE MOST AGREEABLE PEOPLE AT OUR PARTY.
EXPECT YOU AT MY SISTER JUNE'S BUFFET SUPPER NEXT SUNDAY.
STELLA WALKER CALMAN

The blood rushed fast through his veins for a feverish minute. Incredulously he read the telegram over.

"Well, that's the sweetest thing I ever heard of in my life!"

3

CRAZY SUNDAY AGAIN. Joel slept until eleven, then he read a newspaper to catch up with the past week. He lunched in his room on trout, avocado salad and a pint of California wine. Dressing for the tea, he selected a pin-check suit, a blue shirt, a burnt-orange tie. There were dark circles of fatigue under his eyes. In his second-hand car he drove to the Riviera apartments. As he was introducing himself to Stella's sister, Miles and Stella arrived in riding clothes – they had been quarrelling fiercely most of the afternoon on all the dirt roads back of Beverly Hills.

Miles Calman, tall, nervous, with a desperate humour and the unhappiest eyes Joel ever saw, was an artist from the top of his curiously shaped head to his niggerish feet. Upon these last he stood firmly – he had never made a cheap picture, though he had sometimes paid heavily for the luxury of making experimental flops. In spite of his excellent company, one could not be with him long without realizing that he was not a well man.

From the moment of their entrance, Joel's day bound itself up inextricably with theirs. As he joined the group around them, Stella turned away from it with an impatient little tongue click – and Miles Calman said to the man who happened to be next to him:

"Go easy on Eva Goebel. There's hell to pay about her at home." Miles turned to Joel: "I'm sorry I missed you at the office yesterday. I spent the afternoon at the analyst's."

"You being psychoanalysed?"

"I have been for months. First I went for claustrophobia, now I'm trying to get my whole life cleared up. They say it'll take over a year."

"There's nothing the matter with your wife," Joel assured him.

"Oh, no? Well, Stella seems to think so. Ask anybody – they can all tell you about it," he said bitterly.

A girl perched herself on the arm of Miles's chair; Joel crossed to Stella, who stood disconsolately by the fire.

"Thank you for your telegram," he said. "It was darn sweet. I can't imagine anybody as good-looking as you are being so good-humoured."

She was a little lovelier than he had ever seen her and perhaps the unstinted admiration in his eyes prompted her to unload on him – it did not take long, for she was obviously at the emotional bursting point.

"...and Miles has been carrying on this thing for two years, and I never knew. Why, she was one of my best friends, always in the house. Finally, when people began to come to me, Miles had to admit it."

She sat down vehemently on the arm of Joel's chair. Her riding breeches were the colour of the chair, and Joel saw that the mass of her hair was made up of some strands of red gold and some of pale gold, so that it could not be dyed, and that she had on no make-up. She was that good-looking...

Still quivering with the shock of her discovery, Stella found unbearable the spectacle of a new girl hovering over Miles; she led Joel into a bedroom and, seated at either end of a big bed, they went on talking. People on their way to the washroom glanced in and made wisecracks, but Stella, emptying out her story, paid no attention. After a while Miles stuck his head in the door and said, "There's no use trying to explain something to Joel in half an hour that I don't understand myself and the psychoanalyst says will take a whole year to understand."

She talked on as if Miles were not there. She loved Miles, she said – under considerable difficulties she had always been faithful to him.

"The psychoanalyst told Miles that he had a mother complex. In his first marriage he transferred his mother complex to his wife, you see – and then his sex turned to me. But when we married the thing repeated itself – he transferred his mother complex to me and all his libido turned towards this other woman."

Joel knew that this probably wasn't gibberish – yet it sounded like gibberish. He knew Eva Goebel; she was a motherly person, older and probably wiser than Stella, who was a golden child.

Miles now suggested impatiently that Joel come back with them, since Stella had so much to say, so they drove out to the mansion in Beverly Hills. Under the high ceilings the situation seemed more dignified and tragic. It was an eerie bright night with the dark very clear outside of all the windows and Stella all rose-gold raging and crying around the room. Joel did not quite believe in picture actresses' grief. They have other preoccupations – they are beautiful rose-gold figures blown full of life by writers and directors, and after hours they sit around and talk in whispers and giggle innuendoes, and the ends of many adventures flow through them.

Sometimes he pretended to listen and instead thought how well she was got up – sleek breeches with a matched set of legs in them, an Italian-coloured sweater with a little high neck, and a short brown chamois coat. He couldn't decide whether she was an imitation of an English lady or an English lady was an imitation of her. She hovered somewhere between the realest of realities and the most blatant of impersonations.

"Miles is so jealous of me that he questions everything I do," she cried scornfully. "When I was in New York I wrote him that I'd been to the theatre with Eddie Baker. Miles was so jealous he phoned me ten times in one day."

"I was wild." Miles snuffled sharply, a habit he had in times of stress. "The analyst couldn't get any results for a week."

Stella shook her head despairingly. "Did you expect me just to sit in the hotel for three weeks?"

"I don't expect anything. I admit that I'm jealous. I try not to be. I worked on that with Doctor Bridgebane, but it didn't do any good. I was jealous of Joel this afternoon when you sat on the arm of his chair."

"You were?" She started up. "You were! Wasn't there somebody on the arm of your chair? And did you speak to me for two hours?"

"You were telling your troubles to Joel in the bedroom."

"When I think that that woman" – she seemed to believe that to omit Eva Goebel's name would be to lessen her reality – "used to come here—"

"All right... all right," said Miles wearily. "I've admitted everything and I feel as bad about it as you do." Turning to Joel he began talking about pictures, while Stella moved restlessly along the far walls, her hands in her breeches pockets.

"They've treated Miles terribly," she said, coming suddenly back into the conversation as if they'd never discussed her personal affairs. "Dear, tell him about old Beltzer trying to change your picture."

As she stood hovering protectively over Miles, her eyes flashing with indignation in his behalf, Joel realized that he was in love with her. Stifled with excitement he got up to say goodnight.

With Monday the week resumed its workaday rhythm, in sharp contrast to the theoretical discussions, the gossip and scandal of Sunday; there was the endless detail of script revision – "Instead of a lousy dissolve, we can leave her voice on the soundtrack and cut to a medium shot of the taxi from Bell's angle or we can simply pull the camera back to include the station, hold it a minute and then pan to the row of taxis" – by Monday afternoon Joel had again forgotten that people whose business was to provide entertainment were ever privileged to be entertained. In the evening he phoned Miles's house. He asked for Miles but Stella came to the phone.

"Do things seem better?"

"Not particularly. What are you doing next Saturday evening?"

"Nothing."

"The Perrys are giving a dinner and theatre party and Miles won't be here – he's flying to South Bend to see the Notre Dame-California game, I thought you might go with me in his place."

After a long moment Joel said, "Why... surely. If there's a conference I can't make dinner, but I can get to the theatre."

"Then I'll say we can come."

Joel walked his office. In view of the strained relations of the Calmans, would Miles be pleased, or did she intend that Miles shouldn't know of it? That would be out of the question – if Miles didn't mention it, Joel would. But it was an hour or more before he could get down to work again.

Wednesday there was a four-hour wrangle in a conference room crowded with planets and nebulae of cigarette smoke. Three men and a woman paced the carpet in turn, suggesting or condemning, speaking sharply or persuasively, confidently or despairingly. At the end Joel lingered to talk to Miles.

The man was tired – not with the exaltation of fatigue, but life-tired, with his lids sagging and his beard prominent over the blue shadows near his mouth.

"I hear you're flying to the Notre Dame game."

Miles looked beyond him and shook his head.

"I've given up the idea."

"Why?"

"On account of you." Still he did not look at Joel.

"What the hell, Miles?"

"That's why I've given it up." He broke into a perfunctory laugh at himself. "I can't tell what Stella might do just out of spite – she's invited you to take her to the Perrys', hasn't she? I wouldn't enjoy the game."

The fine instinct that moved swiftly and confidently on the set muddled so weakly and helplessly through his personal life.

"Look, Miles," Joel said frowning. "I've never made any passes whatsoever at Stella. If you're really seriously cancelling your trip on account of me, I won't go to the Perrys' with her. I won't see her. You can trust me absolutely."

Miles looked at him, carefully now.

"Maybe." He shrugged his shoulders. "Anyhow there'd just be somebody else. I wouldn't have any fun."

"You don't seem to have much confidence in Stella. She told me she'd always been true to you."

"Maybe she has." In the last few minutes, several more muscles had sagged around Miles's mouth. "But how can I ask anything of her after what's happened? How can I expect her…" He broke off and his face grew harder as he said, "I'll tell you one thing: right or wrong and no matter what I've done, if I ever had anything on her I'd divorce her. I can't have my pride hurt – that would be the last straw."

His tone annoyed Joel, but he said:

"Hasn't she calmed down about the Eva Goebel thing?"

"No." Miles snuffled pessimistically. "I can't get over it either."

"I thought it was finished."

"I'm trying not to see Eva again, but you know it isn't easy just to drop something like that – it isn't some girl I kissed last night in a taxi! The psychoanalyst says—"

"I know," Joel interrupted. "Stella told me." This was depressing. "Well, as far as I'm concerned, if you go to the game I won't see Stella. And I'm sure Stella has nothing on her conscience about anybody."

"Maybe not," Miles repeated listlessly. "Anyhow I'll stay and take her to the party. Say," he said suddenly, "I wish you'd come too. I've got to have somebody sympathetic to talk to. That's the trouble – I've influenced Stella in everything. Especially I've influenced her so that she likes all the men I like – it's very difficult."

"It must be," Joel agreed.

4

J OEL COULD NOT GET TO THE DINNER. Self-conscious in his silk hat against the unemployment, he waited for the others in front of the Hollywood Theatre and watched the evening parade: obscure replicas of bright, particular picture stars, spavined men in polo coats, a stomping dervish with the beard and staff of an apostle, a pair of chic Filipinos in collegiate clothes, reminder that this comer of the Republic opened to the seven seas, a long fantastic carnival of young shouts which proved to be a fraternity initiation. The line split to pass two smart limousines that stopped at the kerb.

There she was, in a dress like ice water, made in a thousand pale-blue pieces, with icicles trickling at the throat. He started forward.

"So you like my dress?"

"Where's Miles?"

"He flew to the game after all. He left yesterday morning – at least I think…" She broke off. "I just got a telegram from South Bend saying that he's starting back. I forgot – you know all these people?"

The party of eight moved into the theatre.

Miles had gone after all and Joel wondered if he should have come. But during the performance, with Stella a profile under the pure grain of light hair, he thought no more about Miles. Once he turned and looked at her and she looked back at him, smiling and meeting his eyes for as long as he wanted. Between the acts they smoked in the lobby and she whispered:

"They're all going to the opening of Jack Johnson's night club – I don't want to go, do you?"

"Do we have to?"

"I suppose not." She hesitated. "I'd like to talk to you. I suppose we could go to our house – if I were only sure…"

Again she hesitated and Joel asked:

"Sure of what?"

"Sure that... oh, I'm haywire I know, but how can I be sure Miles went to the game?"

"You mean you think he's with Eva Goebel?"

"No, not so much that – but supposing he was here watching everything I do. You know Miles does odd things sometimes. Once he wanted a man with a long beard to drink tea with him and he sent down to the casting agency for one, and drank tea with him all afternoon."

"That's different. He sent you a wire from South Bend – that proves he's at the game."

After the play they said goodnight to the others at the kerb and were answered by looks of amusement. They slid off along the golden garish thoroughfare through the crowd that had gathered around Stella.

"You see, he could arrange the telegrams," Stella said, "very easily."

That was true. And with the idea that perhaps her uneasiness was justified, Joel grew angry: if Miles had trained a camera on them he felt no obligations towards Miles. Aloud he said:

"That's nonsense."

There were Christmas trees already in the shop windows and the full moon over the boulevard was only a prop, as scenic as the giant boudoir lamps of the corners. On into the dark foliage of Beverly Hills that flamed as eucalyptus by day, Joel saw only the flash of a white face under his own, the arc of her shoulder. She pulled away suddenly and looked up at him.

"Your eyes are like your mother's," she said. "I used to have a scrapbook full of pictures of her."

"Your eyes are like your own and not a bit like any other eyes," he answered.

Something made Joel look out into the grounds as they went into the house, as if Miles were lurking in the shrubbery. A telegram waited on the hall table. She read aloud:

CHICAGO.

HOME TOMORROW NIGHT. THINKING OF YOU. LOVE.

MILES.

"You see," she said, throwing the slip back on the table, "he could easily have faked that." She asked the butler for drinks and sandwiches and ran upstairs, while Joel walked into the empty reception rooms. Strolling about he wandered to the piano, where he had stood in disgrace two Sundays before.

"Then we could put over," he said aloud, "a story of divorce, the younger generators and the Foreign Legion."

His thoughts jumped to another telegram.

"You were one of the most agreeable people at our party…"

An idea occurred to him. If Stella's telegram had been purely a gesture of courtesy, then it was likely that Miles had inspired it, for it was Miles who had invited him. Probably Miles had said:

"Send him a wire – he's miserable – he thinks he's queered himself."

It fitted in with: "I've influenced Stella in everything. Especially I've influenced her so that she likes all the men I like." A woman would do a thing like that because she felt sympathetic – only a man would do it because he felt responsible.

When Stella came back into the room he took both her hands.

"I have a strange feeling that I'm a sort of pawn in a spite game you're playing against Miles," he said.

"Help yourself to a drink."

"And the odd thing is that I'm in love with you anyhow."

The telephone rang and she freed herself to answer it.

"Another wire from Miles," she announced. "He dropped it, or it says he dropped it, from the airplane at Kansas City."

"I suppose he asked to be remembered to me."

"No, he just said he loved me. I believe he does. He's so very weak."

"Come sit beside me," Joel urged her.

146

It was early. And it was still a few minutes short of midnight a half-hour later, when Joel walked to the cold hearth and said tersely:

"Meaning that you haven't any curiosity about me?"

"Not at all. You attract me a lot and you know it. The point is that I suppose I really do love Miles."

"Obviously."

"And tonight I feel uneasy about everything."

He wasn't angry – he was even faintly relieved that a possible entanglement was avoided. Still, as he looked at her, the warmth and softness of her body thawing her cold blue costume, he knew she was one of the things he would always regret.

"I've got to go," he said. "I'll phone a taxi."

"Nonsense – there's a chauffeur on duty."

He winced at her readiness to have him go and, seeing this, she kissed him lightly and said, "You're sweet, Joel." Then suddenly three things happened: he took down his drink at a gulp, the phone rang loud through the house and a clock in the hall struck in trumpet notes.

Nine – ten – eleven – twelve…

5

I T WAS SUNDAY AGAIN. Joel realized that he had come to the theatre this evening with the work of the week still hanging about him like cerements. He had made love to Stella as he might attack some matter to be cleaned up hurriedly before the day's end. But this was Sunday – the lovely, lazy perspective of the next twenty-four hours unrolled before him – every minute was something to be approached with lulling indirection, every moment held the germ of innumerable possibilities. Nothing was impossible – everything was just beginning. He poured himself another drink.

With a sharp moan, Stella slipped forward inertly by the telephone. Joel picked her up and laid her on the sofa. He squirted soda water on a handkerchief and slapped it over her face. The telephone mouthpiece was still grinding and he put it to his ear.

"…the plane fell just this side of Kansas City. The body of Miles Calman has been identified and—"

He hung up the receiver.

"Lie still," he said, stalling, as Stella opened her eyes.

"Oh, what's happened?" she whispered. "Call them back. Oh, what's happened?"

"I'll call them right away. What's your doctor's name?"

"Did they say Miles was dead?"

"Lie quiet – is there a servant still up?"

"Hold me – I'm frightened."

He put his arm around her.

"I want the name of your doctor," he said sternly. "It may be a mistake, but I want someone here."

"It's Doctor… Oh, God, is Miles dead?"

Joel ran upstairs and searched through strange medicine cabinets for spirits of ammonia. When he came down Stella cried:

"He isn't dead – I know he isn't. This is part of his scheme. He's torturing me. I know he's alive. I can feel he's alive."

"I want to get hold of some close friend of yours, Stella. You can't stay here alone tonight."

"Oh, no," she cried. "I can't see anybody. You stay. I haven't got any friend." She got up, tears streaming down her face. "Oh, Miles is my only friend. He's not dead – he can't be dead. I'm going there right away and see. Get a train. You'll have to come with me."

"You can't. There's nothing to do tonight. I want you to tell me the name of some woman I can call: Lois? Joan? Carmel? Isn't there somebody?"

Stella stared at him blindly.

"Eva Goebel was my best friend," she said.

Joel thought of Miles, his sad and desperate face in the office two days before. In the awful silence of his death all was clear about him. He was the only American-born director with both an interesting temperament and an artistic conscience. Meshed in an industry, he had paid with his ruined nerves for having no resilience, no healthy cynicism, no refuge – only a pitiful and precarious escape.

There was a sound at the outer door – it opened suddenly, and there were footsteps in the hall.

"Miles!" Stella screamed. "Is it you, Miles? Oh, it's Miles."

A telegraph boy appeared in the doorway.

"I couldn't find the bell. I heard you talking inside."

The telegram was a duplicate of the one that had been phoned. While Stella read it over and over, as though it were a black lie, Joel telephoned. It was still early and he had difficulty getting anyone; when finally he succeeded in finding some friends, he made Stella take a stiff drink.

"You'll stay here, Joel," she whispered, as though she were half asleep. "You won't go away. Miles liked you – he said you…" She shivered violently. "Oh, my God, you don't know how alone I feel." Her eyes closed, "Put your arms around me. Miles had a suit like that." She started bolt upright. "Think of what he must have felt. He was afraid of almost everything, anyhow."

She shook her head dazedly. Suddenly she seized Joel's face and held it close to hers.

"You won't go. You like me – you love me, don't you? Don't call up anybody. Tomorrow's time enough. You stay here with me tonight."

He stared at her, at first incredulously, and then with shocked understanding. In her dark groping Stella was trying to keep Miles alive by sustaining a situation in which he had figured – as if Miles's mind could not die so long as the possibilities that had worried him still existed. It was a distraught and tortured effort to stave off the realization that he was dead.

Resolutely Joel went to the phone and called a doctor.

"Don't, oh, don't call anybody!" Stella cried. "Come back here and put your arms around me."

"Is Doctor Bales in?"

"Joel," Stella cried. "I thought I could count on you. Miles liked you. He was jealous of you – Joel, come here."

Ah then – if he betrayed Miles she would be keeping him alive – for if he were really dead how could he be betrayed?

"...has just had a very severe shock. Can you come at once, and get hold of a nurse?"

"Joel!"

Now the doorbell and the telephone began to ring intermittently, and automobiles were stopping in front of the door.

"But you're not going," Stella begged him. "You're going to stay, aren't you?"

"No," he answered. "But I'll be back, if you need me."

Standing on the steps of the house, which now hummed and palpitated with the life that flutters around death like protective leaves, he began to sob a little in his throat.

"Everything he touched he did something magical to," he thought. "He even brought that little gamin alive and made her a sort of masterpiece."

And then:

"What a hell of a hole he leaves in this damn wilderness – already!"

And then with a certain bitterness, "Oh, yes, I'll be back – I'll be back!"

One Intern

1

TRADITIONALLY, THE COCCIDIAN CLUB SHOW is given on the hottest night of spring, and that year was no exception. Two hundred doctors and students sweltered in the reception rooms of the old narrow house and another two hundred students pressed in at the doors, effectually sealing out any breezes from the Maryland night. The entertainment reached these latter clients only dimly, but refreshment was relayed back to them by a busy bucket brigade. Down cellar, the janitor made his annual guess that the sagging floors would hold up one more time.

Bill Tulliver was the coolest man in the hall. For no special reason he wore a light tunic and carried a crook during the only number in which he took part, the rendition of the witty, scurrilous and interminable song which described the failings and eccentricities of the medical faculty. He sat in comparative comfort on the platform and looked out over the hot sea of faces. The most important doctors were in front – Doctor Ruff, the ophthalmologist; Doctor Lane, the brain surgeon; Doctor Georgi, the stomach specialist; Doctor Barnett, the alchemist of internal medicine; and on the end of the row, with his saint-like face undisturbed by the rivulets of perspiration that poured down the long dome of his head, Doctor Norton, the diagnostician.

Like most young men who had sat under Norton, Bill Tulliver followed him with the intuition of the belly, but with a difference. He knelt to him selfishly as a sort of great giver of life. He wanted less to win his approval than to compel it. Engrossed in his own career, which would begin in earnest when he entered the hospital as an intern in July, his whole life was pointed towards the day when his own guess would be right and Doctor Norton's would be wrong. In that moment he would emancipate himself – he need not base himself on the adding machine-calculating machine-probability machine-St Francis of Assisi machine any longer.

Bill Tulliver had not arrived unprovoked at this pitch of egotism. He was the fifth in an unbroken series of Doctor William Tullivers who had practised with distinction in the city. His father died last winter; it was not unnatural that even from the womb of school this last scion of a medical tradition should clamour for "self-expression".

The faculty song, immemorially popular, went on and on. There was a verse about the sanguinary Doctor Lane, about the new names Doctor Brune made up for the new diseases he invented, about the personal idiosyncrasies of Doctor Schwartze and the domestic embroilments of Doctor Gillespie. Doctor Norton, as one of the most popular men on the staff, got off easy. There were some new verses – several that Bill had written himself:

> "Herpes Zigler, sad and tired,
>   Will flunk you out or kill ya,
> If you forget Alfonso wired
>   For dope on haemophilia.
> *Bum*tiddy-bum-bum,
> Tiddy-bum-bum.
> Three thousand years ago,
> Three thousand years ago."

He watched Doctor Zigler and saw the wince that puckered up under the laugh. Bill wondered how soon there would be a verse about him, Bill Tulliver, and he tentatively composed one as the chorus thundered on.

After the show the older men departed, the floors were sloshed with beer and the traditional rough house usurped the evening. But Bill had fallen solemn and, donning his linen suit, he watched for ten minutes and then left the hot hall. There was a group on the front steps, breathing the sparse air, and another group singing around the lamp-post at the corner. Across the street arose the great bulk of the hospital about which his life revolved. Between the Michael's Clinic and the Ward's Dispensary arose a round full moon.

The girl – she was hurrying – reached the loiterers at the lamp-post at the same moment as Bill. She wore a dark dress and a dark, flopping hat, but Bill got an impression that there was a gaiety of cut, if not of colour, about her clothes. The whole thing happened in less than a minute; the man turning about – Bill saw that he was not a member of the grand confraternity – and was simply hurling himself into her arms, like a child at its mother.

The girl staggered backward with a frightened cry; and everyone in the group acted at once.

"Are you sure you're all right?"

"Oh, yes," she gasped. "I think he just passed out and didn't realize he was grabbing at a girl."

"We'll take him over to the emergency ward and see if he can swallow a stomach pump."

Bill Tulliver found himself walking along beside the girl.

"Are you sure you're all right?"

"Oh, yes." She was still breathing hard; her bosom rose, putting out its eternal promises, as if the breath she had taken in were the last breather left in the world.

"Oh, catch it… oh, catch it and take it… oh, catch it," she sighed. "I realized right away that they were students. I shouldn't have gone by there tonight."

Her hair, dark and drawn back to her ears, brushed her shoulders. She laughed uncontrollably.

"He was so helpless," she said. "Lord knows I've seen men helpless – hundreds of them just helpless – but I'll never forget the expression in his face when he decided to… to lean on me."

Her dark eyes shone with mirth, and Bill saw that she was really self-reliant. He stared at her, and the impression of her beauty grew until, uncommitted by a word, by even a formal introduction, he felt himself going out towards her, watching the turn of her lips and the shifting of her cheeks when she smiled…

All this was in the three or four minutes that he walked beside her; not till afterwards did he realize how profound the impression had been.

As they passed the church-like bulk of the administration building, an open cabriolet slowed down beside them and a man of about thirty-five jumped out. The girl ran towards him.

"Howard!" she cried with excited gaiety. "I was attacked. There were some students in front of the Coccidian Club building—"

The man swung sharply and menacingly towards Bill Tulliver.

"Is this one of them?" he demanded.

"No, no; he's all right."

Simultaneously Bill recognized him – it was Doctor Howard Durfee, brilliant among the younger surgeons, heartbreaker and swashbuckler of the staff.

"You haven't been bothering Miss—"

She stopped him, but not before Bill had answered angrily:

"I don't bother people."

Unappeased, as if Bill were in some way responsible, Doctor Durfee got into his car; the girl got in beside him.

"So long," she said. "And thanks." Her eyes shone at Bill with friendly interest, and then, just before the car shot away, she did something else with them – narrowed them a little and then widened them, recognizing by this sign the uniqueness of their relationship. "I see you," it seemed to say. "You registered. Everything's possible."

With the faint fanfare of a new motor, she vanished back into the spring night.

2

BILL WAS TO ENTER THE HOSPITAL in July with the first contingent of newly created doctors. He passed the intervening months at Martha's Vineyard, swimming and fishing with Schoatze, his classmate, and returned tense with health and enthusiasm to begin his work.

The red square broiled under the Maryland sun. Bill went in through the administration building, where a gigantic Christ gestured in marble pity over the entrance hall. It was by this same portal that Bill's father had entered on his internship thirty years before.

Suddenly Bill was in a condition of shock, his tranquillity was rent asunder, he could not have given a rational account as to why he was where he was. A dark-haired girl with great, luminous eyes had started up from the very shadow of the statue, stared at him just long enough to effect this damage, and then with an explosive "Hello!" vanished into one of the offices.

He was still gazing after her, stricken, haywire, scattered and dissolved – when Doctor Norton hailed him:

"I believe I'm addressing William Tulliver the Fifth…"

Bill was glad to be reminded who he was.

"…looking somewhat interested in Doctor Durfee's girl," continued Norton.

"Is she?" Bill asked sharply. Then: "Oh, howdedo, Doctor?"

Doctor Norton decided to exercise his wit, of which he had plenty. "In fact we know they spend their days together, and gossip adds the evenings."

"Their days? I should think he'd be too busy."

"He is. As a matter of fact, Miss Singleton induces the state of coma during which he performs his internal sculpture. She's an anaesthetist."

"I see. Then they are… thrown together all day."

"If you regard that as a romantic situation." Doctor Norton looked at him closely. "Are you settled yet? Can you do something for me right now?"

"Yes, indeed."

"I know you don't go on the ward till tomorrow, but I'd like you to go to East Michael and take a PE and a history."

"Certainly."

"Room 312. I've put your methodical friend Schoatze on the trail of another mystery next door."

Bill hurried to his room on the top of Michael, jumped into a new white uniform, equipped himself with instruments. In his haste he forgot that this was the first time he had performed an inquisition unaided. Outside the door he smoothed himself into a calm, serious manner. He was almost a white apostle when he walked into the room; at least he tried to be.

A paunchy, sallow man of forty was smoking a cigarette in bed.

"Good morning," Bill said heartily. "How are you this morning?"

"Rotten," the man said. "That's why I'm here."

Bill set down his satchel and approached him like a young cat after its first sparrow.

"What seems to be the trouble?"

"Everything. My head aches, my bones ache, I can't sleep, I don't eat, I've got fever. My chauffeur ran over me, I mean ran over me, I mean ran me, if you know what I mean. I mean from Washington this morning. I can't stand those Washington doctors; they don't talk about anything but politics."

Bill clapped a thermometer in his mouth and took his pulse. Then he made the routine examination of chest, stomach, throat and the rest. The reflexes were sluggish to the little rubber hammer. Bill sat down beside the bed.

"I'd trade hearts with you any day," he promised.

"They all say I've got a good heart," agreed the man. "What did you think of Hoover's speech?"

"I thought you were tired of politics."

"That's true, but I got thinking of Hoover while you went over me."

"About Hoover?"

"About me. What did you find out?"

"We'll want to make some tests. But you seem pretty sound really."

"I'm not sound," the patient snapped. "I'm not sound. I'm a sick man."

Bill took out a PE form and a fountain pen.

"What's your name?" he began.

"Paul B. Van Schaik."

"Your nearest relative?"

There was nothing in the case history on which to form any opinion. Mr Van Schaik had had several children's diseases. Yesterday morning he was unable to get out of bed, and his valet had taken his temperature and found fever.

Bill's thermometer registered no fever.

"Now we're going to make just a little prick in your thumb," he said, preparing glass slides, and when this had been accomplished to the tune of a short, dismal howl from the patient, he added: "We want just a little specimen from your upper arm."

"You want everything but my tears," protested the patient.

"We have to investigate all the possibilities," said Bill sternly, plunging the syringe into the soft upper arm, inspiring more explosive protests from Mr Van Schaik.

Reflectively Bill replaced his instruments. He had obtained no clue as to what was the matter and he eyed the patient reproachfully. On a chance, he looked for enlarged cervical glands, and asked him if his parents were alive, and took a last look at throat and teeth.

"Eyes normally prominent," he wrote down, with a feeling of futility. "Pupils round and equal."

"That's all for the moment," he said. "Try and get some rest."

"Rest!" cried Mr Van Schaik indignantly. "That's just the trouble. I haven't been able to sleep for three days. I feel worse every minute."

As Bill went out into the hall, George Schoatze was just emerging from the room next door. His eyes were uncertain and there was sweat upon his brow.

"Finished?" Bill asked.

"Why, yes, in a way. Did Doctor Norton set you a job too?"

"Yeah. Kind of puzzling case in here – contradictory symptoms," he lied.

"Same here," said George, wiping his brow. "I'd rather have started out on something more clearly defined, like the ones Robinson gave us in class last year – you know, where there were two possibilities and one probability."

"Unobliging lot of patients," agreed Bill.

A student nurse approached him.

"You were just in 312," she said in a low voice. "I better tell you. I unpacked for the patient, and there was one empty bottle of whisky and one half empty. He asked me to pour him a drink, but I didn't like to do that without asking a doctor."

"Quite right," said Bill stiffly, but he wanted to kiss her hand in gratitude.

Dispatching the specimens to the laboratory, the two interns went in search of Doctor Norton, whom they found in his office.

"Through already? What luck, Tulliver?"

"He's been on a bust and he's got a hangover," Bill blurted out. "I haven't got the laboratory reports yet, but my opinion is that's all."

"I agree with you," said Doctor Norton. "All right, Schoatze: how about the lady in 314?"

"Well, unless it's too deep for me, there's nothing the matter with her at all."

"Right you are," agreed Doctor Norton. "Nerves – and not even enough of them for the Ward clinic. What'll we do with them?"

"Throw 'em out," said Bill promptly.

"Let them stay," corrected Doctor Norton. "They can afford it. They come to us for protection they don't need, so let them pay for a couple of really sick people over in the free wards. We're not crowded."

Outside the office, Bill and George fastened eyes.

"Humbling us a little," said Bill rather resentfully. "Let's go up to the operating rooms; I want to convince myself all over again that this is a serious profession." He swore. "I suppose for the next few months we'll be feeling the bellies of four-flushers and taking the case histories of women who aren't cases."

"Never mind," said George cautiously. "I was just as glad to start with something simple like… like…"

"Like what?"

"Why, like nothing."

"You're easily pleased," Bill commented.

Ascertaining from a bulletin board that Doctor Howard Durfee was at work in No. 4, they took the elevator to the operating rooms. As they slipped on the gowns, caps and then the masks, Bill realized how quickly he was breathing.

He saw her before he saw anything else in the room, except the bright vermilion spot of the operation itself, breaking the universal whiteness of the scene. There was a sway of eyes towards the two interns as they came into the gallery, and Bill picked out her eyes, darker than ever in contrast with the snowy cap and mask, as she sat working the gas machine at the patient's invisible head. The room was small. The platform on which they stood was raised about four feet, and by leaning out on a glass screen like a windshield, they brought their eyes to within two yards of the surgeon's busy hands.

"It's a neat appendix – not a cut in the muscle," George whispered. "That guy can play lacrosse tomorrow."

Doctor Durfee, busy with catgut, heard him.

"Not this patient," he said. "Too many adhesions."

His hands, trying the catgut, were sure and firm – the fine hands of a pianist, the tough hands of a pitcher combined. Bill thought how insecure, precariously involved the patient would seem to a layman, and yet how safe he was with those sure hands in an atmosphere so made safe from time itself. Time had stopped at the door of the operating room, too profane to enter here.

Thea Singleton guarded the door of the patient's consciousness, a hand on a pulse, another turning the wheels of the gas machine, as if they were the stops on a silent organ.

There *were* others in attendance – an assisting surgeon, a nurse who passed instruments, a nurse who made liaison between the table and the supplies – but Bill was absorbed in what subtle relationship there was between Howard Durfee and Thea Singleton; he felt a wild jealousy towards the mask with the brilliant, agile hands.

"I'm going," he said to George.

He saw her that afternoon, and again it was in the shadow of the great stone Christ in the entrance hall. She was in street clothes, and she looked slick and fresh and tantalizingly excitable.

"Of course. You're the man the night of the Coccidian show. And now you're an intern. Wasn't it you who came into Room 4 this morning?"

"Yes. How did it go?"

"Fine. It was Doctor Durfee."

"Yes," he said with emphasis. "I know it was Doctor Durfee."

He met her by accident or contrivance half a dozen times in the next fortnight, before he judged he could ask her for a date.

"Why, I suppose so." She seemed a little surprised. "Let's see. How about next week – either Tuesday or Wednesday?"

"How about tonight?"

"Oh, not possibly."

When he called Tuesday at the little apartment she shared with a woman musician from the Peabody Institute, he said:

"What would you like to do? See a picture?"

"No," she answered emphatically. "If I knew you better I'd say let's drive about a thousand miles into the country and go swimming in some quarry." She looked at him quizzically. "You're not one of those very impulsive interns, are you, that just sweep poor nurses off their feet?"

"On the contrary, I'm scared to death of you," Bill admitted.

It was a hot night, but the white roads were cool. They found out a little about each other: she was the daughter of an army officer and had grown up in the Philippines, and in the black-and-silver water of the abandoned quarry she surprised him with such diving as he had never seen a girl do. It was ghostly inside of the black shadow that ringed the glaring moonlight, and their voices echoed loud when they called to each other.

Afterwards, with their heads wet and their bodies stung alive, they sat for a while, unwilling to start back. Suddenly she smiled, and then looked at him without speaking, her lips just barely parted. There was the starlight set upon the brilliant darkness, and there were her pale cool cheeks, and Bill let himself be lost in love for her, as he had so wanted to do.

"We must go," she said presently.

"Not yet."

"Oh, *yet* – *very* yet – exceedingly yet."

"Because," he said after a moment, "you're Doctor Durfee's girl?"

"Yes," she admitted after a moment, "I suppose I'm Doctor Durfee's girl."

"Why are you?" he cried.

"Are you in love with me?"

"I suppose I am. Are you in love with Durfee?"

She shook her head. "No, I'm not in love with anybody. I'm just… his girl."

So the evening that had been at first ecstatic was finally unsatisfactory. This feeling deepened when he found that for his date he had to thank the fact that Durfee was out of town for a few days.

With August and the departure of more doctors on vacation, he found himself very busy. During four years he had dreamt of such work as he was doing, and now it was all disturbed by the ubiquity of "Durfee's girl". In vain he searched among the girls in the city, on those Sundays when he could go into the city, for some who would soften the hurt of his unreciprocated emotion. But the city seemed empty of girls, and in the hospital the little probationers in short cuffs had no appeal for him. The truth of his situation was that his initial idealism which had been centred in Doctor Norton had transferred itself to Thea. Instead of a God, it was now a Goddess who symbolized for him the glory and the devotion of his profession; and that she was caught up in an entanglement that bound her away from him played havoc with his peace of mind.

Diagnosis had become a workaday matter – almost. He had made a few nice guesses, and Doctor Norton had given him full credit.

"Nine times out of ten I'll be right," Norton said. "The rare thing is so rare that I'm out of the habit of looking for it. That's where you young men come in; you're cocked for the rare thing and that one time in ten you find it."

"It's a great feeling," said Bill. "I got a big kick out of that actinomycosis business."

"You look tired for your age," said Doctor Norton suddenly. "At twenty-five you shouldn't be existing entirely on nervous energy, Bill, and that's what you're doing. The people you grew up with say they never see you. Why not take a couple of hours a week away from the hospital, if only for the sake of your patients? You took so many chemistry tests of Mr Doremus that we almost had to give him blood transfusions to build him up again."

"I was right," said Bill eagerly.

"But a little brutal. Everything would have developed in a day or two. Take it gently, like your friend Schoatze. You're going to know a lot about internal medicine some day, but you're trying to rush things."

But Bill was a man driven; he tried more Sunday afternoons with current debutantes, but in the middle of a conversation he would find his mind drifting back to those great red building blocks of an Idea, where alone he could feel the pulse of life.

The news that a famous character in politics was leaving the Coast and coming to the hospital for the diagnosis of some obscure malady had the effect of giving him a sudden interest in politics. He looked up the record of the man and followed his journey east, which occupied half a column daily in the newspapers; party issues depended on his survival and eventual recovery.

Then one August afternoon there was an item in the society column which announced the engagement of *Helen*, debutante daughter of Mrs Truby Ponsonby Day, to Doctor Howard Durfee. Bill's reconciled world turned upside down. After an amount of very real suffering, he had accepted the fact that Thea was the mistress of a brilliant surgeon, but that Doctor Durfee should suddenly cut loose from her was simply incredible.

Immediately he went in search of her, found her issuing from the nurses' ward in street clothes. Her lovely face, with the eyes that held for him all the mystery of people trying, all the splendour of a goal, all reward, all purpose, all satisfaction, was harried with annoyance: she had been stared at and pitied.

"If you like," she answered, when he asked if he could run her home, and then: "Heaven help women! The amount of groaning over my body that took place this afternoon would have been plenty for a war."

"I'm going to help you," he said. "If that guy has let you down—"

"Oh, shut up! Up to a few weeks ago I could have married Howard Durfee by nodding my head – that's just what I wouldn't tell those women this afternoon. I think you've got discretion, and that'll help you a lot when you're a doctor."

"I am a doctor," he said somewhat stiffly.

"No, you're just an intern."

He was indignant, and they drove in silence. Then, softening, she turned towards him and touched his arm.

"You happen to be a gentleman," she said, "which is nice sometimes – though I prefer a touch of genius."

"I've got that," Bill said doggedly. "I've got everything, except you."

"Come up to the apartment and I'll tell you something that no one else in this city knows."

It was a modest apartment, but it told him that at some time she had lived in a more spacious world. It was all reduced, as if she had hung on to several cherished things, a Duncan Phyfe table, a brass by Brâncuși,* two oil portraits of the '50s.

"I was engaged to John Gresham," she said. "Do you know who he was?"

"Of course," he said. "I took up the subscription for the bronze tablet to him."

John Gresham had died by inches from radium poisoning, got by his own experiments.

"I was with him till the end," Thea went on quickly, "and just before he died he wagged his last finger at me and said, 'I forbid you to go to pieces. That doesn't do any good.' So, like a good little girl, I didn't go to pieces, but I toughened up instead. Anyhow, that's why I never could love Howard Durfee the way he wanted to be loved, in spite of his nice swagger and his fine hands."

"I see." Overwhelmed by the revelation, Bill tried to adjust himself to it. "I knew there was something far off about you, some sort of... oh, dedication to something I didn't know about."

"I'm pretty hard." She got up impatiently. "Anyhow, I've lost a good friend today and I'm cross, so go before I show it. Kiss me goodbye if you like."

"It wouldn't mean anything at this moment."

"Yes, it would," she insisted. "I like to be close to you. I like your clothes."

Obediently he kissed her, but he felt far off from her and very rebuffed and young as he went out the door.

He awoke next morning with the sense of something important hanging over him; then he remembered. Senator Billings, relayed by crack trains, airplanes and ambulances, was due to arrive during the morning, and the ponderous body which had housed and expelled so much nonsense in thirty years was to be at the mercy of the rational at last.

"I'll diagnose the old boy," he thought grimly, "if I have to invent a new disease."

He went about his routine work with a sense of fatigue that morning. Perhaps Doctor Norton would keep this plum to himself and Bill wouldn't have a chance at him. But at eleven o'clock he met his senior in a corridor.

"The senator's come," he said. "I've formed a tentative opinion. You might go in and get his history. Go over him quickly and give him the usual laboratory work-up."

"All right," said Bill, but there was no eagerness in his voice. He seemed to have lost all his enthusiasm. With his instruments and a block of history paper, he repaired to the senator's room.

"Good morning," he began. "Feeling a little tired after your trip?"

The big barrel of a man rolled towards him.

"Exhausted," he squeaked unexpectedly. "All in."

Bill didn't wonder; he felt rather that way himself, as if he had travelled thousands of miles in all sorts of conveyances until his insides, including his brains, were all shaken up together.

He took the case history.

"What's your profession?"

"Legislator."

"Do you use any alcohol?"

The senator raised himself on one arm and thundered, "See here, young man; I'm not going to be heckled! As long as the Eighteenth Amendment…" He subsided.

"Do you use any alcohol?" Bill asked again patiently.

"Why, yes."

"How much?"

"A few drinks every day. I don't count them. Say, if you look in my suitcase you'll find an X-ray of my lungs, taken a few years ago."

Bill found it and stared at it with a sudden feeling that everything was getting a little crazy.

"This is an X-ray of a woman's stomach," he said.

"Oh… well, it must have got mixed up," said the senator. "It must be my wife's."

Bill went into the bathroom to wash his thermometer. When he came back he took the senator's pulse, and was puzzled to find himself regarded in a curious way.

"What's the idea?" the senator demanded. "Are you the patient or am I?" He jerked his hand angrily away from Bill. "Your hand's like ice. And you've put the thermometer in your own mouth."

Only then did Bill realize how sick he was. He pressed the nurse's bell and staggered back to a chair with wave after wave of pain chasing across his abdomen.

3

HE AWOKE WITH A SENSE that he had been in bed for many hours. There was fever bumping in his brain, a pervasive weakness in his body, and what had wakened him was a new series of pains in his stomach. Across the room in an armchair sat Doctor George Schoatze, and on his knee was the familiar case-history pad.

"What the hell?" Bill said weakly. "What the hell's the matter with me? What happened?"

"You're all right," said George. "You just lie quiet."

Bill tried to sit upright, but found he was too weak.

"Lie quiet!" he repeated incredulously. "What do you think I am – some dumb patient? I asked you what's the matter with me?"

"That's exactly what we're trying to find out. Say, what is your exact age?"

"My age!" Bill cried. "A hundred and ten in the shade! My name's Al Capone and I'm an old hophead. Stick that on your goddamn paper and mail it to Santa Claus. I asked you what's the matter with me."

"And I say that's what we're trying to find out," said George, staunch, but a little nervous. "Now, you take it easy."

"Take it easy!" cried Bill. "When I'm burning up with fever and a half-wit intern sits there and asks me how many fillings I've got in my teeth! You take my temperature, and take it right away!"

"All right... all right," said George conciliatingly. "I was just going to."

He put the thermometer in Bill's mouth and felt for the pulse, but Bill mumbled, "I'll shake my owd pulse," and pulled his hand away. After two minutes George deftly extracted the thermometer and walked with it to the window, an act of treachery that brought Bill's legs out of bed.

"I want to read that thermometer!" he cried. "Now, you look here! I want to know what's on that thermometer!"

George shook it down quickly and put it in its case.

"That isn't the way we do things here," he said.

"Oh, isn't it? Well, then, I'll go somewhere where they've got some sense."

George prepared a syringe and two small plates of glass.

Bill groaned. "Do you think for a moment I'm going to let you do that? I taught you everything you know about blood chemistry. By God, I used to do your lessons for you, and you come here to make some clumsy stab into my arm!"

Perspiring fluently, as was his wont under strain, George rang for a nurse, with the hope that a female presence would have a calming effect on Bill. But it was not the right female.

"Another nitwit!" Bill cried as she came in. "Do you think I'm going to lie here and stand more of this nonsense? Why doesn't somebody do something? Where's Doctor Norton?"

"He'll be here this afternoon."

"This afternoon! I'll probably be dead by this afternoon. Why isn't he here this morning? Off on some social bat – and I lie here surrounded by morons who've lost their heads and don't know what to do about it. What are you writing there – that my 'tongue protrudes in mid-line without tremor'? Give me my slippers and bathrobe. I'm going to report you two as specimens for the nerve clinic."

They pressed him down in bed, whence he looked up at George with infinite reproach.

"You, that I explained a whole book of toxicology to, you're presuming to diagnose *me*. Well, then, *do* it! What have I got? Why is my stomach burning up? Is it appendicitis? What's the white count?"

"How can I find out the white count when—"

With a sigh of infinite despair at the stupidity of mankind, Bill relaxed, exhausted.

Doctor Norton arrived at two o'clock. His presence should have been reassuring, but by this time the patient was too far gone in nervous tension.

"Look here, Bill," he said sternly. "What's all this about not letting George look into your mouth?"

"Because he deliberately gagged me with that stick," Bill cried. "When I get out of this I'm going to stick a plank down that ugly trap of his."

"Now, that'll do. Do you know little Miss Cary has been crying? She says she's going to give up nursing. She says she's never been so disillusioned in her life."

"The same with me. Tell her I'm going to give it up too. After this, I'm going to kill people instead of curing them. Now when I need it nobody has even tried to cure me."

An hour later Doctor Norton stood up.

"Well, Bill, we're going to take you at your word and tell you what's what. I'm laying my cards on the table when I say we don't know what's the matter with you. We've just got the X-rays from this morning, and it's pretty certain it's not the gall bladder. There's a possibility of acute food poisoning or mesenteric thrombosis, or it may be something we haven't thought of yet. Give us a chance, Bill."

With an effort and with the help of a sedative, Bill got himself in comparative control; only to go to pieces again in the morning, when George Schoatze arrived to give him a hypodermoclysis.

"But I can't stand it," he raged. "I never could stand being pricked, and you have as much right with a needle as a year-old baby with a machine gun."

"Doctor Norton has ordered that you get nothing by mouth."

"Then give it intravenously."

"This is best."

"What I'll do to you when I get well! I'll inject stuff into you until you're as big as a barrel! I will! I'll hire somebody to hold you down!"

Forty-eight hours later, Doctor Norton and Doctor Schoatze had a conference in the former's office.

"So there we are," George was saying gloomily. "He just flatly refuses to submit to the operation."

"H'm." Doctor Norton considered. "That's bad."

"There's certainly danger of a perforation."

"And you say that his chief objection—"

"—that it was my diagnosis. He says I remembered the word 'volvulus' from some lecture and I'm trying to wish it on him." George added uncomfortably: "He always was domineering, but I never saw anything like *this*. Today he claims it's acute pancreatitis, but he doesn't have any convincing reasons."

"Does he know I agree with your opinion?"

"He doesn't seem to believe in *any*body," said George uncomfortably. "He keeps fretting about his father; he keeps thinking he could help him if he was alive."

"I wish that there was someone outside the hospital he had some faith in," Norton said. An idea came to him: "I wonder…" He picked up the telephone and said to the operator: "I wish you'd locate Miss Singleton, Doctor Durfee's anaesthetist. And when she's free, ask her to come and see me."

Bill opened his eyes wearily when Thea came into his room at eight that night.

"Oh, it's you," he murmured.

She sat on the side of his bed and put her hand on his arm.

"H'lo, Bill," she said.

"H'lo."

Suddenly he turned in bed and put both arms around her arm. Her free hand touched his hair.

"You've been bad," she said.

"I can't help it."

She sat with him silently for half an hour; then she changed her position so that her arm was under his head. Stooping over him, she kissed him on the brow. He said:

"Being close to you is the first rest I've had in four days."

After a while she said: "Three months ago Doctor Durfee did an operation for volvulus and it was entirely successful."

"But it isn't volvulus!" he cried. "Volvulus is when a loop of the intestine gets twisted on itself. It's a crazy idea of Schoatze's! He wants to make a trick diagnosis and get a lot of credit."

"Doctor Norton agrees with him. You must give in, Bill. I'll be right beside you, as close as I am now."

Her soft voice was a sedative; he felt his resistance growing weaker; two long tears rolled from his eyes. "I feel so helpless," he admitted. "How do I know whether George Schoatze has any sense?"

"That's just childish," she answered gently. "You'll profit more by submitting to this than Doctor Schoatze will from his lucky guess."

He clung to her suddenly. "Afterwards, will you be my girl?"

She laughed. "The selfishness! The bargainer! You wouldn't be very cheerful company if you went around with a twisted intestine."

He was silent for a moment. "Yesterday I made my will," he said. "I divided what I have between an old aunt and you."

She put her face against his. "You'll make me weep, and it really isn't that serious at all."

"All right then." His white, pinched face relaxed. "Get it over with."

* * *

Bill was wheeled upstairs an hour later. Once the matter was decided, all nervousness left him, and he remembered how the hands of Doctor Durfee had given him such a sense of surety last July, and remembered who would be at his head watching over him. His* last thought as the gas began was sudden jealousy that Thea and Howard Durfee would be awake and near each other while he was asleep...

...When he awoke he was being wheeled down a corridor to his room. Doctor Norton and Doctor Schoatze, seeming very cheerful, were by his side.

"H'lo, hello," cried Bill in a daze. "Say, what did they finally discover about Senator Billings?"

"It was only a common cold, Bill," said Doctor Norton. "They've shipped him back west – by dirigible, helicopter and freight elevator."

"Oh," said Bill – and then, after a moment: "I feel terrible."

"You're not terrible," Doctor Norton assured him. "You'll be up on deck in a week. George here is certainly a swell guesser."

"It was a beautiful operation," said George modestly. "That loop would have perforated in another six hours."

"Good anaesthesia job, too," said Doctor Norton, winking at George. "Like a lullaby."

Thea slipped in to see Bill next morning, when he was rested and the soreness was eased and he felt weak but himself again. She sat beside him on the bed.

"I made an awful fool of myself," he confessed.

"A lot of doctors do when they get sick the first time. They go neurotic."

"I guess everybody's off me."

"Not at all. You'll be in for some kidding probably. Some bright young one wrote this for the Coccidian Club show." She read from a scrap of paper:

"Intern Tulliver, chloroformed,
    Had dreams above his station;
He woke up thinking he'd performed
    His own li'l operation."

"I guess I can stand it," said Bill. "I can stand anything when you're around; I'm so in love with you. But I suppose after this you'll always see me as about high-school age."

"If you'd had your first sickness at forty you'd have acted the same way."

"I hear your friend Durfee did a brilliant job, as usual," he said resentfully.

"Yes," she agreed; after a minute she added: "He wants to break his engagement and marry me on my own terms."

His heart stopped beating. "And what did you say?"

"I said no."

Life resumed itself again.

"Come closer," he whispered. "Where's your hand? Will you, anyhow, go swimming with me every night all the rest of September?"

"Every other night."

"Every night."

"Well, every hot night," she compromised.

Thea stood up.

He saw her eyes fix momentarily on some distant spot, linger there for a moment as if she were drawing support from it; then she leant over him and kissed his hungry lips goodbye, and faded back into her own mystery, into those woods where she hunted, with an old suffering and with a memory he could not share.

But what was valuable in it she had distilled; she knew how to pass it along so that it would not disappear. For the moment Bill had had more than his share, and reluctantly he relinquished her.

"This has been my biggest case so far," he thought sleepily.

The verse to the Coccidian Club song passed through his mind, and the chorus echoed on, singing him into deep sleep:

"Bumtiddy, bum-bum,
Tiddy-bum-bum.
Three thousand years ago,
Three thousand years ago."

More than Just a House

1

THIS WAS THE SORT OF THING Lew was used to – and he'd been around a good deal already. You came into an entrance hall, sometimes narrow New England Colonial, sometimes cautiously spacious. Once in the hall, the host said: "Clare" – or Virginia, or Darling – "this is Mr Lowrie." The woman said, "How do you do, Mr Lowrie," and Lew answered, "How do you do, Mrs Woman." Then the man suggested, "How about a little cocktail?" And Lew lifted his brows apart and said, "Fine," in a tone that implied: "What hospitality – consideration – attention!" Those delicious canapés. "M'm'm! Madame, what are they – broiled feathers? Enough to spoil a stronger appetite than mine."

But Lew was on his way up, with six new suits of clothes, and he was getting into the swing of the thing. His name was up for a downtown club and he had his eye on a very modern bachelor apartment full of wrought-iron swinging gates – as if he were a baby inclined to topple downstairs – when he saved the life of the Gunther girl and his tastes underwent revision.

This was back in 1925, before the Spanish-American... No, before whatever it is that has happened since then. The Gunther girls had got off the train on the wrong side and were walking along arm in arm, with Amanda in the path of an approaching donkey engine. Amanda was rather tall, golden and proud, and the donkey engine was very squat and dark and determined. Lew had no time to speculate upon their respective chances in the approaching encounter; he lunged at Jean, who was nearest him, and as the two sisters clung together, startled, he pulled

Amanda out of the iron pathway by such a hair's breadth that a piston cylinder touched her coat.

And so Lew's taste was changed in regard to architecture and interior decoration. At the Gunther house they served tea, hot or iced, sugar buns, gingerbread and hot rolls at half-past four. When he first went there he was embarrassed by his heroic status – for about five minutes. Then he learnt that during the Civil War the grandmother had been saved by her own grandmother from a burning house in Montgomery County, that Father had once saved ten men at sea and been recommended for the Carnegie medal, that when Jean was little a man had saved her from the surf at Cape May – that, in fact, all the Gunthers had gone on saving and being saved for the last fifty years and that their real debt to Lew was that now there would be no gap left in the tradition.

This was on the very wide, vine-curtained veranda ("The first thing I'd do would be tear off that monstrosity," said a visiting architect) which almost completely bounded the big square box of the house, *circa* 1880. The sisters, three of them, appeared now and then during the time Lew drank tea and talked to the older people. He was only twenty-six himself and he wished Amanda would stay uncovered long enough for him to look at her, but only Bess, the sixteen-year-old sister, was really in sight; in front of the two others interposed a white-flannel screen of young men.

"It was the quickness," said Mr Gunther, pacing the long straw rug, "that second of coordination. Suppose you'd tried to warn them – never. Your subconscious mind saw that they were joined together – saw that if you pulled one, you pulled them both. One second, one thought, one motion. I remember in 1904—"

"Won't Mr Lowrie have another piece of gingerbread?" asked the grandmother.

"Father, why don't you show Mr Lowrie the apostles' spoons?" Bess proposed.

"What?" Her father stopped pacing. "Is Mr Lowrie interested in old spoons?"

Lew was thinking at the moment of Amanda twisting somewhere between the glare of the tennis courts and the shadow of the veranda, through all the warmth and graciousness of the afternoon.

"Spoons? Oh, I've got a spoon, thank you."

"Apostles' spoons," Bess explained. "Father has one of the best collections in America. When he likes anybody enough he shows them the spoons. I thought, since you saved Amanda's life—"

He saw little of Amanda that afternoon – talked to her for a moment by the steps while a young man standing near tossed up a tennis racket and caught it by the handle with an impatient bend of his knees at each catch. The sun shopped among the yellow strands of her hair, poured around the rosy tan of her cheeks and spun along the arms that she regarded abstractedly as she talked to him.

"It's hard to thank a person for saving your life, Mr Lowrie," she said. "Maybe you shouldn't have. Maybe it wasn't worth saving."

"Oh yes, it was," said Lew, in a spasm of embarrassment.

"Well, I'd like to think so." She turned to the young man. "Was it, Allen?"

"It's a good enough life," Allen admitted, "if you go in for woolly blondes."

She turned her slender smile full upon Lew for a moment, and then aimed it a little aside, like a pocket torch that might dazzle him. "I'll always feel that you own me, Mr Lowrie; my life is forfeit to you. You'll always have the right to take me back and put me down in front of that engine again. "

Her proud mouth was a little overgracious about being saved, though Lew didn't realize it; it seemed to Amanda that it might at least have been someone in her own crowd. The Gunthers were a haughty family – haughty beyond all logic, because Mr Gunther had once been presented at the Court of St James's and remained slightly convalescent ever since. Even Bess was haughty, and it was Bess, eventually, who led Lew down to his car.

"It's a nice place," she agreed. "We've been going to modernize it, but we took a vote and decided to have the swimming pool repaired instead."

Lew's eyes lifted over her – she was like Amanda, except for the slightness of her and the childish disfigurement of a small wire across her teeth – up to the house with its decorative balconies outside the windows, its fickle gables, its gold-lettered, Swiss-chalet mottoes, the bulging projections of its many bays. Uncritically he regarded it; it seemed to him one of the finest houses he had ever known.

"Of course, we're miles from town, but there's always plenty of people. Father and Mother go south after the Christmas holidays when we go back to school."

It was more than just a house, Lew decided as he drove away. It was a place where a lot of different things could go on at once – a private life for the older people, a private romance for each girl. Promoting himself, he chose his own corner – a swinging seat behind one of the drifts of vines that cut the veranda into quarters. But this was in 1925, when the ten thousand a year that Lew had come to command did not permit an indiscriminate crossing of social frontiers. He was received by the Gunthers and held at arm's length by them, and then gradually liked for the qualities that began to show through his awkwardness. A good-looking man on his way up can put directly into action the things he learns; Lew was never again quite so impressed by the suburban houses whose children lived upon rolling platforms in the street.

It was September before he was invited to the Gunthers' on an intimate scale – and this largely because Amanda's mother insisted upon it.

"He saved your life. I want him asked to this one little party."

But Amanda had not forgiven him for saving her life.

"It's just a dance for friends," she complained. "Let him come to Jean's debut in October – everybody'll think he's a business acquaintance of Father's. After all, you can be nice to somebody without falling into their arms."

Mrs Gunther translated this correctly as: "You can be awful to some-body without their knowing it" – and brusquely overrode her: "You can't have advantages without responsibilities," she said shortly.

Life had been opening up so fast for Lew that he had a black dinner coat instead of a purple one. Asked for dinner, he came early; and thinking to give him his share of attention when it was most conveni-ent, Amanda walked with him into the tangled, out-of-hand garden. She wanted to be bored, but his gentle vitality disarmed her, made her look at him closely for almost the first time.

"I hear everywhere that you're a young man with a future," she said.

Lew admitted it. He boasted a little; he did not tell her that he had analysed the spell which the Gunther house exerted upon him – his father had been gardener on a similar Maryland estate when he was a boy of five. His mother had helped him to remember that when he told her about the Gunthers. And now this garden was shot bright with sunset, with Amanda one of its own flowers in her flowered dress; he told her, in a rush of emotion, how beautiful she was, and Amanda, excited by the prospect of impending hours with another man, let herself encourage him. Lew had never been so happy as in the moment before she stood up from the seat and put her hand on his arm lightly.

"I do like you," she said. "You're very handsome. Do you know that?"

The harvest dance took place in an L-shaped space formed by the clearing of three rooms. Thirty young people were there, and a dozen of their elders, but there was no crowding, for the big windows were opened to the veranda and the guests danced against the wide, illimit-able night. A country orchestra alternated with the phonograph, there was mildly calculated cider punch, and an air of safety beside the open bookshelves of the library and the oil portraits of the living room, as though this were one of an endless series of dances that had taken place here in the past and would take place again.

"Thought you never would cut in," Bess said to Lew. "You'd be foolish not to. I'm the best dancer of us three, and I'm much the smartest one. Jean is the jazzy one, the most chic, but I think it's passé to be jazzy and play the traps and neck every second boy. Amanda is the beauty, of course. But I'm going to be the Cinderella, Mr Lowrie. They'll be the two wicked sisters, and gradually you'll find I'm the most attractive and get all hot and bothered about me."

There was an interval of intervals before Lew could manoeuvre Amanda to his chosen segment of the porch. She was all radiant and shimmering. More than content to be with him, she tried to relax with the creak of the settee. Then instinct told her that something was about to happen.

Lew, remembering a remark of Jean's – "He asked me to marry him, and he hadn't even kissed me" – could yet think of no graceful way to assault Amanda; nevertheless he was determined to tell her tonight that he was in love with her.

"This'll seem sudden," he ventured, "but you might as well know. Please put me down on the list of those who'd like to have a chance."

She was not surprised but, being deep in herself at the moment, she was rather startled. Giving up the idea of relaxing, she sat upright.

"Mr Lowrie – can I call you by your first name? – can I tell you something? No, I won't – yes, I will, because I like you now. I didn't like you at first. How's that for frankness?"

"Is that what you wanted to tell me?"

"No. Listen. You met Mr Horton – the man from New York – the tall man with the rather old-looking hair?"

"Yes." Lew felt a pang of premonition in his stomach.

"I'm engaged to him. You're the first to know – except Mother suspects. Whee! Now I told you because you saved my life, so you do sort of own me – I wouldn't be here to be engaged, except for you." Then she was honestly surprised at his expression. "Heavens, don't look like that!"

She regarded him, pained. "Don't tell me you've been secretly in love with me all these months. Why didn't I know? And now it's too late."

Lew tried a laugh.

"I hardly know you," he confessed. "I haven't had time to fall in love with you."

"Maybe I work quick. Anyhow, if you did, you'll have to forget it and be my friend." Finding his hand, she squeezed it. "A big night for this little girl, Mr Lew; the chance of a lifetime. I've been afraid for two days that his bureau drawer would stick or the hot water would give out and he'd leave for civilization."

They were silent for a moment; then he asked:

"You very much in love with him?"

"Of course I am. I mean, I don't know. You tell me. I've been in love with so many people; how can I answer that? Anyhow, I'll get away from this old barn."

"This house? You want to get away from here? Why, this is a lovely old house."

She was astonished now, and then suddenly explosive:

"This old tomb! That's the chief reason I'm marrying George Horton. Haven't I stood it for twenty years? Haven't I begged Mother and Father on my knees to move into town? This – shack – where everybody can hear what everybody else says three rooms off, and Father won't allow a radio, and not even a phone till last summer. I'm afraid even to ask a girl down from school – probably she'd go crazy listening to the shutters on a stormy night."

"It's a darn nice old house," he said automatically.

"Nice and quaint," she agreed. "Glad you like it. People who don't have to live here generally do, but you ought to see us alone in it – if there's a family quarrel you have to stay with it for hours. It all comes down to father wanting to live fifty miles from anywhere, so we're condemned to rot. I'd rather live in a three-room apartment in town!" Shocked by her own vehemence, she broke off. "Anyhow," she insisted, "it may seem nice to you, but it's a nuisance to us."

A man pulled the vines apart and peered at them, claimed her and pulled her to her feet; when she was gone, Lew went over the railing with a handhold and walked into the garden; he walked far enough away so that the lights and music from the house were blurred into one entity like a stage effect, like an approaching port viewed from a deck at night.

"I only saw her four times," he said to himself. "Four times isn't much. Eeney-meeney-miney-moe – what could I expect in four times? I shouldn't feel anything at all." But he was engulfed by fear. What had he just begun to know that now he might never know? What had happened in these moments in the garden this afternoon, what was the excitement that had blacked out in the instant of its birth? The scarcely emergent young image of Amanda – he did not want to carry it with him for ever. Gradually he realized a truth behind his grief: he had come too late for her; unknown to him, she had been slipping away through the years. With the odds against him, he had managed to found himself on solid rock, and then, looking around for the girl, discovered that she had just gone. "Sorry, just gone out; just left; just gone." Too late in every way – even for the house. Thinking over her tirade, Lew saw that he had come too late for the house; it was the house of a childhood from which the three girls were breaking away, the house of an older generation, sufficient unto them. To a younger generation it was pervaded with an aura of completion and fulfilment beyond their own power to add to. It was just old.

Nevertheless, he recalled the emptiness of many grander mansions built in more spectacular fashions – empty to him, at any rate, since he had first seen the Gunther place three months before. Something humanly valuable would vanish with the break-up of this family. The house itself, designed for reading long Victorian novels around an open fire of the evening, didn't even belong to an architectural period worthy of restoration.

Lew circled an outer drive and stood quiet in the shadow of a rose-bush as a pair of figures strolled down from the house; by their voices he recognized Jean and Allen Parks.

"Me, I'm going to New York," Jean said, "whether they let me or not… No, not now, you nut. I'm not in that mood."

"Then what mood are you in?"

"Not in any mood. I'm only envious of Amanda because she's hooked this M'sieur, and now she'll go to Long Island and live in a house instead of a mousetrap. Oh, Jake, this business of being simple and swell…"

They passed out of hearing. It was between dances, and Lew saw the colours of frocks and the quick white of shirt fronts in the window panes as the guests flowed onto the porch. He looked up at the second floor as a light went on there – he had a conception of the second floor as walled with crowded photographs; there must be bags full of old materials, and trunks with costumes and dress-making forms, and old dolls' houses, and an overflow, everywhere along the vacant walls, of books for all generations – many childhoods side by side drifting into every corner.

Another couple came down the walk from the house and, feeling that inadvertently he had taken up too strategic a position, Lew moved away; but not before he had identified the pair as Amanda and her man from New York.

"What would you think if I told you I had another proposal tonight?"

"…be surprised at all."

"A very worthy young man. Saved my life… Why weren't you there on that occasion, Bubbles? You'd have done it on a grand scale, I'm sure."

Standing square in front of the house, Lew looked at it more search-ingly. He felt a kinship with it – not precisely that, for the house's use-fulness was almost over and his was just beginning; rather, the sense of superior unity that the thoughtful young feel for the old sense of the grandparent. More than only a house. He would like to be that much used up himself before being thrown out on the ash heap at the end.

And then, because he wanted to do some courteous service to it while he could, if only to dance with the garrulous little sister, he pulled a brash pocket comb through his hair and went inside.

2

THE MAN WITH THE SMILING SCAR approached Lew once more. "This is probably," he announced, "the biggest party ever given in New York."

"I even heard you the first time you told me," agreed Lew cheerfully.

"But, on the other hand," qualified the man, "I thought the same thing at a party two years ago, in 1927. Probably they'll go on getting bigger and bigger. You play polo, don't you?"

"Only in the backyard," Lewis assured him. "I said I'd like to play. I'm a serious businessman."

"Somebody told me you were the polo star." The man was somewhat disappointed. "I'm a writer myself. A humani... a humanitarian. I've been trying to help out a girl over there in that room where the champagne is. She's a lady. And yet, by golly, she's the only one in the room that can't take care of herself. "

"Never try to take care of anybody," Lew advised him. "They hate you for it."

But although the apartment, or rather the string of apartments and penthouses pressed into service for the affair, represented the best resources of the New York skyline, it was only limited metropolitan space at that, and, moving among the swirls of dancers, thinned with dawn, Lew found himself finally in the chamber that the man had spoken of. For a moment he did not recognize the girl who had assumed the role of entertaining the glassy-eyed citizenry, chosen by natural selection to personify dissolution; then, as she issued a blanket invitation to a squad of Gaiety beauties to come south and recuperate on her Maryland estates, he recognized Jean Gunther.

She was the dark Gunther – dark and shining and driven. Lew, living in New York now, had seen none of the family since Amanda's marriage four years ago. Driving her home a quarter of an hour later, he extracted what news he could; and then left her in the dawn at the door of her apartment, mussed and awry, yet still proud, and tottering with absurd formality as she thanked him and said goodnight.

He called next afternoon and took her to tea in Central Park.

"I am," she informed him, "the child of the century. Other people claim to be the child of the century, but I'm actually the child of the century. And I'm having the time of my life at it."

Thinking back to another period – of young men on the tennis courts and hot buns in the afternoon, and of wisteria and ivy climbing along the ornate railings of a veranda – Lew became as moral as it was possible to be in that well-remembered year of 1929.

"What are you getting out of it? Why don't you invest in some reliable man – just a sort of background?"

"Men are good to invest money for you," she dodged neatly. "Last year one darling spun out my allowance so it lasted ten months instead of three."

"But how about marrying some candidate?"

"I haven't got any love," she said. "Actually, I know four… five… I know six millionaires I could maybe marry. This little girl from Carroll County. It's just too many. Now, if somebody that had everything came along…" She looked at Lew appraisingly. "You've improved, for example."

"I should say I have," admitted Lew, laughing. "I even go to first nights. But the most beautiful thing about me is I remember my old friends, and among them are the lovely Gunther girls of Carroll County."

"You're very nice," she said. "Were you terribly in love with Amanda?"

"I thought so, anyhow."

"I saw her last week. She's super-Park Avenue and very busy having Park Avenue babies. She considers me rather disreputable and tells her friends about our magnificent plantation in the old South."

"Do you ever go down to Maryland?"

"Do I though? I'm going Sunday night, and spend two months there saving enough money to come back on. When Mother died" – she paused – "I suppose you knew Mother died – I came into a little cash, and I've still got it, but it has to be stretched, see?" She pulled her napkin cornerwise. "By tactful investing. I think the next step is a quiet summer on the farm."

Lew took her to the theatre the next night, oddly excited by the encounter. The wild flush of the times lay upon her; he was conscious of her physical pulse going at some abnormal rate, but most of the young women he knew were being hectic, save the ones caught up tight in domesticity.

He had no criticism to make – behind that lay the fact that he would not have dared to criticize her. Having climbed from a nether rung of the ladder, he had perforce based his standards on what he could see from where he was at the moment. Far be it from him to tell Jean Gunther how to order her life.

Getting off the train in Baltimore three weeks later, he stepped into the peculiar heat that usually preceded an electric storm. He passed up the regular taxis and hired a limousine for the long ride out to Carroll County, and as he drove through rich foliage, moribund in midsummer, between the white fences that lined the rolling road, many years fell away and he was again the young man, starved for a home, who had first seen the Gunther house four years ago. Since then he had occupied a twelve-room apartment in New York, rented a summer mansion on Long Island, but his spirit, warped by loneliness and grown gypsy with change, turned back persistently to this house.

Inevitably it was smaller than he had expected, a small, big house, roomy rather than spacious. There was a rather intangible neglect about it – the colour of the house had never been anything but a brown-green relict of the sun; Lew had never known the stable to lean otherwise than as the Tower of Pisa, nor the garden to grow any other way than plebeian and wild.

Jean was on the porch – not, as she had prophesied, in the role of gingham queen or rural equestrienne, but very Rue de la Paix against the dun cushions of the swinging settee. There was the stout, coloured butler whom Lew remembered and who pretended, with racial guile, to remember Lew delightedly. He took the bag to Amanda's old room, and Lew stared around it a little before he went downstairs. Jean and Bess were waiting over a cocktail on the porch.

It struck him that Bess had made a leaping change out of childhood into something that was not quite youth. About her beauty there was a detachment, almost an impatience, as though she had not asked for the gift and considered it rather a burden; to a young man, the gravity of her face might have seemed formidable.

"How is your father?" Lew asked.

"He won't be down tonight," Bess answered. "He's not well. He's over seventy, you know. People tire him. When we have guests, he has dinner upstairs."

"It would be better if he ate upstairs all the time," Jean remarked, pouring the cocktails.

"No, it wouldn't," Bess contradicted her. "The doctors said it wouldn't. There's no question about that."

Jean turned in a rush to Lew. "For over a year Bess has hardly left this house. We could—"

"What junk!" her sister said impatiently. "I ride every morning."

"—we could get a nurse who would do just as well."

Dinner was formal, with candles on the table and the two young women in evening dresses. Lew saw that much was missing – the feeling that the house was bursting with activity, with expanding life – all this had gone. It was difficult for the diminished clan to do much more than inhabit the house. There was not a moving-up into vacated places; there was simply an anachronistic staying on between a vanishing past and an incalculable future.

Midway through dinner, Lew lifted his head at a pause in the conversation, but what he had confused with a mutter of thunder was a long groan from the floor above, followed by a measured speech, whose words were interrupted by the quick clatter of Bess's chair.

"You know what I ordered. Just so long as I am the head of—"

"It's Father." Momentarily Jean looked at Lew as if she thought the situation was faintly humorous, but at his concerned face, she continued seriously, "You might as well know. It's senile dementia. Not dangerous. Sometimes he's absolutely himself. But it's hard on Bess."

Bess did not come down again; after dinner, Lew and Jean went into the garden, splattered with faint drops before the approaching rain. Through the vivid green twilight Lew followed her long dress, spotted with bright-red roses – it was the first of that fashion he had ever seen; in the tense hush he had an illusion of intimacy with her, as though they shared the secrets of many years and, when she caught at his arm suddenly at a rumble of thunder, he drew her around slowly with his other arm and kissed her shaped, proud mouth.

"Well, at least you've kissed one Gunther girl," Jean said lightly. "How was it? And don't you think you're taking advantage of us, being unprotected out here in the country?"

He looked at her to see if she were joking, and with a swift laugh she seized his arm again. It was raining in earnest, and they fled towards the house – to find Bess on her knees in the library, setting light to an open fire.

"Father's all right," she assured them. "I don't like to give him the medicine till the last minute. He's worrying about some man that lent him twenty dollars in 1892." She lingered, conscious of being a third party, and yet impelled to play her mother's role and impart an initial solidarity before she retired. The storm broke, shrieking in white at the windows, and Bess took the opportunity to fly to the windows upstairs, calling down after a moment:

"The telephone's trying to ring. Do you think it's safe to answer it?"

"Perfectly," Jean called back, "or else they wouldn't ring." She came close to Lewis in the centre of the room, away from the white, quivering windows.

"It's strange having you here right now. I don't mind saying I'm glad you're here. But if you weren't, I suppose we'd get along just as well."

"Shall I help Bess close the windows?" Lew asked.

Simultaneously, Bess called downstairs:

"Nobody seemed to be on the phone, and I don't like holding it."

A ripping crash of thunder shook the house, and Jean moved into Lew's arm, breaking away as Bess came running down the stairs with a yelp of dismay.

"The lights are out up there," she said. "I never used to mind storms when I was little. Father used to make us sit on the porch sometimes, remember?"

There was a dazzle of light around all the windows of the first floor, reflecting itself back and forth in mirrors, so that every room was pervaded with a white glare; there followed a sound as of a million matches struck at once, so loud and terrible that the thunder rolling down seemed secondary; then a splintering noise separated itself out, and Bess's voice:

"That struck!"

Once again came the sickening lightning, and through a rolling pandemonium of sound they groped from window to window till Jean cried: "It's William's room! There's a tree on it!"

In a moment, Lew had flung wide the kitchen door and saw, in the next glare, what had happened: the great tree, in falling, had divided the lean-to from the house proper.

"Is William there?" he demanded.

"Probably. He should be."

Gathering up his courage, Lew dashed across the twenty feet of new marsh, and with a waffle iron smashed in the nearest window. Inundated with sheet rain and thunder, he yet realized that the storm had moved off from overhead, and his voice was strong as he called: "William! You all right?"

No answer.

"William!"

He paused, and there came a quiet answer:

"Who dere?"

"You all right?"

"I wanna know who dere."

"The tree fell on you. Are you hurt?"

There was a sudden peal of laughter from the shack as William emerged mentally from dark and atavistic suspicions of his own. Again and again the pealing laughter rang out.

"Hurt? Not me hurt. Nothin' hurt me. I'm never better, as they say. Nothin' hurt me."

Irritated by his melting clothes, Lew said brusquely:

"Well, whether you know it or not, you're penned up in there. You've got to try and get out this window. That tree's too big to push off tonight. "

Half an hour later, in his room, Lew shed the wet pulp of his clothing by the light of a single candle. Lying naked on the bed, he regretted that he was in poor condition, unnecessarily fatigued with the exertion of pulling a fat man out a window. Then, over the dull rumble of the thunder, he heard the phone again in the hall, and Bess's voice – "I can't hear a word. You'll have to get a better connection" – and for thirty seconds he dozed, to wake with a jerk at the sound of his door opening.

"Who's that?" he demanded, pulling the quilt up over himself.

The door opened slowly.

"Who's that?"

There was a chuckle; a last pulse of lightning showed him three tense, blue-veined fingers, and then a man's voice whispered: "I only wanted to know whether you were in for the night, dear. I worry... I worry."

The door closed cautiously, and Lew realized that old Gunther was on some nocturnal round of his own. Aroused, he slipped into his sole change of clothes, listening to Bess for the third time at the phone.

"…in the morning," she said. "Can't it wait? We've got to get a connection ourselves."

Downstairs he found Jean surprisingly sprightly before the fire. She made a sign to him, and he went and stood above her, indifferent suddenly to her invitation to kiss her. Trying to decide how he felt, he brushed his hand lightly along her shoulder.

"Your father's wandering around. He came in my room. Don't you think you ought to—"

"Always does it," Jean said. "Makes the nightly call to see if we're in bed."

Lew stared at her sharply; a suspicion that had been taking place in his subconscious assumed tangible form. A bland, beautiful expression stared back at him; but his ears lifted suddenly up the stairs to Bess still struggling with the phone.

"All right. I'll try to take it that way… P-ay-double ess-ee-dee – 'p-a-s-s-e-d'. All right; ay-double you-ay-why. 'Passed away?'" Her voice, as she put the phrase together, shook with sudden panic. "What did you say – 'Amanda Gunther passed away'?"

Jean looked at Lew with funny eyes.

"Why does Bess try to take that message now? Why not—"

"Shut up!" he ordered. "This is something serious."

"I don't see…"

Alarmed by the silence that seeped down the stairs, Lew ran up and found Bess sitting beside the telephone table holding the receiver in her lap, just breathing and staring, breathing and staring. He took the receiver and got the message:

"Amanda passed away quietly, giving life to a little boy."

Lew tried to raise Bess from the chair, but she sank back, full of dry sobbing.

"Don't tell Father tonight."

How did it matter if this was added to that old store of confused memories? It mattered to Bess, though.

"Go away," she whispered. "Go tell Jean."

Some premonition had reached Jean, and she was at the foot of the stairs while he descended.

"What's the matter?"

He guided her gently back into the library.

"Amanda is dead," he said, still holding her.

She gathered up her forces and began to wail, but he put his hand over her mouth.

"You've been drinking!" he said. "You've got to pull yourself together. You can't put anything more on your sister."

Jean pulled herself together visibly – first her proud mouth and then her whole body – but what might have seemed heroic under other conditions seemed to Lew only reptilian, a fine animal effort – all he had begun to feel about her went out in a few ticks of the clock.

In two hours the house was quiet under the simple ministrations of a retired cook whom Bess had sent for; Jean was put to sleep with a sedative by a physician from Ellicott City. It was only when Lew was in bed at last that he thought really of Amanda, and broke suddenly, and only for a moment. She was gone out of the world, his second – no, his third love – killed in single combat. He thought rather of the dripping garden outside, and nature so suddenly innocent in the clearing night. If he had not been so tired he would have dressed and walked through the long-stemmed, clinging ferns, and looked once more impersonally at the house and its inhabitants – the broken old, the youth breaking and growing old with it, the other youth escaping into dissipation. Walking through broken dreams, he came in his imagination to where the falling tree had divided William's bedroom from the house, and paused there in the dark shadow, trying to piece together what he thought about the Gunthers.

"It's degenerate business," he decided – "all this hanging-on to the past. I've been wrong. Some of us are going ahead, and these people and the roof over them are just pushovers for time. I'll be glad to leave it for good and get back to something fresh and new and clean in Wall Street tomorrow."

Only once was he wakened in the night, when he heard the old man quavering querulously about the twenty dollars that he had borrowed in '92. He heard Bess's voice soothing him – and then, just before he went to sleep, the voice of the old Negress blotting out both voices.

3

LEW'S BUSINESS TOOK HIM FREQUENTLY to Baltimore, but with the years it seemed to change back into the Baltimore that he had known before he met the Gunthers. He thought of them often, but after the night of Amanda's death he never went there. By 1933, the role that the family had played in his life seemed so remote – except for the unforgettable fact that they had formed his ideas about how life was lived – that he could drive along the Frederick Road to where it dips into Carroll County before a feeling of recognition crept over him. Impelled by a formless motive, he stopped his car.

It was deep summer; a rabbit crossed the road ahead of him and a squirrel did acrobatics on an arched branch. The Gunther house was up the next crossroad and five minutes away – in half an hour he could satisfy his curiosity about the family; yet he hesitated. With painful consequences, he had once tried to repeat the past, and now, in normal times, he would have driven on with a feeling of leaving the past well behind him; but he had come to realize recently that life was not always a progress, nor a search for new horizons, nor a going-away. The Gunthers were part of him; he would not be able to bring to new friends the exact things that he had brought to the Gunthers. If the memory of them became extinct, then something in himself became extinct also.

The squirrel's flight on the branch, the wind nudging at the leaves, the cock splitting distant air, the creep of sunlight transpiring through the immobility lulled him into an adolescent trance, and he sprawled back against the leather for a moment without problems. He loafed for ten minutes before the "k-dup, k-dup, k-dup" of a walking horse came around the next bend of the road. The horse bore a girl in Jodhpur breeches and, bending forward, Lew recognized Bess Gunther.

He scrambled from the car. The horse shied as Bess recognized Lew and pulled up. "Why, Mr Lowrie!... Hey! Hoo-oo there, girl!... Where did you arrive from? Did you break down?"

It was a lovely face, and a sad face, but it seemed to Lew that some new quality made it younger – as if she had finally abandoned the cosmic sense of responsibility which had made her seem older than her age four years ago.

"I was thinking about you all," he said. "Thinking of paying you a visit." Detecting a doubtful shadow in her face, he jumped to a conclusion and laughed. "I don't mean a visit; I mean a call. I'm solvent – sometimes you have to add that these days."

She laughed too. "I was only thinking the house was full and where would we put you."

"I'm bound for Baltimore anyhow. Why not get off your rocking horse and sit in my car a minute."

She tied the mare to a tree and got in beside him.

He had not realized that flashing fairness could last so far into the twenties – only when she didn't smile he saw from three small thoughtful lines that she was always a grave girl – he had a quick recollection of Amanda on an August afternoon, and looking at Bess, he recognized all that he remembered of Amanda.

"How's your father?"

"Father died last year. He was bedridden a year before he died." Her voice was in the sing-song of something often repeated. "It was just as well."

"I'm sorry. How about Jean? Where is she?"

"Jean married a Chinaman – I mean she married a man who lives in China. I've never seen him."

"Do you live alone, then?"

"No, there's my aunt." She hesitated. "Anyhow, I'm getting married next week."

Inexplicably, he had the old sense of loss in his diaphragm.

"Congratulations! Who's the unfortunate—"

"From Philadelphia. The whole party went over to the races this afternoon. I wanted to have a last ride with Juniper."

"Will you live in Philadelphia?"

"Not sure. We're thinking of building another house on the place, tear down the old one. Of course, we might remodel it."

"Would that be worth doing?"

"Why not?" she said hastily. "We could use some of it, the architects think."

"You're fond of it, aren't you?"

Bess considered.

"I wouldn't say it was just my idea of modernity. But I'm a sort of a home girl." She accentuated the words ironically. "I never went over very big in Baltimore, you know – the family failure. I never had the sort of thing Amanda and Jean had."

"Maybe you didn't want it."

"I thought I did when I was young."

The mare neighed peremptorily, and Bess backed out of the car.

"So that's the story, Lew Lowrie, of the last Gunther girl. You always did have a sort of yen for us, didn't you?"

"Didn't I! If I could possibly stay in Baltimore, I'd insist on coming to your wedding."

At the lost expression on her face, he wondered to whom she was handing herself, a very precious self. He knew more about people now, and he felt the steel beneath the softness in her, the girders showing through the gentle curves of cheek and chin. She was an exquisite person, and he hoped that her husband would be a good man.

When she had ridden off into a green lane, he drove tentatively towards Baltimore. This was the end of a human experience, and it released old images that regrouped themselves about him – if he had married one of the sisters; supposing... The past, slipping away under the wheels of his car, crunched awake his acuteness.

"Perhaps I was always an intruder in that family... But why on earth was that girl riding in bedroom slippers?"

At the crossroads store he stopped to get cigarettes. A young clerk searched the case with country slowness.

"Big wedding up at the Gunther place," Lew remarked.

"Hah? Miss Bess getting married?"

"Next week. The wedding party's there now."

"Well, I'll be dog! Wonder what they're going to sleep on, since Mark H. Bourne took the furniture away?"

"What's that? What?"

"Month ago Mark H. Bourne took all the furniture and everything else while Miss Bess was out riding – they mortgaged on it just before Gunther died. They say around here she ain't got a stitch except them riding clothes. Mark H. Bourne was good and sore. His claim was they sold off all the best pieces of furniture without his knowing it... Now, that's ten cents I owe you."

"What do she and her aunt live on?"

"Never heard about an aunt – I only been here a year. She works the truck garden herself; all she buys from us is sugar, salt and coffee."

Anything was possible these times, yet Lew wondered what incredibly fantastic pride had inspired her to tell that lie.

He turned his car around and drove back to the Gunther place. It was a desperately forlorn house he came to, and a jungled garden; one side of the veranda had slipped from the brick pillars and sloped to the ground; a shingle job, begun and abandoned, rotted paintless on the roof, a broken pane gaped from the library window.

Lew went in without knocking. A voice challenged him from the dining room, and he walked towards it, his feet loud on the rugless floor, through rooms empty of stick and book, empty of all save casual dust. Bess Gunther, wearing the cheapest of house dresses, rose from the packing box on which she sat, with fright in her eyes; a tin spoon rattled on the box she was using as a table.

"Have you been kidding me?" he demanded. "Are you actually living like this?"

"It's you." She smiled in relief; then, with visible effort, she spurred herself into amenities:

"Take a box, Mr Lowrie. Have a canned-goods box – they're superior; the grain is better. And welcome to the open spaces. Have a cigar, a glass of champagne, have some rabbit stew and meet my fiancé."

"Stop that."

"All right," she agreed.

"Why didn't you go and live with some relatives?"

"Haven't got any relatives. Jean's in China."

"What are you doing? What do you expect to happen?"

"I was waiting for you, I guess."

"What do you mean?"

"You always seemed to turn up. I thought if you turned up, I'd make a play for you. But when it came to the point, I thought I'd better lie. I seem to lack the SA my sisters had."

Lew pulled her up from the box and held her with his fingers by her waist.

"Not to me."

In the hour since Lew had met her on the road the vitality seemed to have gone out of her; she looked up at him very tired.

"So you liked the Gunthers," she whispered. "You liked us all."

Lew tried to think, but his heart beat so quick that he could only sit her back on the box and pace along the empty walls.

"We'll get married," he said. "I don't know whether I love you – I don't even know you – I know the notion of your being in want or trouble makes me physically sick." Suddenly he went down on both knees in front of her so that she would not seem so unbearably small and helpless. "Miss Bess Gunther, so it was you I was meant to love all the while."

"Don't be so anxious about it," she laughed. "I'm not used to being loved. I wouldn't know what to do; I never got the trick of it." She looked down at him, shy and fatigued. "So here we are. I told you years ago that I had the makings of Cinderella."

He took her hand; she drew it back instinctively and then replaced it in his. "Beg your pardon. Not even used to being touched. But I'm not afraid of you, if you stay quiet and don't move suddenly."

It was the same old story of reserve Lew could not fathom, motives reaching back into a past he did not share. With the three girls, facts seemed to reveal themselves precipitately, pushing up through the gay surface; they were always unsuspected things, currents and predilections alien to a man who had been able to shoot in a straight line always.

"I was the conservative sister," Bess said. "I wasn't any less pleasure-loving, but with three girls, somebody has to play the boy, and gradually that got to be my part... Yes, touch me like that. Touch my cheek. I want to be touched; I want to be held. And I'm glad it's you; but you've got to go slow; you've got to be careful. I'm afraid I'm the kind of person that's for ever. I'll live with you and die for you, but I never knew what halfway meant... Yes, that's the wrist. Do you like it? I've had a lot of fun looking at myself in the last month, because there's one long mirror upstairs that was too big to take out."

Lew stood up. "All right, we'll start like that. I'll be so healthy that I'll make you all healthy again."

"Yes, like that," she agreed.

"Suppose we begin by setting fire to this house."

"Oh, no!" She took him seriously. "In the first place, it's insured. In the second place—"

"All right, we'll just get out. We'll get married in Baltimore, or Ellicott City if you'd rather."

"How about Juniper? I can't go off and leave her."

"We'll leave her with the young man at the store."

"The house isn't mine. It's all mortgaged away, but they let me live here – I guess it was remorse after they took even our old music, and our old scrapbooks. They didn't have a chance of getting a tenant, anyhow."

Minute by minute, Lew found out more about her, and liked what he found, but he saw that the love in her was all encrusted with the sacrificial years, and that he would have to be gardener to it for a while. The task seemed attractive.

"You lovely," he told her. "You lovely! We'll survive, you and I, because you're so nice and I'm so convinced about it."

"And about Juniper – will she survive if we go away like this?"

"Juniper too."

She frowned and then smiled – and this time really smiled – and said: "Seems to me you're falling in love."

"Speak for yourself. My opinion is that this is going to be the best thing ever happened."

"I'm going to help. I insist on…"

They went out together – Bess changed into her riding habit, but there wasn't another article that she wanted to bring with her. Backing through the clogging weeds of the garden, Lew looked at the house over his shoulder. "Next week or so we'll decide what to do about that."

It was a bright sunset – the creep of rosy light that played across the blue fenders of the car and across their crazily happy faces moved across the house too – across the paralysed door of the ice house, the rusting tin gutters, the loose-swinging shutter, the cracked cement of the front walk, the burnt place of last year's rubbish back of the tennis court. Whatever its further history, the whole human effort of collaboration was done now. The purpose of the house was achieved – finished and folded – it was an effort towards some commonweal, an effort difficult to estimate, so closely does it press against us still.

The Fiend

O N 3 R D J U N E 1895, on a country road near Stillwater, Minnesota, Mrs Crenshaw Engels and her seven-year-old son, Mark, were waylaid and murdered by a fiend, under circumstances so atrocious that, fortunately, it is not necessary to set them down here.

Crenshaw Engels, the husband and father, was a photographer in Stillwater. He was a great reader and considered "a little unsafe", for he had spoken his mind frankly about the railroad-agrarian struggles of the time – but no one denied that he was a devoted family man, and the catastrophe visited upon him hung over the little town for many weeks. There was a move to lynch the perpetrator of the horror, for Minnesota did not permit the capital punishment it deserved, but the instigators were foiled by the big stone penitentiary close at hand.

The cloud hung over Engels's home so that folks went there only in moods of penitence, of fear or guilt, hoping that they would be visited in turn should their lives ever chance to trek under a black sky. The photography studio suffered also: the routine of being posed, the necessary silences and pauses in the process, permitted the clients too much time to regard the prematurely aged face of Crenshaw Engels, and high-school students, newly married couples, mothers of new babies were always glad to escape from the place into the open air. So Crenshaw's business fell off and he went through a time of hardship – finally liquidating the lease, the apparatus and the goodwill, and wearing out the money obtained. He sold his house for a little more than its two mortgages, went to board and took a position clerking in Radamacher's Department Store.

In the sight of his neighbours he had become a man ruined by adversity, a man *manqué,* a man emptied. But in the last opinion they were wrong – he was empty of all save one thing. His memory was long as a Jew's, and though his heart was in the grave he was sane as when his wife and son had started on their last walk that summer morning. At the first trial he lost control and got at the Fiend, seizing him by the necktie – and then had been dragged off with the Fiend's tie in such a knot that the man was nearly garrotted.

At the second trial Crenshaw cried aloud once. Afterwards he went to all the members of the state legislature in the county and handed them a bill he had written himself for the introduction of capital punishment in the state – the bill to be retroactive on criminals condemned to life imprisonment. The bill fell through; it was on the day Crenshaw heard this that he got inside the penitentiary by a ruse and was only apprehended in time to be prevented from shooting the Fiend in his cell.

Crenshaw was given a suspended sentence, and for some months it was assumed that the agony was fading gradually from his mind. In fact, when he presented himself to the warden in another role a year after the crime, the official was sympathetic to his statement that he had had a change of heart and felt he could only emerge from the Valley of Shadow by forgiveness, that he wanted to help the Fiend, show him the True Path by means of good books and appeals to his buried better nature. So, after being carefully searched, Crenshaw was permitted to sit for half an hour in the corridor outside the Fiend's cell.

But had the warden suspected the truth he would not have permitted the visit – for, far from forgiving, Crenshaw's plan was to wreak upon the Fiend a mental revenge to replace the physical one of which he was subducted.

When he faced the Fiend, Crenshaw felt his scalp tingle. From behind the bars a roly-poly man, who somehow made his convict's uniform resemble a business suit, a man with thick brown-rimmed glasses and the trim air of an insurance salesman, looked at him uncertainly. Feeling faint, Crenshaw sat down in the chair that had been brought for him.

"The air around you stinks!" he cried suddenly. "This whole corridor, this whole prison."

"I suppose it does," admitted the Fiend, "I noticed it too."

"You'll have time to notice it," Crenshaw muttered. "All your life you'll pace up and down stinking in that little cell, with everything getting blacker and blacker. And after that there'll be hell waiting for you. For all eternity you'll be shut in a little space, but in hell it'll be so small that you can't stand up or stretch out."

"*Will* it now?" asked the Fiend, concerned.

"It will!" said Crenshaw. "You'll be alone with your own vile thoughts in that little space, for ever and ever and ever. You'll itch with corruption so that you can never sleep, and you'll always be thirsty, with water just out of reach."

"*Will* I now?" repeated the Fiend, even more concerned. "I remember once—"

"All the time you'll be full of horror," Crenshaw interrupted. "You'll be like a person just about to go crazy but can't go crazy. All the time you'll be thinking that it's for ever and ever."

"That's bad," said the Fiend, shaking his head gloomily. "That's real bad."

"Now listen here to me," went on Crenshaw. "I've brought you some books you're going to read. It's arranged that you get no books or papers except what I bring you."

As a beginning Crenshaw had brought half a dozen books, which his vagarious curiosity had collected over as many years. They comprised a German doctor's thousand case histories of sexual abnormality – cases with no cures, no hopes, no prognoses, cases listed cold; a series of sermons by a New England Divine of the Great Revival which pictured the tortures of the damned in hell; a collection of horror stories; and a volume of erotic pieces from each of which the last two pages, containing the consummations, had been torn out; a volume of detective stories mutilated in the same manner. A tome of the Newgate calendar completed the batch. These Crenshaw handed through the bars – the Fiend took them and put them on his iron cot.

This was the first of Crenshaw's long series of fortnightly visits. Always he brought with him something sombre and menacing to say, something dark and terrible to read – save that once, when the Fiend had had nothing to read for a long time, he brought him four inspiringly titled books – that proved to have nothing but blank paper inside. Another time, pretending to concede a point, he promised to bring newspapers – he brought ten copies of the yellowed journal that had reported the crime and the arrest. Sometimes he obtained medical books that showed in colour the red and blue and green ravages of leprosy and skin disease, the mounds of shattered cells, the verminous tissue and brown corrupted blood.

And there was no sewer of the publishing world from which he did not obtain records of all that was gross and vile in man.

Crenshaw could not keep this up indefinitely, both because of the expense and because of the exhaustibility of such books. When five years had passed he leant towards another form of torture. He built up false hopes in the Fiend with protests of his own change of heart and manoeuvres for a pardon, and then dashed the hopes to pieces. Or else he pretended to have a pistol with him, or an inflammatory substance that would make the cell a raging Inferno and consume the Fiend in two minutes – once he threw a dummy bottle into the cell and listened in delight to the screams as the Fiend ran back and forth waiting for the explosion. At other times he would pretend grimly that the legislature had passed a new law which provided that the Fiend would be executed in a few hours.

A decade passed. Crenshaw was grey at forty – he was white at fifty when the alternating routine of his fortnightly visits to the graves of his loved ones and to the penitentiary had become the only part of his life

– the long days at Radamacher's were only a weary dream. Sometimes he went and sat outside the Fiend's cell, with no word said during the half-hour he was allowed to be there. The Fiend too had grown white in twenty years. He was very respectable-looking with his horn-rimmed glasses and his white hair. He seemed to have a great respect for Crenshaw, and even when the latter, in a renewal of diminishing vitality, promised him one day that on his very next visit he was going to bring a revolver and end the matter, he nodded gravely as if in agreement, said, "I suppose so. Yes, I suppose you're perfectly right," and did not mention the matter to the guards. On the occasion of the next visit he was waiting with his hands on the bars of the cell looking at Crenshaw both hopefully and desperately. At certain tensions and strains, death takes on, indeed, the quality of a great adventure, as any soldier can testify.

Years passed. Crenshaw was promoted to floor manager at Radamacher's – there were new generations now that did not know of his tragedy and regarded him as an austere nonentity. He came into a little legacy and bought new stones for the graves of his wife and son. He knew he would soon be retired, and while a third decade lapsed through the white winters, the short sweet smoky summers, it became more and more plain to him that the time had come to put an end to the Fiend; to avoid any mischance by which the other would survive him.

The moment he fixed upon came at the exact end of thirty years. Crenshaw had long owned the pistol with which it would be accomplished; he had fingered the shells lovingly and calculated the lodgement of each in the Fiend's body, so that death would be sure but lingering – he studied the tales of abdominal wounds in the war news and delighted in the agony that made victims pray to be killed.

After that, what happened to *him* did not matter.

When the day came, he had no trouble in smuggling the pistol into the penitentiary. But to his surprise he found the Fiend scrunched up upon his iron cot, instead of waiting for him avidly by the bars.

"I'm sick," the Fiend said. "My stomach's been burning me up all morning. They gave me a physic, but now it's worse and nobody comes."

Crenshaw fancied momentarily that this was a premonition in the man's bowels of a bullet that would shortly ride ragged through that spot.

"Come up to the bars," he said mildly.

"I can't move."

"Yes, you can."

"I'm doubled up. All doubled up."

"Come doubled up then."

With an effort the Fiend moved himself, only to fall on his side on the cement floor. He groaned and then lay quiet for a minute, after which, still bent in two, he began to drag himself a foot at a time towards the bars.

Suddenly Crenshaw set off at a run towards the end of the corridor.

"I want the prison doctor," he demanded of the guard. "That man's sick – *sick,* I tell you."

"The doctor has—"

"Get him – get him now!"

The guard hesitated, but Crenshaw had become a tolerated, even privileged person around the prison, and in a moment the guard took down his phone and called the infirmary.

All that afternoon Crenshaw waited in the bare area inside the gates, walking up and down with his hands behind his back. From time to time he went to the front entrance and demanded of the guard:

"Any news?"

"Nothing yet. They'll call me when there's anything."

Late in the afternoon, the warden appeared at the door, looked about and spotted Crenshaw. The latter, all alert, hastened over.

"He's dead," the warden said. "His appendix burst. They did every-thing they could."

"Dead," Crenshaw repeated.

"I'm sorry to bring you this news. I know how—"

"It's all right," said Crenshaw, and licking his lips. "So he's dead."

The warden lit a cigarette.

"While you're here, Mr Engels, I wonder if you can let me have that pass that was issued to you – I can turn it in to the office. That is – I suppose you won't need it any more."

Crenshaw took the blue card from his wallet and handed it over. The warden shook hands with him.

"One thing more," Crenshaw demanded as the warden turned away. "Which is the... the window of the infirmary?"

"It's on the interior court, you can't see it from here."

"Oh."

When the warden had gone, Crenshaw still stood there a long time, the tears running out down his face. He could not collect his thoughts and he began by trying to remember what day it was; Saturday, the day, every other week, on which he came to see the Fiend.

He would not see the Fiend two weeks from now.

In a misery of solitude and despair he muttered aloud: "So he is dead. He has left me." And then with a long sigh of mingled grief and fear: "So I have lost him – my only friend – now I am alone."

He was still saying that to himself as he passed through the outer gate, and as his coat caught in the great swing of the outer door and the guard opened up to release it, he heard a reiteration of the words:

"I'm alone. At last – at last I am alone."

Once more he called on the Fiend, after many weeks.

"But he's dead," the warden told him kindly.

"Oh, yes," Crenshaw said. "I guess I must have forgotten."

And he set off back home, his boots sinking deep into the white diamond surface of the flats.

The Night at Chancellorsville

I TELL YOU I DIDN'T HAVE any notion what I was getting into or I wouldn't of gone down there. They can have their army – it seems to me they were all a bunch of yella-bellies. But my friend Nell said to me: "Nora, Philly is as dead as Baltimore and we've got to eat this summer." She just got a letter from a girl that said they were living fine down there in "Ole Virginia". The soldiers were getting big pay-offs and figuring maybe they'd stay there all summer, at least till the Johnny Rebs* gave up. They got their pay regular too, and a good clean-looking girl could ask... well, I forget now, because, after what happened to us, I guess you can't expect me to remember anything.

I've always been used to decent treatment – somehow when I meet a man, no matter how fresh he is in the beginning, he comes to respect me in the end, and I've never had things done to me like some girls – getting left in a strange town or had my purse stolen.

Well, I started to tell you how I went down to the army in "Ole Virginia". Never again! Wait'll you hear.

I was used to travelling nice – once when I was a little girl my daddy took me on the cars to Baltimore – we lived in York, PA. And we couldn't have been more comfortable; we had pillows and the men came through with baskets of oranges and apples. You know, singing out: "Want to buy some oranges or apples – or beer?"

You know what they sell – but I never took any beer because...

Oh I know, I'll go on... You only want to talk about the war, like all you men. But if this is your idea what a war is...

Well, they stuck us all in one car and a fresh fella took our tickets, and winked and said:

"Oh, you're going down to Hooker's army."*

The lights were terrible in the car, smoky and full of bugs, so everything looked sort of yella. And say, that car was so old it was falling to pieces.

There must of been forty gay girls in it, a lot of them from Baltimore and Philly. Only there were three or four that weren't gay – I mean they were more, oh, you know, rich people, and sat up front. Every once an' a while an officer would pop in from the next car and ask them if they wanted anything. I was in the seat behind with Nell, and we heard him whisper: "You're in terrible company, but we'll be there in a few hours. And we'll go right to headquarters, and I guarantee you some solid comfort."

I never will forget that night. None of us had any food except some girls behind us had some sausages and bread, and they gave us what they had left. There was a spigot you turned, but no water came out. After about two hours – stopping every two minutes it seemed to me – a couple of lieutenants, drunk as monkeys, came in from the next car and offered Nell and me some whiskey out of a bottle. Nell took some and I pretended to, and they set on the side of our seats. One of them started to make up to Nell, but just then the officer that had spoken to the women, pretty high up I guess, a major or a general, came back again and asked:

"You all right? Anything I can do?"

One of the ladies kind of whispered to him, and he turned to the one that was talking to Nell and made him go back in the other car. After that there was only one officer with us; he wasn't really so drunk, just feeling sick.

"This certainly is a happy-looking gang," he said. "It's good you can hardly see them in this light. They look as if their best friend just died."

"What if they do?" Nell answered back quick. "How would you look yourself if you come all the way from Philly and then got in a buggy like this?"

"I come all the way from the Seven Days, sister," he answered. "Maybe I'd be more pretty for you if I hadn't lost an eye at Gaines's Mill."*

Then we noticed he *had* lost an eye. He kept it sort of closed, so we hadn't remarked it before. Pretty soon he left and said he'd try and get us some water or coffee: that was what we wanted most.

The car kept rocking, and it made us both feel funny. Some of the girls was sick and some was asleep on each other's shoulders.

"Hey, where *is* this army?" Nell said. "Down in Mexico?"

I was kind of half asleep myself by that time and didn't answer.

The next thing I knew I was woke up by a storm, the car was stopped again, and I said, "It's raining."

"Raining!" said Nell. "That's cannons – they're having a battle."

"Oh!" I got awake. "Well, after *this* ride I don't care who wins."

It seemed to get louder all the time, but out the windows you couldn't see anything on account of the mist.

In about half an hour another officer came in the car – he looked pretty messy, as if he'd just crawled out of bed: his coat was still unbuttoned and he kept hitching up his trousers as if he didn't have any suspenders on.

"All you ladies outside," he said. "We need this car for the wounded."

"Hey!"

"We paid for our tickets, didn't we?"

"We need all the cars for the wounded and the other cars are filled up."

"Hey! We didn't come down to fight in any battle!"

"It doesn't matter what you came down for – you're in a hell of a battle."

I was scared, I can tell *you*. I thought maybe the Rebs would capture us and send us down to one of those prisons you hear about, where they starve you to death unless you sing 'Dixie' all the time and kiss niggers.

"Hurry up!"

But another officer had come in who looked more nice.

"Stay where you are, ladies," he said. And then he said to the officer, "What do you want to do? leave them standing on the siding! If Sedgwick's Corps* is broken, like they say, the Rebs may come up in this direction!"

Some of the girls began crying out loud.

"These are Northern women after all," he said.

"These are—"

"Shut up and go back to your command! I'm detailed to this transportation job – I'm taking these girls back to Washington with us."

I thought they were going to hit each other, but they both walked off together. And we girls sat wondering what we were going to do.

What happened next I don't remember exact. The cannons were sometimes very loud, and then sometimes more far away, but there was firing of shots right near us – and a girl down the car had her window smashed like a hole in the centre, sort of, all smashed you know, not like when you break a glass, more like ice in cold weather, just a hole and streaks around – you know. I heard a whole bunch of horses gallop by our windows, but I still couldn't see anything.

That went on half an hour – galloping and more shots. We couldn't tell how far away, but they sounded like up by the engine.

Then it got quiet – and two men came into our car – we all knew right away they were Rebels, not officers, just plain private ones, with muskets. One had on an old brown blouse sort of thing and one had on a blue thing – all spotted – I know I could never of let *that* man make love to me. It had spots – it was too short – anyway, it was out of style. Oh, it was disgusting. I was surprised, because I thought they always wore grey. They were disgusting-looking and very dirty; one had a big pot of jam smeared all over his face, and the other one had a big box of crackers.

"Hi ladies."

"What you gals doin' down here?"

"Cain't you see, Steve, this is old Joe Hooker's staff."

"Reckin we ought to take 'em back to the General?"

They talked outlandish like that – I could hardly understand, they talked so funny.

One of the girls got historical she was so scared, and that made them kind of shy. They were just kids under those beards, and one of them tipped his hat or cap or whatever the old thing was.

"We're not fixin' to hurt you."

At that moment there was a whole bunch more shooting down by the engine and the Rebs turned and ran.

We were glad, I can tell you.

Then, about fifteen minutes later, in came one of our officers. This was another new one.

"You better duck down!" he shouted to us. "They may fire on this train. We're starting you off as soon as we unload two more ambulances."

Half of us was on the floor already. The rich women sitting ahead of Nell and me had gone up into the car ahead, where the wounded were – to see if they could do anything. Nell thought she'd look in too, but she came back holding her nose. She said it smelt awful in there.

It was lucky she didn't go in, because two of the girls did from our car. People that is sick can never seem to get much consideration for other people who happen to be well. The nurses sent them right back – as if they was dirt under their feet.

After I don't know how long, the train began to move. A soldier come in and poured oil out of all our lights except one, and took it into the wounded car. So now we could hardly see at all.

If the trip down was slow, the trip back was slower... The wounded began making so much noise, grunting and all, that we could hear it and couldn't get a decent sleep.

We stopped everywhere.

When we got in Washington at last, there was a lot of people in the station and they were all anxious about what had happened to the army, but I said, "You can search me." All I wanted was my little old room and my little old bed. I never been treated like that in my life.

One of the girls said she was going to write to President Lincoln about it.

And in the papers next day they never said anything about how our train got attacked, or about us girls at all! Can you beat it?

Afternoon of an Author

1

WHEN HE WOKE UP, he felt better than he had for many weeks, a fact that became plain to him negatively – he did not feel ill. He leant for a moment against the door frame between his bedroom and bath till he could be sure he was not dizzy. Not a bit, not even when he stooped for a slipper under the bed.

It was a bright April morning, he had no idea what time, because his clock was long unwound, but as he went back through the apartment to the kitchen he saw that his daughter had breakfasted and departed and that the mail was in, so it was after nine.

"I think I'll go out today," he said to the maid.

"Do you good – it's a lovely day." She was from New Orleans, with the features and colouring of an Arab.

"I want two eggs like yesterday and toast, orange juice and tea."

He lingered for a moment in his daughter's end of the apartment and read his mail. It was an annoying mail with nothing cheerful in it – mostly bills and advertisements with the diurnal Oklahoma schoolboy and his gaping autograph album. Sam Goldwyn might do a ballet picture with Spessiwitza* and might not – it would all have to wait till Mr Goldwyn got back from Europe, when he might have half a dozen new ideas. Paramount wanted a release on a poem that had appeared in one of the author's books, as they didn't know whether it was an original or quoted. Maybe they were going to get a title from it. Anyhow he had no more equity in that property – he had sold the silent rights many years ago and the sound rights last year.

"Never any luck with movies," he said to himself. "Stick to your last, boy."

He looked out the window during breakfast at the students changing classes on the college campus across the way.

"Twenty years ago I was changing classes," he said to the maid. She laughed her debutante's laugh.

"I'll need a cheque," she said, "if you're going out."

"Oh, I'm not going out yet. I've got two or three hours' work. I meant late this afternoon."

"Going for a drive?"

"I wouldn't drive that old junk – I'd sell it for fifty dollars. I'm going on the top of a bus."

After breakfast he lay down for fifteen minutes. Then he went into the study and began to work.

The problem was a magazine story that had become so thin in the middle that it was about to blow away. The plot was like climbing endless stairs, he had no element of surprise in reserve, and the characters who started so bravely day before yesterday couldn't have qualified for a newspaper serial.

"Yes, I certainly need to get out," he thought. "I'd like to drive down the Shenandoah Valley, or go to Norfolk on the boat."

But both of these ideas were impractical – they took time and energy and he had not much of either – what there was must be conserved for work. He went through the manuscript underlining good phrases in red crayon and, after tucking these into a file, slowly tore up the rest of the story and dropped it in the wastebasket. Then he walked the room and smoked, occasionally talking to himself.

"Wee-l, let's see…"

"Nau-ow, the next thing… would be…"

"Now let's see, now…"

After a while he sat down thinking:

"I'm just stale – I shouldn't have touched a pencil for two days."

He looked through the heading "Story Ideas" in his notebook until the maid came to tell him his secretary was on the phone – part-time secretary since he had been ill.

"Not a thing," he said. "I just tore up everything I'd written. It wasn't worth a damn. I'm going out this afternoon."

"Good for you. It's a fine day."

"Better come up tomorrow afternoon – there's a lot of mail and bills."

He shaved, and then as a precaution rested five minutes before he dressed. It was exciting to be going out – he hoped the elevator boys wouldn't say they were glad to see him up and he decided to go down the back elevator, where they did not know him. He put on his best suit with the coat and trousers that didn't match. He had bought only two suits in six years, but they were the very best suits – the coat alone of this one had cost a hundred and ten dollars. As he must have a destination – it wasn't good to go places without a destination – he put a tube of shampoo ointment in his pocket for his barber to use, and also a small phial of luminol.

"The perfect neurotic," he said, regarding himself in the mirror. "Byproduct of an idea, slag of a dream."

2

H E WENT INTO THE KITCHEN and said goodbye to the maid as if he were going to Little America. Once in the war he had commandeered an engine on sheer bluff and had it driven from New York to Washington to keep from being AWOL. Now he stood carefully on the street corner waiting for the light to change, while young people hurried past him with a fine disregard for traffic. On the bus corner under the trees it was green and cool and he thought of Stonewall Jackson's last words: "Let us cross over the river and rest under the shade of the trees."* Those Civil War leaders seemed to have realized very suddenly how tired they were – Lee shrivelling into another man, Grant with his desperate memoir-writing at the end.*

The bus was all he expected – only one other man on the roof and the green branches ticking against each window through whole blocks. They would probably have to trim those branches, and it seemed a pity. There was so much to look at – he tried to define the colour of one line of houses and could only think of an old opera cloak of his mother's that was full of tints and yet was of no tint – a mere reflector of light. Somewhere church bells were playing *Venite adoremus** and he wondered why, because Christmas was eight months off. He didn't like bells, but it had been very moving when they played 'Maryland, My Maryland' at the governor's funeral.

On the college football field men were working with rollers, and a title occurred to him: *Turf-Keeper* or else *The Grass Grows*, something about a man working on turf for years and bringing up his son to go to college and play football there. Then the son dying in youth and the man's going to work in the cemetery and putting turf over his son instead of under his feet. It would be the kind of piece that is often placed in anthologies, but not his sort of thing – it was sheer swollen antithesis, as formalized as a popular magazine story and easier to write. Many people, however, would consider it excellent because it was melancholy, had digging in it and was simple to understand.

The bus went past a pale Athenian railroad station brought to life by the blue-shirted redcaps out in front. The street narrowed as the business section began, and there were suddenly brightly dressed girls, all very beautiful – he thought he had never seen such beautiful girls. There were men too, but they all looked rather silly, like himself in the mirror, and there were old undecorative women – and presently, too, there were plain and unpleasant faces among the girls; but in general they were lovely, dressed in real colours all the way from six to thirty, no plans or struggles in their faces, only a state of sweet suspension, provocative and serene. He loved life terribly for a minute, not wanting to give it up at all. He thought perhaps he had made a mistake in coming out so soon.

He got off the bus, holding carefully to all the railings, and walked a block to the hotel barber shop. He passed a sporting-goods store and looked in the window, unmoved except by a first baseman's glove which was already dark in the pocket. Next to that was a haberdasher's, and here he stood for quite a while looking at the deep shade of shirts and the ones of chequer and plaid. Ten years ago, on the summer Riviera, the author and some others had bought dark-blue workmen's shirts, and probably that had started that style. The chequered shirts were nice-looking, bright as uniforms, and he wished he were twenty and going to a beach club all dolled up like a Turner sunset or Guido Reni's *Dawn*.*

The barbershop was large, shining and scented – it had been several months since the author had come downtown on such a mission, and he found that his familiar barber was laid up with arthritis; however, he explained to another man how to use the ointment, refused a newspaper and sat, rather happy and sensually content at the strong fingers on his scalp, while a pleasant mingled memory of all the barber shops he had ever known flowed through his mind.

Once he had written a story about a barber. Back in 1929 the proprietor of his favourite shop in the city where he was then living had made a fortune of $300,000 on tips from a local industrialist and was about to retire. The author had no stake in the market, in fact was about to sail for Europe for a few years with such accumulation as he had, and that autumn, hearing how the barber had lost all his fortune, he was prompted to write a story, thoroughly disguised in every way yet hinging on the fact of a barber rising in the world and then tumbling; he heard, nevertheless, that the story had been identified in the city and caused some hard feelings.

The shampoo ended. When he came out into the hall, an orchestra had started to play in the cocktail room across the way, and he stood for

217

a moment in the door listening. So long since he had danced, perhaps two evenings in five years, yet a review of his last book had mentioned him as being fond of nightclubs; the same review had also spoken of him as being indefatigable. Something in the sound of the word in his mind broke him momentarily and, feeling tears of weakness behind his eyes, he turned away. It was like in the beginning fifteen years ago, when they said he had "fatal facility", and he laboured like a slave over every sentence so as not to be like that.

"I'm getting bitter again," he said to himself. "That's no good, no good... I've got to go home."

The bus was a long time coming, but he didn't like taxis and he still hoped that something would occur to him on that upper-deck passing through the green leaves of the boulevard. When it came finally he had some trouble climbing the steps, but it was worth it, for the first thing he saw was a pair of high-school kids, a boy and a girl, sitting without any self-consciousness on the high pedestal of the Lafayette statue, their attention fast upon each other. Their isolation moved him, and he knew he would get something out of it professionally, if only in contrast to the growing seclusion of his life and the increasing necessity of picking over an already well-picked past. He needed reforestation and he was well aware of it, and he hoped the soil would stand one more growth. It had never been the very best soil, for he had had an early weakness for showing off instead of listening and observing.

Here was the apartment house – he glanced up at his own windows on the top floor before he went in.

"The residence of the successful writer," he said to himself. "I wonder what marvellous books he's tearing off up there. It must be great to have a gift like that – just sit down with pencil and paper. Work when you want – go where you please."

His child wasn't home yet, but the maid came out of the kitchen and said:

"Did you have a nice time?"

"Perfect," he said. "I went roller-skating and bowled and played around with Man Mountain Dean* and finished up in a Turkish bath. Any telegrams?"

"Not a thing."

"Bring me a glass of milk, will you?"

He went through the dining room and turned into his study, struck blind for a moment with the glow of his two thousand books in the late sunshine. He was quite tired – he would lie down for ten minutes and then see if he could get started on an idea in the two hours before dinner.

Financing Finnegan

1

FINNEGAN AND I HAVE THE SAME literary agent to sell our writings for us – but though I'd often been in Mr Cannon's office just before and just after Finnegan's visits, I had never met him. Likewise we had the same publisher and often when I arrived there Finnegan had just departed. I gathered from a thoughtful sighing way in which they spoke of him – "Ah... Finnegan..." "Oh yes, Finnegan was here." – that the distinguished author's visit had been not uneventful. Certain remarks implied that he had taken something with him when he went – manuscripts, I supposed, one of those great successful novels of his. He had taken "it" off for a final revision, a last draft, of which he was rumoured to make ten in order to achieve that facile flow, that ready wit which distinguished his work. I discovered only gradually that most of Finnegan's visits had to do with money.

"I'm sorry you're leaving," Mr Cannon would tell me. "Finnegan will be here tomorrow." Then, after a thoughtful pause: "I'll probably have to spend some time with him."

I don't know what note in his voice reminded me of a talk with a nervous bank president when Dillinger* was reported in the vicinity. His eyes looked out into the distance and he spoke as to himself:

"Of course he may be bringing a manuscript. He has a novel he's working on, you know. And a play too."

He spoke as though he were talking about some interesting but remote events of the Cinquecento; but his eyes became more hopeful as he added: "Or maybe a short story."

"He's very versatile, isn't he?" I said.

"Oh yes." Mr Cannon perked up. "He can do anything – anything – when he puts his mind to it. There's never been such a talent."

"I haven't seen much of his work lately."

"Oh, but he's working hard. Some of the magazines have stories of his that they're holding."

"Holding for what?"

"Oh, for a more appropriate time – an upswing. They like to think they have something of Finnegan's."

His was indeed a name with ingots in it. His career had started brilliantly, and if it had not kept up to its first exalted level, at least it started brilliantly all over again every few years. He was the perennial man of promise in American letters – what he could actually do with words was astounding; they glowed and coruscated – he wrote sentences, paragraphs, chapters that were masterpieces of fine weaving and spinning. It was only when I met some poor devil of a screenwriter who had been trying to make a logical story out of one of his books that I realized he had his enemies.

"It's all beautiful when you read it," this man said disgustedly, "but when you write it down plain it's like a week in the nuthouse."

From Mr Cannon's office I went over to my publishers on Fifth Avenue, and there too I learnt in no time that Finnegan was expected tomorrow.

Indeed he had thrown such a long shadow before him that the luncheon where I expected to discuss my own work was largely devoted to Finnegan. Again I had the feeling that my host, Mr George Jaggers, was talking not to me but to himself.

"Finnegan's a great writer," he said.

"Undoubtedly."

"And he's really quite all right, you know."

As I hadn't questioned the fact, I enquired whether there was any doubt about it.

"Oh no," he said hurriedly. "It's just that he's had such a run of hard luck lately…"

I shook my head sympathetically. "I know. That diving into a half-empty pool was a tough break."

"Oh, it wasn't half empty. It was full of water. Full to the brim. You ought to hear Finnegan on the subject – he makes a side-splitting story of it. It seems he was in a run-down condition and just diving from the side of the pool, you know…" Mr Jaggers pointed his knife and fork at the table. "And he saw some young girls diving from the fifteen-foot board. He says he thought of his lost youth and went up to do the same and made a beautiful swan dive – but his shoulder broke while he was still in the air." He looked at me rather anxiously. "Haven't you heard of cases like that – a ball player throwing his arm out of joint?"

I couldn't think of any orthopaedic parallels at the moment.

"And then," he continued dreamily, "Finnegan had to write on the ceiling."

"On the ceiling?"

"Practically. He didn't give up writing – he has plenty of guts, that fellow, though you may not believe it. He had some sort of arrangement built that was suspended from the ceiling, and he lay on his back and wrote in the air."

I had to grant that it was a courageous arrangement.

"Did it affect his work?" I enquired. "Did you have to read his stories backward – like Chinese?"

"They were rather confused for a while," he admitted, "but he's all right now. I got several letters from him that sounded more like the old Finnegan – full of life and hope and plans for the future…"

The faraway look came into his face, and I turned the discussion to affairs closer to my heart. Only when we were back in his office did the subject recur – and I blush as I write this, because it includes confessing something I seldom do – reading another man's telegram. It happened because Mr Jaggers was intercepted in the hall, and when I went into his office and sat down it was stretched out open before me:

WITH FIFTY I COULD AT LEAST PAY TYPIST AND GET HAIRCUT AND PENCILS LIFE HAS BECOME IMPOSSIBLE AND I EXIST ON DREAM OF GOOD NEWS DESPERATELY FINNEGAN

I couldn't believe my eyes – fifty dollars, and I happened to know that Finnegan's price for short stories was somewhere around three thousand. George Jaggers found me still staring dazedly at the telegram. After he read it he stared at me with stricken eyes.

"I don't see how I can conscientiously do it," he said.

I started and glanced around to make sure I was in the prosperous publishing office in New York. Then I understood – I had misread the telegram. Finnegan was asking for fifty thousand as an advance – a demand that would have staggered any publisher, no matter who the writer was.

"Only last week," said Mr Jaggers disconsolately, "I sent him a hundred dollars. It puts my department in the red every season, so I don't dare tell my partners any more. I take it out of my own pocket – give up a suit and a pair of shoes."

"You mean Finnegan's broke?"

"Broke!" He looked at me and laughed soundlessly – in fact I didn't exactly like the way that he laughed. My brother had a nervous... but that is afield from this story. After a minute he pulled himself together. "You won't say anything about this, will you? The truth is Finnegan's been in a slump, he's had blow after blow in the past few years, but now

he's snapping out of it and I know we'll get back every cent we've…"
He tried to think of a word, but "given him" slipped out. This time it
was he who was eager to change the subject.

Don't let me give the impression that Finnegan's affairs absorbed me
during a whole week in New York – it was inevitable, though, that being
much in the offices of my agent and my publisher, I happened in on a lot.
For instance, two days later, using the telephone in Mr Cannon's office, I
was accidentally switched in on a conversation he was having with George
Jaggers. It was only partly eavesdropping, you see, because I could only
hear one end of the conversation, and that isn't as bad as hearing it all.

"But I got the impression he was in good health… he did say something
about his heart a few months ago, but I understood it got well… yes, and
he talked about some operation he wanted to have – I think he said it was
cancer… Well, I felt like telling him I had a little operation up my sleeve
too, that I'd have had by now if I could afford it… No, I didn't say it. He
seemed in such good spirits that it would have been a shame to bring him
down. He's starting a story today, he read me some of it on the phone…

"…I did give him twenty-five because he didn't have a cent in his pocket…
oh, yes – I'm sure he'll be all right now. He sounds as if he means business."

I understood it all now. The two men had entered into a silent conspiracy
to cheer each other up about Finnegan. Their investment in him, in his
future, had reached a sum so considerable that Finnegan belonged to them.
They could not bear to hear a word against him – even from themselves.

2

I SPOKE MY MIND TO MR CANNON. "If this Finnegan is a four-flusher,
you can't go on indefinitely giving him money. If he's through he's
through, and there's nothing to be done about it. It's absurd that you
should put off an operation when Finnegan's out somewhere diving into
half-empty swimming pools."

"It was full," said Mr Cannon patiently – "full to the brim."

"Well, full or empty, the man sounds like a nuisance to me."

"Look here," said Cannon, "I've got a talk to Hollywood due on the wire. Meanwhile you might glance over that." He threw a manuscript into my lap. "Maybe it'll help you understand. He brought it in yesterday."

It was a short story. I began it in a mood of disgust, but before I'd read five minutes I was completely immersed in it, utterly charmed, utterly convinced and wishing to God I could write like that. When Cannon finished his phone call, I kept him waiting while I finished it, and when I did there were tears in these hard old professional eyes. Any magazine in the country would have run it first in any issue.

But then nobody had ever denied that Finnegan could write.

3

MONTHS PASSED BEFORE I went again to New York, and then, so far as the offices of my agent and my publisher were concerned, I descended upon a quieter, more stable world. There was at last time to talk about my own conscientious if uninspired literary pursuits, to visit Mr Cannon in the country and to kill summer evenings with George Jaggers, where the vertical New York starlight falls like lingering lightning into restaurant gardens. Finnegan might have been at the North Pole – and as a matter of fact he was. He had quite a group with him, including three Bryn Mawr anthropologists, and it sounded as if he might collect a lot of material there. They were going to stay several months, and if the thing had somehow the ring of a promising little house party about it, that was probably due to my jealous, cynical disposition.

"We're all just delighted," said Cannon. "It's a godsend for him. He was fed up and he needed just this… this—"

"Ice and snow," I supplied.

"Yes, ice and snow. The last thing he said was characteristic of him. Whatever he writes is going to be pure white – it's going to have a blinding glare about it."

"I can imagine it will. But tell me – who's financing it? Last time I was here I gathered the man was insolvent."

"Oh, he was really very decent about that. He owed me some money, and I believe he owed George Jaggers a little too" – he "believed", the old hypocrite; he knew damn well – "so before he left he made most of his life insurance over to us. That's in case he doesn't come back – those trips are dangerous of course."

"I should think so," I said, "especially with three anthropologists."

"So Jaggers and I are absolutely covered in case anything happens – it's as simple as that."

"Did the life-insurance company finance the trip?"

He fidgeted perceptibly.

"Oh, no. In fact when they learnt the reason for the assignments they were a little upset. George Jaggers and I felt that when he had a specific plan like this with a specific book at the end of it, we were justified in backing him a little further."

"I don't see it," I said flatly.

"You don't?" The old harassed look came back into his eyes. "Well, I'll admit we hesitated. In principle I know it's wrong. I used to advance authors small sums from time to time, but lately I've made a rule against it – and kept it. It's only been waived once in the last two years, and that was for a woman who was having a bad struggle – Margaret Trahill, do you know her? She was an old girl of Finnegan's, by the way."

"Remember, I don't even know Finnegan."

"That's right. You must meet him when he comes back – if he does come back. You'd like him – he's utterly charming."

Again I departed from New York, to imaginative North Poles of my own, while the year rolled through summer and fall. When the first snap of November was in the air, I thought of the Finnegan expedition with a sort of shiver, and any envy of the man departed. He was probably earning any loot, literary or anthropological, he might bring back. Then, when I hadn't been back in New York three days, I read in the paper that he and some other members of his party had walked off into a snowstorm when the food supply gave out, and the Arctic had claimed another sacrifice.

I was sorry for him, but practical enough to be glad that Cannon and Jaggers were well protected. Of course, with Finnegan scarcely cold – if such a simile is not too harrowing – they did not talk about it, but I gathered that the insurance companies had waived habeas corpus or whatever it is in their lingo, and it seemed quite sure that they would collect.

His son, a fine-looking young fellow, came into George Jaggers's office while I was there, and from him I could guess at Finnegan's charm – a shy frankness together with an impression of a very quiet brave battle going on inside of him that he couldn't quite bring himself to talk about – but that showed as heat lightning in his work.

"The boy writes well too," said George after he had gone. "He's brought in some remarkable poems. He's not ready to step into his father's shoes, but there's a definite promise."

"Can I see one of his things?"

"Certainly – here's one he left just as he went out."

George took a paper from his desk, opened it and cleared his throat. Then he squinted and bent over a little in his chair.

"*Dear Mr Jaggers,*" he began, "*I didn't like to ask you this in person...*" Jaggers stopped, his eyes reading ahead rapidly.

"How much does he want?" I enquired.

He sighed.

"He gave me the impression that this was some of his work," he said in a pained voice.

"But it is," I consoled him. "Of course he isn't quite ready to step into his father's shoes."

I was sorry afterwards to have said this, for after all Finnegan had paid his debts, and it was nice to be alive now that better times were back and books were no longer rated as unnecessary luxuries. Many authors I knew who had skimped along during the Depression were now making long-deferred trips or paying off mortgages or turning out the more finished kind of work that can only be done with a certain leisure and security. I had just got a thousand dollars' advance for a venture in Hollywood and was going to fly out with all the verve of the old days when there was chicken feed in every pot. Going in to say goodbye to Cannon and collect the money, it was nice to find he too was profiting – wanted me to go along and see a motor boat he was buying.

But some last-minute stuff came up to delay him, and I grew impatient and decided to skip it. Getting no response to a knock on the door of his sanctum, I opened it anyhow.

The inner office seemed in some confusion. Mr Cannon was on several telephones at once and dictating something about an insurance company to a stenographer. One secretary was getting hurriedly into her hat and coat as upon an errand, and another was counting bills from her purse.

"It'll be only a minute," said Cannon, "it's just a little office riot – you never saw us like this."

"Is it Finnegan's insurance?" I couldn't help asking. "Isn't it any good?"

"His insurance – oh, perfectly all right, perfectly. This is just a matter of trying to raise a few hundred in a hurry. The banks are closed and we're all contributing."

"I've got that money you just gave me," I said. "I don't need all of it to get to the coast." I peeled off a couple of hundred. "Will this be enough?"

"That'll be fine – it just saves us. Never mind, Miss Carlsen. Mrs Mapes, you needn't go now."

"I think I'll be running along," I said.

"Just wait two minutes," he urged. "I've only got to take care of this wire. It's really splendid news. Bucks you up."

It was a cablegram from Oslo, Norway – before I began to read I was full of a premonition.

AM MIRACULOUSLY SAFE HERE BUT DETAINED BY AUTHORITIES PLEASE WIRE PASSAGE MONEY FOR FOUR PEOPLE AND TWO HUNDRED EXTRA I AM BRINGING BACK PLENTY GREETINGS FROM THE DEAD.

FINNEGAN

"Yes, that's splendid," I agreed. "He'll have a story to tell now."

"Won't he though," said Cannon. "Miss Carlsen, will you wire the parents of those girls – and you'd better inform Mr Jaggers."

As we walked along the street a few minutes later, I saw that Mr Cannon, as if stunned by the wonder of this news, had fallen into a brown study, and I did not disturb him, for after all I did not know Finnegan and could not wholeheartedly share his joy. His mood of silence continued until we arrived at the door of the motor-boat show. Just under the sign he stopped and stared upward, as if aware for the first time where we were going.

"Oh my," he said, stepping back. "There's no use going in here now. I thought we were going to get a drink."

We did. Mr Cannon was still a little vague, a little under the spell of the vast surprise – he fumbled so long for the money to pay his round that I insisted it was on me.

I think he was in a daze during that whole time because, though he is a man of the most punctilious accuracy, the two hundred I handed him in his office has never shown to my credit in the statements he has sent me. I imagine, though, that some day I will surely get it, because some day Finnegan will click again and I know that people will clamour to read what he writes. Recently I've taken it upon myself to investigate some of the stories about him, and I've found that they're mostly as false as the half-empty pool. That pool was full to the brim.

So far there's only been a short story about the polar expedition, a love story. Perhaps it wasn't as big a subject as he expected. But the movies are interested in him – if they can get a good long look at him first – and I have every reason to think that he will come through. He'd better.

The Lost Decade*

ALL SORTS OF PEOPLE came into the offices of the news weekly and Orrison Brown had all sorts of relations with them. Outside of office hours he was "one of the editors" – during work time he was simply a curly-haired man who a year before had edited the Dartmouth *Jack-o'-Lantern* and was now only too glad to take the undesirable assignments around the office, from straightening out illegible copy to playing call boy without the title.

He had seen this visitor go into the editor's office – a pale, tall man of forty with blond statuesque hair and a manner that was neither shy nor timid, nor other-worldly like a monk, but something of all three. The name on his card, Louis Trimble, evoked some vague memory but, having nothing to start on, Orrison did not puzzle over it – until a buzzer sounded on his desk, and previous experience warned him that Mr Trimble was to be his first course at lunch.

"Mr Trimble – Mr Brown," said the Source of all luncheon money. "Orrison – Mr Trimble's been away a long time. Or he *feels* it's a long time – almost twelve years. Some people would consider themselves lucky to've missed the last decade."

"That's so," said Orrison.

"I can't lunch today," continued his chief. "Take him to Voisin or 21 or anywhere he'd like. Mr Trimble feels there're lots of things he hasn't seen."

Trimble demurred politely.

"Oh, I can get around."

"I know it, old boy. Nobody knew this place like you did once – and if Brown tries to explain the horseless carriage, just send him back here to me. And you'll be back yourself by four, won't you?"

Orrison got his hat.

"You've been away ten years?" he asked while they went down in the elevator.

"They'd begun the Empire State Building," said Trimble. "What does that add up to?"

"About 1928. But as the chief said, you've been lucky to miss a lot." As a feeler he added, "Probably had more interesting things to look at."

"Can't say I have."

They reached the street, and the way Trimble's face tightened at the roar of traffic made Orrison take one more guess.

"You've been out of civilization?"

"In a sense." The words were spoken in such a measured way that Orrison concluded this man wouldn't talk unless he wanted to – and simultaneously wondered if he could have possibly spent the Thirties in a prison or an insane asylum.

"This is the famous 21," he said. "Do you think you'd rather eat somewhere else?"

Trimble paused, looking carefully at the brownstone house.

"I can remember when the name 21 got to be famous," he said, "about the same year as Moriarity's." Then he continued almost apologetically, "I thought we might walk up Fifth Avenue about five minutes and eat wherever we happened to be. Some place with young people to look at. "

Orrison gave him a quick glance, and once again thought of bars and grey walls and bars; he wondered if his duties included introducing Mr Trimble to complaisant girls. But Mr Trimble didn't look as if that was in his mind – the dominant expression was of absolute and deep-seated curiosity – and Orrison attempted to connect the name with Admiral Byrd's hideout at the South Pole* or flyers lost in Brazilian jungles. He was, or he had been, quite a fellow – that was obvious. But the only definite clue to his environment – and to Orrison the clue that led nowhere – was his countryman's obedience to the traffic lights and his predilection for walking on the side next to the shops and not the street. Once, he stopped and gazed into a haberdasher's window.

"Crêpe ties," he said. "I haven't seen one since I left college."

"Where'd you go?"

"Massachusetts Tech."

"Great place."

"I'm going to take a look at it next week. Let's eat somewhere along here" – they were in the upper Fifties – "you choose."

There was a good restaurant with a little awning just around the corner.

"What do you want to see most?" Orrison asked, as they sat down.

Trimble considered.

"Well… the back of people's heads," he suggested. "Their necks – how their heads are joined to their bodies. I'd like to hear what those two little girls are saying to their father. Not exactly what they're saying but whether the words float or submerge, how their mouths shut when they've finished speaking. Just a matter of rhythm – Cole Porter came back to the States in 1928* because he felt that there were new rhythms around."

Orrison was sure he had his clue now, and with nice delicacy did not pursue it by a millimetre – even suppressing a sudden desire to say there was a fine concert in Carnegie Hall tonight.

"The weight of spoons," said Trimble, "so light. A little bowl with a stick attached. The cast in that waiter's eye. I knew him once, but he wouldn't remember me."

But as they left the restaurant the same waiter looked at Trimble rather puzzled, as if he almost knew him. When they were outside, Orrison laughed:

"After ten years people will forget."

"Oh, I had dinner there last May…" He broke off in an abrupt manner.

It was all kind of nutsy, Orrison decided – and changed himself suddenly into a guide.

"From here you get a good candid focus on Rockefeller Center" – he pointed out with spirit – "and the Chrysler Building and the Armistead Building, the daddy of all the new ones."

"The Armistead Building." Trimble rubbernecked obediently. "Yes – I designed it."

Orrison shook his head cheerfully – he was used to going out with all kinds of people. But that stuff about having been in the restaurant last May...

He paused by the brass entablature in the cornerstone of the building. "Erected 1928", it said.

Trimble nodded.

"But I was taken drunk that year – every-which-way drunk. So I never saw it before now."

"Oh." Orrison hesitated. "Like to go in now?"

"I've been in it – lots of times. But I've never seen it. And now it isn't what I want to see. I wouldn't ever be able to see it now. I simply want to see how people walk and what their clothes and shoes and hats are made of. And their eyes and hands. Would you mind shaking hands with me?"

"Not at all, sir."

"Thanks. Thanks. That's very kind. I suppose it looks strange – but people will think we're saying goodbye. I'm going to walk up the avenue for a while, so we *will* say goodbye. Tell your office I'll be in at four."

Orrison looked after him when he started out, half-expecting him to turn into a bar. But there was nothing about him that suggested or ever had suggested drink.

"Jesus," he said to himself. "Drunk for ten years."

He felt suddenly of the texture of his own coat and then he reached out and pressed his thumb against the granite of the building by his side.

Last Kiss

THE SOUND OF REVELRY FELL SWEET upon James Leonard's ear. He alighted, a little awed by his new limousine, and walked down the red carpet through the crowd. Faces strained forward, weird in the split glare of the drum lights – but after a moment they lost interest in him. Once Jim had been annoyed by his anonymity in Hollywood. Now he was pleased with it.

Elsie Donohue, a tall, lovely, gangling girl, had a seat reserved for him at her table. "If I had no chance before," she said, "what chance have I got now that you're so important?" She was half teasing – but only half.

"You're a stubborn man," she said. "When we first met, you put me in the 'undesirable class'. Why?" She tossed her shoulders despairingly as Jim's eyes lingered on a little Chinese beauty at the next table. "You're looking at Ching Loo Poo-poo, Ching Loo Poo-poo! And for five long years I've come out to this ghastly town—"

"They couldn't keep you away," Jim objected. "It's on your swing-around – the Stork Club, Palm Beach and Dave Chasen's."

Tonight something in him wanted to be quiet. Jim was thirty-five and suddenly on the winning side of all this. He was one of those who said how pictures should go, what they should say. It was a fine pure feeling to be on top.

One was very sure that everything was for the best, that the lights shone upon fair ladies and brave men, that pianos dripped the right notes and that the young lips singing them spoke for happy hearts.

They absolutely must be happy, these beautiful faces. And then in a twilight rumba, a face passed Jim's table that was not quite happy. It had gone before Jim formulated this opinion, yet it remained fixed on his memory for some seconds. It was the head of a girl almost as tall as he was, with opaque brown eyes and cheeks as porcelain as those of the little Chinese.

"At least you're back with the white race," said Elsie, following his eyes.

Jim wanted to answer sharply: "You've had your day – three husbands. How about me? Thirty-five and still trying to match every woman with a childhood love who died, still finding fatally in every girl the similarities and not the differences."

The next time the lights were dim, he wandered through the tables to the entrance hall. Here and there friends hailed him – more than the usual number of course, because his rise had been in the *Reporter* that morning, but Jim had made other steps up and he was used to that. It was a charity ball, and by the stairs was the man who imitated wallpaper about to go in and do a number, and Bob Bordley with a sandwich board on his back:

At Ten Tonight

In the Hollywood Bowl

SONJA HEINE

Will Skate on

HOT SOUP.

By the bar, Jim saw the producer whom he was displacing tomorrow having an unsuspecting drink with the agent who had contrived his ruin. Next to the agent was the girl whose face had seemed sad as she danced by in the rumba.

"Oh, Jim," said the agent, "Pamela Knighton – your future star."

She turned to him with professional eagerness. What the agent's voice had said to her was: "Look alive! This *is* somebody."

"Pamela's joined my stable," said the agent. "I want her to change her name to Boots."

"I thought you said Toots," the girl laughed.

"Toots or Boots. It's the *oo-oo* sound. Cutie shoots Toots. Judge Hoots. No conviction possible. Pamela is English. Her real name is Sybil Higgins."

It seemed to Jim that the deposed producer was looking at him with an infinite something in his eyes – not hatred, not jealousy, but a profound and curious astonishment that asked: Why? Why? For Heaven's sake, why? More disturbed by this than by enmity, Jim surprised himself by asking the English girl to dance. As they faced each other on the floor, his exultation of the early evening came back.

"Hollywood's a good place," he said, as if to forestall any criticism from her. "You'll like it. Most English girls do – they don't expect too much. I've had luck working with English girls."

"Are you a director?"

"I've been everything – from press agent on. I've just signed a producer's contract that begins tomorrow."

"I like it here," she said after a minute. "You can't help expecting things. But if they don't come, I could always teach school again."

Jim leant back and looked at her – his impression was of pink-and-silver frost. She was so far from a schoolmarm, even a schoolmarm in a Western, that he laughed. But again he saw that there was something sad and a little lost within the triangle formed by lips and eyes.

"Whom are you with tonight?" he asked.

"Joe Becker," she answered, naming the agent. "Myself and three other girls."

"Look – I have to go out for half an hour. To see a man – this is not phoney. Believe me. Will you come along for company and night air?"

She nodded.

On the way they passed Elsie Donohue, who looked inscrutably at the girl and shook her head slightly at Jim. Out in the clear California night he liked his big car for the first time, liked it better than driving himself. The streets through which they rolled were quiet at this hour. Miss Knighton waited for him to speak.

"What did you teach in school?" he asked.

"Sums. Two and two are four and all that."

"It's a long jump from that to Hollywood."

"It's a long story."

"It can't be very long – you're about eighteen."

"Twenty." Anxiously she asked: "Do you think that's too old?"

"Lord, no! It's a beautiful age. I know – I'm twenty-one myself and the arteries haven't hardened much."

She looked at him gravely, estimating his age and keeping it to herself.

"I want to hear the long story," he said.

She sighed. "Well, a lot of old men fell in love with me. Old, old men – I was an old man's darling."

"You mean old gaffers of twenty-two?"

"They were between sixty and seventy. This is all true. So I became a gold-digger and dug enough money out of them to go to New York. I walked into 21 the first day and Joe Becker saw me."

"Then you've never been in pictures?" he asked.

"Oh yes – I had a test this morning," she told him.

Jim smiled. "And you don't feel bad taking money from all those old men?" he enquired.

"Not really," she said, matter-of-fact. "They enjoyed giving it to me. Anyhow it wasn't really money. When they wanted to give me presents I'd send them to a certain jeweller, and afterwards I'd take the presents back to the jeweller and get four fifths of the cash."

"Why, you little chiseller!"

"Yes," she admitted. "Somebody told me how. I'm out for all I can get."

"Didn't they mind – the old men, I mean – when you didn't wear their presents?"

"Oh, I'd wear them – once. Old men don't see very well, or remember. But that's why I haven't any jewellery of my own." She broke off. "This I'm wearing is rented."

Jim looked at her again and then laughed aloud.

"I wouldn't worry about it. California's full of old men."

They had twisted into a residential district. As they turned a corner, Jim picked up the speaking tube. "Stop here." He turned to Pamela. "I have some dirty work to do."

He looked at his watch, got out and went up the street to a building with the names of several doctors on a sign. He went past the building walking slowly, and presently a man came out of the building and followed him. In the darkness between two lamps Jim went close, handed him an envelope and spoke concisely. The man walked off in the opposite direction and Jim returned to the car.

"I'm having all the old men bumped off," he explained. "There're some things worse than death."

"Oh, I'm not free now," she assured him. "I'm engaged."

"Oh." After a minute he asked: "To an Englishman?"

"Well – naturally. Did you think…" She stopped herself, but too late.

"Are we that uninteresting?" he asked.

"Oh no." Her casual tone made it worse. And when she smiled, at the moment when a street light shone in and dressed her beauty up to a white radiance, it was more annoying still.

"Now you tell *me* something," she asked. "Tell me the mystery."

"Just money," he answered almost absently. "That little Greek doctor keeps telling a certain lady that her appendix is bad – we need her in a picture. So we bought him off. It's the last time I'll ever do anyone else's dirty work."

She frowned. "Does she really need her appendix out?"

He shrugged. "Probably not. At least that rat wouldn't know. He's her brother-in-law and he wants the money."

After a long time, Pamela spoke judicially. "An Englishman wouldn't do that."

"Some would," he said shortly – "and some Americans wouldn't."

"An English gentleman wouldn't," she insisted.

"Aren't you getting off on the wrong foot," he suggested, "if you're going to work here?"

"Oh, I like Americans all right – the civilized ones."

From her look Jim took this to include him, but far from being appeased he had a sense of outrage. "You're taking chances," he said. "In fact I don't see how you dared come out with me. I might have had feathers under my hat."

"You didn't bring a hat," she said placidly. "Besides, Joe Becker said to. There might be something in it for me."

After all, he was a producer, and you didn't reach eminence by losing your temper – except on purpose. "I'm sure there's something in it for you," he said, listening to a stealthily treacherous purr creep into his voice.

"Are you?" she demanded. "Do you think I'll stand out at all – or am I just one of the thousands?"

"You stand out already," he continued on the same note. "Everyone at the dance was looking at you." He wondered if this was even faintly true. Was it only he who had fancied some uniqueness? "You're a new type," he went on, "A face like yours might give American pictures a... a more civilized tone."

This was his arrow – but to his vast surprise it glanced off.

"Oh, do you think so?" she cried. "Are you going to give me a chance?"

"Why, certainly." It was hard to believe that the irony in his voice was missing its mark. "But after tonight there'll be so much competition that—"

"Oh, I'd rather work for you," she declared. "I'll tell Joe Becker—"

"Don't tell him anything," he interrupted.

"Oh, I won't. I'll do just as you say," she promised.

Her eyes were wide and expectant. Disturbed, he felt that words were being put in his mouth or slipping from him unintended. That so much innocence and so much predatory toughness could go side by side behind this gentle English voice...

"You'd be wasted in bits," he began. "The thing is to get a fat part..." He broke off and started again: "You've got such a strong personality that—"

"Oh don't!" He saw tears blinking in the corners of her eyes. "Let me just keep this to sleep on tonight. You call me in the morning – or when you need me."

The car came to rest at the carpet strip in front of the dance. Seeing Pamela, the crowd bulged forward grotesquely, autograph books at the ready. Failing to recognize her, it sighed back behind the ropes.

In the ballroom he danced her to Becker's table.

"I won't say a word," she whispered. From her evening case she took a card with the name of her hotel pencilled on it. "If any other offers come, I'll refuse them."

"Oh no," he said quickly.

"Oh yes." She smiled brightly at him, and for an instant the feeling Jim had had on seeing her came back. It was an impression of a rich warm sympathy, of youth and suffering side by side. He braced himself for a final quick slash to burst the scarcely created bubble.

"After a year or so..." he began. But the music and her voice over-rode him.

"I'll wait for you to call. You're the... you're the most civilized American I've ever met."

She turned her back, as if embarrassed by the magnificence of her compliment. Jim started back to his table – then seeing Elsie Donohue talking to a woman across his empty chair, he turned obliquely away. The room, the evening had gone raucous – the blend of music and voices seemed inharmonious and accidental, and his eyes covering the room saw only jealousies and hatreds – egos tapping like drum beats up to a fanfare. He was not above the battle as he had thought.

He started for the coatroom thinking of the note he would dispatch by waiter to his hostess: "You were dancing". Then he found himself almost upon Pamela Knighton's table, and turning again he took another route towards the door.

A picture executive can do without intelligence, but he cannot do without tact. Tact now absorbed Jim Leonard to the exclusion of everything else. Power should have pushed diplomacy into the background, leaving him free, but instead it intensified all his human relations – with the executives, with the directors, writers, actors and technical men assigned to his unit, with department heads, censors and "men from the East" besides. So the stalling-off of one lone English girl, with no weapon except the telephone and a little note that reached him from the entrance desk, should have been no problem at all.

Just passing by the studio and thought of you and of our ride. There have been some offers, but I keep stalling Joe Becker. If I move I will let you know.

A city full of youth and hope spoke in it – in its two transparent lies, the brave falsity of its tone. It didn't matter to her – all the money and glory beyond the impregnable walls. She had just been passing by – just passing by.

That was after two weeks. In another week, Joe Becker dropped in to see him. "About that little English girl, Pamela Knighton – remember? How'd she strike you?"

"Very nice."

"For some reason she didn't want me to talk to you." Joe looked out the window. "So I suppose you didn't get along so well that night."

"Sure we did."

"The girl's engaged, you see, to some guy in England."

"She told me that," said Jim, annoyed. "I didn't make any passes at her, if that's what you're getting at."

"Don't worry – I understand those things. I just wanted to tell you something about her."

"Nobody else interested?"

"She's only been here a month. Everybody's got to start. I just want to tell you that when she came into 21 that day the barflies dropped like… like flies. Let me tell you – in one minute she was the talk of café society."

"It must have been great," Jim said drily.

"It was. And Lamarr was there that day too. Listen – Pam was all alone, and she had on English clothes, I guess, nothing you'd look at twice – rabbit fur. But she shone through it like a diamond."

"Yeah?"

"Strong women wept into their vichyssoise. Elsa Maxwell—"

"Joe, this is a busy morning."

"Will you look at her test?"

"Tests are for make-up men," said Jim, impatiently. "I never believe a good test. And I always suspect a bad one."

"Got your own ideas, eh?"

"About that," Jim admitted. "There've been a lot of bad guesses in projection rooms."

"Behind desks too," said Joe, rising.

A second note came after another week:

When I phoned yesterday one secretary said you were away and one said you were in conference. If this is a run-around tell me. I'm not

*getting any younger. Twenty-one is staring me in the face – and you
must have bumped off all the old men.*

Her face had grown dim now. He remembered the delicate cheeks, the
haunted eyes, as from a picture seen a long time ago. It was easy to
dictate a letter that told of changed plans, of new casting, of difficulties
which made it impossible…

He didn't feel good about it, but at least it was finished business.
Having a sandwich in his neighbourhood drugstore that night, he
looked back at his month's work as good. He had reeked of tact.
His unit functioned smoothly. The shades who controlled his destiny
would soon see.

There were only a few people in the drugstore. Pamela Knighton was
the girl at the magazine rack. She looked up at him, startled, over a copy
of *The Illustrated London News*.

Knowing of the letter that lay for signature on his desk, Jim wished
he could pretend not to see her. He turned slightly aside, held his
breath, listened. But though she had seen him, nothing happened,
and hating his Hollywood cowardice he turned again presently and
lifted his hat.

"You're up late," he said.

Pamela searched his face momentarily. "I live around the corner," she
said. "I've just moved – I wrote you today."

"I live near here too."

She replaced the magazine in the rack. Jim's tact fled. He felt suddenly
old and harassed and asked the wrong question.

"How do things go?" he asked.

"Oh, very well," she said. "I'm in a play – a real play at the New Faces
Theatre in Pasadena. For the experience."

"Oh, that's very wise."

"We open in two weeks. I was hoping you could come."

They walked out the door together and stood in the glow of the red neon sign. Across the autumn street, newsboys were shouting the result of the night football.

"Which way?" she asked.

"The other way from you," he thought, but when she indicated her direction he walked with her. It was months since he had seen Sunset Boulevard, and the mention of Pasadena made him think of when he had first come to California ten years ago, something green and cool.

Pamela stopped before some tiny bungalows around a central court. "Goodnight," she said. "Don't let it worry you if you can't help me. Joe has explained how things are, with the war and all. I know you wanted to."

He nodded solemnly – despising himself.

"Are you married?" she asked.

"No."

"Then kiss me goodnight."

As he hesitated she said, "I like to be kissed goodnight. I sleep better."

He put his arms around her shyly and bent down to her lips, just touching them – and thinking hard of the letter on his desk which he couldn't send now – and liking holding her.

"You see, it's nothing," she said, "just friendly. Just goodnight."

On his way to the corner Jim said aloud, "Well, I'll be damned," and kept repeating the sinister prophecy to himself for some time after he was in bed.

On the third night of Pamela's play, Jim went to Pasadena and bought a seat in the last row. A likely crowd was jostling into the theatre, and he felt glad that she would play to a full house, but at the door he found that it was a revival of *Room Service** – Pamela's play was in the Experiment Hall up the stairs.

Meekly he climbed to a tiny auditorium and was the first arrival except for fluttering ushers and voices chattering amid the hammers backstage.

* * *

He considered a discreet retirement, but was reassured by the arrival of a group of five, among them Joe Becker's chief assistant. The lights went out; a gong was beaten; to an audience of six the play began.

It was about some Mexicans who were being deprived of relief. Concepcione (Pamela Knighton) was having a child by an oil magnate. In the old Horatio Alger* tradition, Pedro was reading Marx so some day he could be a bureaucrat and have offices at Palm Springs.

PEDRO: We stay here. Better Boss Ford than Renegade Trotsky.
CONCEPCIONE (Miss Knighton): But who will live to inherit?
PEDRO: Perhaps the great-grandchildren, or the grandchildren of the great-grandchildren. *Quién sabe?*

Through the gloomy charade Jim watched Pamela; in front of him the party of five leant together and whispered after her scenes. Was she good? Jim had no notion – he should have taken someone along, or brought in his chauffeur. What with pictures drawing upon half the world for talent there was scarcely such a phenomenon as a "natural". There were only possibilities – and luck. He was luck. He was maybe this girl's luck – if he felt that her pull at his insides was universal.

Stars were no longer created by one man's casual desire as in the silent days, but stock girls were, tests were, chances were. When the curtain finally dropped, domestically as a Venetian blind, he went backstage by the simple process of walking through a door on the side. She was waiting for him.

"I was hoping you wouldn't come tonight," she said. "We've flopped. But the first night it was full and I looked for you."

"You were fine," he said stiffly.

"Oh no. You should have seen me then."

"I saw enough," he said suddenly. "I can give you a little part. Will you come to the studio tomorrow?"

He watched her expression. Once more it surprised him. Out of her eyes, out of the curve of her mouth gleamed a sudden and overwhelming pity.

"Oh," she said. "Oh, I'm terribly sorry. Joe brought some people over and next day I signed up with Bernie Wise."

"You *did*?"

"I knew you wanted me, and at first I didn't realize you were just a sort of supervisor. I thought you had more power – you know?" She could not have chosen sharper words out of deliberate mischief. "Oh, I like you better *personally*," she assured him. "You're much more civilized than Bernie Wise."

All right then, he was civilized. He could at least pull out gracefully. "Can I drive you back to Hollywood?"

They rode through an October night soft as April. When they crossed a bridge, its walls topped with wire screens, he gestured towards it and she nodded.

"I know what it is," she said. "But how stupid! English people don't commit suicide when they don't get what they want."

"I know. They come to America."

She laughed and looked at him appraisingly. Oh, she could do something with him all right. She let her hand rest upon his.

"Kiss tonight?" he suggested after a while.

Pamela glanced at the chauffeur, insulated in his compartment. "Kiss tonight," she said...

He flew East next day, looking for a young actress just like Pamela Knighton. He looked so hard that any eyes with an aspect of lovely melancholy, any bright English voice predisposed him; he wandered as far afield as a stock company in Erie and a student play at Wellesley – it came to seem a desperate matter that he should find someone exactly like this girl. Then, when a telegram called him impatiently back to Hollywood, he found Pamela dumped in his lap.

"You got a second chance, Jim," said Joe Becker. "Don't miss it again."

"What was the matter over there?"

"They had no part for her. They're in a mess – change of management. So we tore up the contract."

Mike Harris, the studio head, investigated the matter. Why was Bernie Wise, a shrewd picture man, willing to let her go?

"Bernie says she can't act," he reported to Jim. "And what's more, she makes trouble. I keep thinking of Simone and those two Austrian girls."

"I've seen her act," insisted Jim. "And I've got a place for her. I don't even want to build her up yet. I want to spot her in this little part and let you see."

A week later, Jim pushed open the padded door of Stage III and walked in. Extras in dress clothes turned towards him in the semi-darkness; eyes widened.

"Where's Bob Griffin?"

"In that bungalow with Miss Knighton."

They were sitting side by side on a couch in the glare of the make-up light, and from the resistance in Pamela's face Jim knew the trouble was serious.

"It's *nothing*," Bob insisted heartily. "We get along like a couple of kittens, don't we, Pam? Sometimes I roll over her, but she doesn't mind."

"You smell of onions," said Pamela.

Griffin tried again. "There's an English way and an American way. We're looking for the happy mean – that's all."

"There's a nice way and a silly way," Pamela said shortly. "I don't want to begin by looking like a fool."

"Leave us alone, will you, Bob?" Jim said.

"Sure. All the time in the world."

Jim had not seen her in this busy week of tests and fittings and rehearsals, and he thought now how little he knew about her and she of them.

"Bob seems to be in your hair," he said.

"He wants me to say things no sane person would say."

"All right – maybe so," he agreed. "Pamela, since you've been working here, have you ever blown up in your lines?"

"Why – everybody does sometimes."

"Listen, Pamela – Bob Griffin gets almost ten times as much money as you do – for a particular reason. Not because he's the most brilliant director in Hollywood – he isn't – but because he never blows up in his lines."

"He's not an actor," she said, puzzled.

"I mean his lines in real life. I picked him for this picture because once in a while I blow up. But not Bob. He signed a contract for an unholy amount of money – which he doesn't deserve, which nobody deserves. But smoothness is the fourth dimension of this business and Bob has forgotten the word 'I'. People of three times his talent – producers and troopers and directors – go down the sink because they can't forget it."

"I know I'm being lectured to," she said uncertainly. "But I don't seem to understand. An actress has her own personality…"

He nodded. "And we pay her five times what she could get for it any-where else – *if* she'll only keep it off the floor where it trips the rest of us up. You're tripping us all up, Pamela."

"I thought you were my friend," her eyes said.

He talked to her a few minutes more. Everything he said he believed with all his heart, but because he had twice kissed those lips, he saw that it was support and protection they wanted from him. All he had done was to make her a little shocked that he was not on her side. Feeling rather baffled, and sorry for her loneliness, he went to the door of the bungalow and called: "Hey, Bob!"

Jim went about other business. He got back to his office to find Mike Harris waiting.

"Again that girl's making trouble."

"I've been over there."

"I mean in the last five minutes!" cried Harris. "Since you left she's made trouble! Bob Griffin had to stop shooting for the day. He's on his way over."

Bob came in. "There's one type you can't seem to get at – can't find what makes them that way. I'm afraid it's either Pamela or me."

There was a moment's silence. Mike Harris, upset by the whole situation, suspected that Jim was having an affair with the girl.

"Give me till tomorrow morning," said Jim. "I think I can find what's back of this."

Griffin hesitated, but there was a personal appeal in Jim's eyes – an appeal to associations of a decade. "All right, Jim," he agreed.

When they had gone, Jim called Pamela's number. What he had almost expected happened, but his heart sank nonetheless when a man's voice answered the phone…

Excepting a trained nurse, an actress is the easiest prey for the unscrupulous male. Jim had learnt that in the background of their troubles or their failures there was often some plausible confidence man, some soured musician, who asserted his masculinity by way of interference, midnight nagging, bad advice. The technique of the man was to belittle the woman's job and to question endlessly the motives and intelligence of those for whom she worked.

Jim was thinking of all this when he reached the bungalow hotel in Beverly Hills where Pamela had moved. It was after six. In the court, a cold fountain splashed senselessly against the December fog and he heard Major Bowes's voice* loud from three radios.

When the door of the apartment opened, Jim stared. The man was old – a bent and withered Englishman with ruddy winter colour dying in his face. He wore an old dressing gown and slippers and he asked Jim to sit down with an air of being at home. Pamela would be in shortly.

"Are you a relative?" Jim asked wonderingly.

"No, Pamela and I met here in Hollywood. We were strangers in a strange land. Are you employed in pictures, Mr... Mr..."

"Leonard," said Jim. "Yes. At present I'm Pamela's boss."

A change came into the man's eyes – the watery blink became conspicuous, there was a stiffening of the old lids. The lips curled down and backward and Jim was gazing into an expression of utter malignancy. Then the features became old and bland again.

"I hope Pamela is being handled properly?"

"You've been in pictures?" Jim asked.

"Till my health broke down. But I am still on the rolls at Central Casting and I know everything about this business and the souls of those who own it..." He broke off.

The door opened and Pamela came in. "Well, hello," she said in surprise. "You've met? The Honourable Chauncey Ward – Mr Leonard."

Her glowing beauty, borne in from outside like something snatched from wind and weather, made Jim breathless for a moment.

"I thought you told me my sins this afternoon," she said with a touch of defiance.

"I wanted to talk to you away from the studio."

"Don't accept a salary cut," the old man said. "That's an old trick."

"It's not that, Mr Ward," said Pamela. "Mr Leonard has been my friend up to now. But today the director tried to make a fool of me, and Mr Leonard backed him up."

"They all hang together," said Mr Ward.

"I wonder..." began Jim. "Could I possibly talk to you alone?"

"I trust Mr Ward," said Pamela, frowning. "He's been over here twenty-five years and he's practically my business manager."

Jim wondered from what deep loneliness this relationship had sprung. "I hear there was more trouble on the set," he said.

"Trouble!" She was wide-eyed. "Griffin's assistant swore at me, and I heard it. So I walked out. And if Griffin sent apologies by you, I don't want them – our relation is going to be strictly business from now on."

"He didn't send apologies," said Jim uncomfortably. "He sent an ultimatum."

"An ultimatum!" she exclaimed. "I've got a contract, and you're his boss, aren't you?"

"To an extent," said Jim – "but of course making pictures is a joint matter—"

"Then let me try another director."

"Fight for your rights," said Mr Ward. "That's the only thing that impresses them."

"You're doing your best to wreck this girl," said Jim quietly.

"You can't frighten me," snapped Ward. "I've seen your type before."

Jim looked again at Pamela. There was exactly nothing he could do. Had they been in love, had it ever seemed the time to encourage the spark between them, he might have reached her now. But it was too late. In the Hollywood darkness outside, he seemed to feel the swift wheels of the industry turning. He knew that when the studio opened tomorrow, Mike Harris would have new plans that did not include Pamela at all.

For a moment longer he hesitated. He was a well-liked man, still young, and with a wide approval. He could buck them about this girl, send her to a dramatic teacher. He could not bear to see her make such a mistake. On the other hand he was afraid that somewhere people had yielded to her too much, spoilt her for this sort of career.

"Hollywood isn't a very civilized place," said Pamela.

"It's a jungle," agreed Mr Ward. "Full of prowling beasts of prey."

Jim rose. "Well, this one will prowl out," he said. "Pam, I'm very sorry. Feeling like you do, I think you'd be wise to go back to England and get married."

For a moment a flicker of doubt was in her eyes. But her confidence, her young egotism, was greater than her judgement – she did not realize that this very minute was opportunity and she was losing it for ever.

For she had lost it when Jim turned and went out. It was weeks before she knew how it happened. She received her salary for some months – Jim saw to that – but she did not set foot on that lot again. Nor on any other. She was placed quietly on that blacklist that is not written down but that functions at backgammon games after dinner, or on the way to the races. Men of influence stared at her with interest at restaurants here and there, but all their enquiries about her reached the same dead end.

She never gave up during the following months – even long after Becker had lost interest and she was in want, and no longer seen in the places where people go to be looked at. It was not from grief or discouragement but only through commonplace circumstances that in June she died...

When Jim heard about it, it seemed incredible and terrible. He learnt accidentally that she was in the hospital with pneumonia – he telephoned and found that she was dead. "Sybil Higgins, actress, English. Age twenty-one."

She had given old Ward as the person to be informed, and Jim managed to get him enough money to cover the funeral expenses, on the pretext that some old salary was still owing. Afraid that Ward might guess the source of the money, he did not go to the funeral, but a week later he drove out to the grave.

It was a long bright June day and he stayed there an hour. All over the city there were young people just breathing and being happy and it seemed senseless that the little English girl was not one of them. He kept on trying and trying to twist things about so that they would come out right for her, but it was too late. He said goodbye aloud and promised that he would come again.

Back at the studio he reserved a projection room and asked for her tests and for the bits of film that had been shot on her picture. He sat in a big leather chair in the darkness and pressed the button for it to begin.

In the test Pamela was dressed as he had seen her that first night at the dance. She looked very happy, and he was glad she had had at least that much happiness. The reel of takes from the picture began and ran jerkily with the sound of Bob Griffin's voice off scene and with prop boys showing the number blocks for the scenes. Then Jim started as the next-to-the-last one came up, and he saw her turn from the camera and whisper: "I'd rather die than do it that way."

Jim got up and went back to his office, where he opened the three notes he had from her and read them again.

...just passing by the studio and thought of you and of our ride.

Just passing by. During the spring she had called him twice on the phone, he knew, and he had wanted to see her. But he could do nothing for her and could not bear to tell her so.

"I am not very brave," Jim said to himself. Even now there was fear in his heart that this would haunt him like that memory of his youth, and he did not want to be unhappy.

Several days later he worked late in the dubbing room, and afterwards he dropped into his neighbourhood drugstore for a sandwich. It was a warm night and there were many young people at the soda counter. He was paying his cheque when he became aware that a figure was standing by the magazine rack looking at him over the edge of a magazine. He stopped – he did not want to turn for a closer look, only to find the resemblance at an end. Nor did he want to go away.

He heard the sound of a page turning, and then out of the corner of his eye he saw the magazine cover, *The Illustrated London News.*

He felt no fear – he was thinking too quickly, too desperately. If this were real and he could snatch her back, start from there, from that night...

"Your change, Mr Leonard."

"Thank you."

Still without looking, he started for the door, and then he heard the magazine close, drop to a pile, and he heard someone breathe close to his side. Newsboys were calling an extra across the street, and after a moment he turned the wrong way, her way, and he heard her following – so plain that he slowed his pace with the sense that she had trouble keeping up with him.

In front of the apartment court he took her in his arms and drew her radiant beauty close.

"Kiss me goodnight," she said. "I like to be kissed goodnight. I sleep better."

Then sleep, he thought as he turned away – sleep. I couldn't fix it. I tried to fix it. When you brought your beauty here, I didn't want to throw it away, but I did somehow. There is nothing left for you now but sleep.

Note on the Texts

The texts of 'Babylon Revisited', 'Family in the Wind', 'Crazy Sunday', 'One Intern', 'The Fiend' and 'The Night at Chancellorsville' are based on the versions published in *Taps at Reveille* (1935). The text of 'A New Leaf' is based on the version published in the *Saturday Evening Post* (4th July 1931). The text of 'A Freeze-out' is based on the version published in the *Saturday Evening Post* (19th December 1931). The text of 'Six of One...' is based on the version published in *Redbook* (February 1932). The text of 'What a Crazy Pair' is based on the version published in the *Saturday Evening Post* (27th August 1932). The text of 'More than Just a House' is based on the version published in the *Saturday Evening Post* (24th June 1933). The text of 'Afternoon of an Author' is based on the version published in *Esquire* (August 1936). The text of 'Financing Finnegan' is based on the version published in *Esquire* (January 1938). The text of 'The Lost Decade' is based on the version published in *Esquire* (December 1939). The text of 'Last Kiss' is based on the version published in *Collier's Weekly* (16th April 1949). The spelling and punctuation have been Anglicized, standardized, modernized and made consistent throughout.

Notes

p. 3, *chasseur*: "Hotel messenger" (French).

p. 5, *La plus que lente*: A 1910 waltz for piano by Claude Debussy (1862–1918).

p. 7, *strapontin*: "Fold-up seat" (French).

p. 7, *Josephine Baker*: Josephine Baker (1906–75) was a world-famous French dancer and entertainer of Afro-American origin.

p. 9, *épinards and chou-fleur...* and *haricots*: "Spinach... cauli-flower... beans" (French).

p. 9, *Qu'elle est mignonne... comme une française*: "How adorable is this little one? She speaks exactly like a French girl" (French).

p. 20, *pneumatique*: "Pneumatic-post message" (French).

p. 22, *bonne à tout faire*: "All-around maid" (French).

p. 27, *The purple noon's... unexpanded bud*: Lines 5–7 of Shelley's 'Stanzas Written in Dejection Near Naples' (1818). The last line has been slightly modified.

p. 37, *Libby Holman's 'This Is How the Story Ends'*: A reference to the song 'Can't We Be Friends?', performed by Libby Holman (1904–71), from a 1929 revue.

p. 44, *Scroll and Key*: A prestigious secret society at Yale University.

p. 45, *from him that hath... even that which he hath*: Matthew 25:29.

p. 46, *Louis Aragon's*: Louis Aragon (1897–1982), French poet, playwright and novelist who was one of the founding members of the Surrealist movement.

p. 47, *the Sioux war... James brothers shot up the main street*: The Sioux war refers to various conflicts between Sioux and their allies and the United States forces between 1854 and 1890, particularly the Great Sioux War of 1876. The notorious outlaws Jesse James (1847–82) and Frank James (1843–1915) attempted a robbery in Northfield, Minnesota, in 1876, which resulted in failure after a shootout. The brothers managed to escape, while other members of their gang were arrested and incarcerated in Stillwater.

p. 47, *the Free Silver Movement*: A late-nineteenth-century campaign to permit the coinage of silver, as well as gold.

p. 47, *killed at Cold Harbor*: The Battle of Cold Harbor of 1864 in Virginia was one of the bloodiest battles in the Civil War, with the Union Forces suffering major losses.

p. 48, *the alien-property scandal*: A scandal in which Thomas W. Miller (1886–1973), the Alien Property Custodian – in charge of seizing and redistributing enemy assets in the US during the First World War – was found guilty of corruption and imprisoned in 1927.

p. 80, *the Sacco-Vanzetti demonstrations*: A reference to the protests following the controversial arrest, trials and execution of the militant anarchists Nicola Sacco (1891–1927) and Bartolomeo Vanzetti (1888–1927).

p. 84, *Pedro the Cruel or Charles the Mad*: Pedro the Cruel is the nickname of King Peter of Castile (1334–69), who had a reputation for despotism and ruthlessness. Charles the Mad was Charles VI of France (1368–1422), who during his reign was the victim of delusional bouts of insanity.

p. 93, *and*: The original text reads "had"; this has been amended by the editors of this edition.

p. 111, *Erminie*: *Erminie* was a successful 1895 opera composed by Erminie is a comic opera in two acts composed by Edward Jakobowski (1856–1929), with a libretto by Claxson Bellamy and Harry Paulton.

p. 112, *His Move on a Gibson pillow*: A reference to a famous illustration by Charles Dana Gibson (1867–1944), whose work was widely reproduced on all manner of merchandising.

p. 131, *Puppenfeen*: "Fairy dolls" (German). A reference to the 1888 Austrian ballet *Die Puppenfee*, in which fairy dolls come to life in a toy shop.

p. 132, *Marion Davies*: Marion Davies (1897–1961) was an American film star and prominent Hollywood socialite.

p. 136, *Menjou... Michael Arlen*: Adolphe Menjou (1890–1963), an American film actor, and Michael Arlen (1895–1956), an Armenian-born British author and scriptwriter.

p. 164, *a Duncan Phyfe table, a brass by Brâncuşi*: Duncan Phyfe (1770–1854) was a famous Scottish-born American cabinet-maker.

Constantin Brâncuşi (1876–1957) was an influential Paris-based Romanian sculptor.

p. 171, *His*: The original text reads "He"; this has been amended by the editors of this edition.

p. 207, *Johnny Rebs*: A colloquial reference to the Confederate soldiers.

p. 208, *Hooker's army*: Major General Joseph Hooker led Union forces to the famous defeat at Chancellorsville in April-May 1863.

p. 209, *the Seven Days... Gaines's Mill*: The Seven Days Battles were a series of battles near Richmond, Virginia, in 1862, one of which was the Battle of Gaines's Mill on 27th June.

p. 210, *Sedgwick's Corps*: John Sedgwick (1813–64) was a Union general.

p. 213, *Spessiwitza*: A reference to Olga Spessivtseva (1895–1991), one of the most famous ballerinas of the twentieth century.

p. 215, *Stonewall Jackson's last words... shade of the trees*: Thomas Jonathan "Stonewall" Jackson (1824–63) was a famous Confederate commander, who died of pneumonia shortly after the Battle of Chancellorsville.

p. 216, *Lee shrivelling... desperate memoir-writing at the end*: The Confederate commander Robert E. Lee (1807–70) and the Union general Ulysses S. Grant (1822–85) both remained in public life after the end of the Civil War in 1865 – the former continuing to be a vocal in US politics after surrendering and the latter becoming President of the United States before writing his memoirs, which were published to great success shortly after his death.

p. 216, *Venite adoremus*: A reference to the hymn 'Adeste Fideles' ('O Come All Ye Faithful').

p. 217, *Guido Reni's Dawn*: A reference to the 1613–14 fresco *Aurora* by the Italian baroque painter Guido Reni (1575–1642).

p. 219, *Man Mountain Dean*: The pseudonym of Frank Simmons Leavitt (1891–1953), a famous professional wrestler.

p. 220, *Dillinger*: The notorious bank robber John Herbert Dillinger (1903–34).

p. 231, *The Lost Decade*: This following fragment is an unfinished story which was published in *Esquire* a year before the author's death.

p. 232, *Admiral Byrd's hideout at the South Pole*: A reference to Admiral Richard E. Byrd (1888–1957), who led several expeditions to Antarctica.

p. 233, *Cole Porter came back to the States in 1928*: Between 1917 and 1928, the composer Cole Porter (1891–1964) lived in Paris and Venice, before moving back ot New York City.

p. 245, *Room Service*: A successful 1937 Broadway play written by Allen Boretz (1900–85) and John Murray (1906–84).

p. 246, *Horatio Alger*: Horatio Alger, Jr (1832–99) was the author of popular rags-to-riches novels aimed at young readers.

p. 250, *Major Bowes's voice*: Edward "Major" Bowes (1874–1946) was the presenter of a popular radio talent show in the 1930s and 1940s.

Extra Material

on

F. Scott Fitzgerald's

Babylon Revisted
and
Other Stories

F. Scott Fitzgerald's Life

Francis Scott Key Fitzgerald was born on 24th September 1896 at 481 Laurel Avenue in St Paul, Minnesota. Fitzgerald, who would always be known as "Scott", was named after Francis Scott Key, the author of 'The Star-Spangled Banner' and his father's second cousin three times removed. His mother, Mary "Mollie" McQuillan, was born in 1860 in one of St Paul's wealthier streets, and would come into a modest inheritance at the death of her father in 1877. His father, Edward Fitzgerald, was born in 1853 near Rockville, Maryland. A wicker-furniture manufacturer at the time of Fitzgerald's birth, his business would collapse in 1898 and he would then take to the road as a wholesale grocery salesman for Procter & Gamble. This change of job necessitated various moves of home and the family initially shifted east to Buffalo, New York, in 1898, and then on to Syracuse, New York, in 1901. By 1903 they were back in Buffalo and in March 1908 they were in St Paul again after Edward lost his job at Procter & Gamble. The *déclassé* Fitzgeralds would initially live with the McQuillans and then moved into a series of rented houses, settling down at 599 Summit Avenue.

This itinerancy would disrupt Fitzgerald's early schooling, isolating him and making it difficult to make many friends at his various schools in Buffalo, Syracuse and St Paul. The first one at which Fitzgerald would settle for a prolonged period was the St Paul Academy, which he entered in September 1908. It was here that Fitzgerald would achieve his first appearance in print, 'The Mystery of the Raymond Mortgage', which appeared in the St Paul Academy school magazine *Now and Then* in October 1909. 'Reade, Substitute Right Half' and 'A Debt of Honor' would follow in the February and March 1910 numbers, and 'The Room with the Green Blinds' in the June 1911 number. His reading at this time was dominated by adventure stories and the other typical literary interests of a turn-of-the-century American teen, with the novels of G.A. Henty, Walter Scott's *Ivanhoe* and Jane Porter's *The Scottish Chiefs* among his favourites; their influence was apparent in the floridly melodramatic tone of his early pieces, though themes that would recur throughout Fitzgerald's mature fiction, such as the social difficulties of the outsider, would be

Early Life

Schooling and Early Writings

introduced in these stories. An interest in the theatre also surfaced at this time, with Fitzgerald writing and taking the lead role in *The Girl from Lazy J*, a play that would be performed with a local amateur-dramatic group, the Elizabethan Drama Club, in August 1911. The group would also produce *The Captured Shadow* in 1912, *The Coward* in 1913 and *Assorted Spirits* in 1914.

At the end of the summer of 1911, Fitzgerald was once again uprooted (in response to poor academic achievements) and moved to the Newman School, a private Catholic school in Hackensack, New Jersey. He was singularly unpopular with the other boys, who considered him aloof and overbearing. This period as a social pariah at Newman was a defining time for Fitzgerald, one that would be echoed repeatedly in his fiction, most straightforwardly in the "Basil" stories, the most famous of which, 'The Freshest Boy', would appear in *The Saturday Evening Post* in July 1928 and is clearly autobiographical in its depiction of a boastful schoolboy's social exclusion.

Hackensack had, however, the advantage of proximity to New York City, and Fitzgerald began to get to know Manhattan, visiting a series of shows, including *The Quaker Girl* and *Little Boy Blue*. His first publication in Newman's school magazine, *The Newman News*, was 'Football', a poem written in an attempt to appease his peers following a traumatic incident on the football field that led to widespread accusation of cowardice, compounding the young writer's isolation. In his last year at Newman he would publish three stories in *The Newman News*.

Father Fay and the Catholic Influence

Also in that last academic year Fitzgerald would encounter the prominent Catholic priest Father Cyril Sigourney Webster Fay, a lasting and formative connection that would influence the author's character, oeuvre and career. Father Fay introduced Fitzgerald to such figures as Henry Adams and encouraged the young writer towards the aesthetic and moral understanding that underpins all of his work. In spite of the licence and debauchery for which Fitzgerald's life and work are often read, a strong moral sense informs all of his fiction – a sense that can be readily traced to Fay and the author's Catholic schooling at Newman. Fay would later appear in thinly disguised form as Amory Blaine's spiritual mentor, and man of the world, Monsignor Darcy, in *This Side of Paradise*.

Princeton

Fitzgerald's academic performance was little improved at Newman, and he would fail four courses in his two years there. In spite of this, in May 1913 Fitzgerald took the entrance exams for Princeton, the preferred destination for Catholic undergraduates in New Jersey. He would go up in September 1913, his fees paid for through a legacy left by his grandmother Louisa McQuillan, who had died in August.

At Princeton Fitzgerald would begin to work in earnest on the process of turning himself into an author: in his first year he met confrères and future collaborators John Peale Bishop and Edmund Wilson. During his freshman year Fitzgerald won a competition to write the book and lyrics for the 1914–15 Triangle Club (the Princeton dramatic society) production *Fie! Fie! Fi-Fi!* He would also co-author, with Wilson, the 1915–16 production, *The Evil Eye*, and the lyrics for *Safety First*, the 1916–17 offering. He also quickly began to contribute to the Princeton humour magazine *The Princeton Tiger*, while his reading tastes had moved on to the social concerns of George Bernard Shaw, Compton Mackenzie and H.G. Wells. His social progress at Princeton also seemed assured as Fitzgerald was approached by the Cottage Club (one of Princeton's exclusive eating clubs) and prominence in the Triangle Club seemed inevitable.

September 1914 and the beginning of Fitzgerald's sophomore year would mark the great calamity of his Princeton education, causing a trauma that Fitzgerald would approach variously in his writing (notably in *This Side of Paradise* and Gatsby's abortive "Oxford" career in *The Great Gatsby*). Poor academic performance meant that Fitzgerald was barred from extra-curricular activities; he was therefore unable to perform in *Fie! Fie! Fi-Fi!*, and took to the road with the production in an attendant capacity. Fitzgerald's progress at the Triangle and Cottage clubs stagnated (he made Secretary at Triangle nonetheless, but did not reach the heights he had imagined for himself), and his hopes of social dominance on campus were dashed.

The second half of the 1914–15 academic year saw a brief improvement and subsequent slipping of Fitzgerald's performance in classes, perhaps in response to a budding romance with Ginevra King, a sixteen-year-old socialite from Lake Forest, Illinois. Their courtship would continue until January 1917. King would become the model for a series of Fitzgerald's characters, including Judy Jones in the 1922 short story 'Winter Dreams', Isabelle Borgé in *This Side of Paradise* and, most famously, Daisy Miller in *The Great Gatsby*. In November 1915 Fitzgerald's academic career was once again held up when he was diagnosed with malaria (though it is likely that this was in fact the first appearance of the tuberculosis that would sporadically disrupt his health for the rest of his life) and left Princeton for the rest of the semester to recuperate. At the same time as all of this disruption, however, Fitzgerald was building a head of steam in terms of his literary production. Publications during this period included stories, reviews and poems for Princeton's *Nassau Literary Magazine*.

The USA entered the Great War in May 1917 and a week later Fitzgerald joined up, at least partly motivated by the fact that his

Ginevra King and Ill Health

Army Commission

uncompleted courses at Princeton would automatically receive credits as he signed up. Three weeks of intensive training and the infantry commission exam soon followed, though a commission itself did not immediately materialize. Through the summer he stayed in St Paul, undertaking important readings in William James, Henri Bergson and others, and in the autumn he returned to Princeton (though not to study) and took lodgings with John Biggs Jr, the editor of the *Tiger*. More contributions appeared in both the *Nassau Literary Magazine* and the *Tiger*, but the commission finally came and in November Fitzgerald was off to Fort Leavenworth, Kansas, where he was to report as a second lieutenant in the infantry. Convinced that he would die in the war, Fitzgerald began intense work on his first novel, *The Romantic Egoist*, the first draft of which would be finished while on leave from Kansas in February 1918. The publishing house Charles Scribner's Sons, despite offering an encouraging appreciation of the novel, rejected successive drafts in August and October 1918.

Zelda Sayre   As his military training progressed and the army readied Fitzgerald and his men for the fighting in Europe, he was relocated, first to Camp Gordon in Georgia, and then on to Camp Sheridan, near Montgomery, Alabama. There, at a dance at the Montgomery Country Club in July, he met Zelda Sayre, a beautiful eighteen-year-old socialite and daughter of a justice of the Alabama Supreme Court. An intense courtship began and Fitzgerald soon proposed marriage, though Zelda was nervous about marrying a man with so few apparent prospects.

As the armistice that ended the Great War was signed on 11th November 1918, Fitzgerald was waiting to embark for Europe, and had already been issued with his overseas uniform. The closeness by which he avoided action in the Great War stayed with Fitzgerald, and gave him another trope for his fiction, with many of his characters, Amory Blaine from *This Side of Paradise* and Jay Gatsby among them, attributed with abortive or ambiguous military careers. Father Fay, who had been involved, and had tried to involve Fitzgerald, in a series of mysterious intelligence operations during the war, died in January 1919, leaving Fitzgerald without a moral guide just as he entered the world free from the restrictions of Princeton and the army. Fay would be the dedicatee of *This Side of Paradise*.

Literary   Fitzgerald's first move after the war was to secure gainful
Endeavours   employment at Barron Collier, an advertising agency, producing copy for trolley-car advertisements. At night he continued to work hard at his fiction, collecting 112 rejection slips over this period. Relief was close at hand, however, with *The Smart Set* printing a revised version of 'Babes in the Wood' (a short story that had previous appeared in *Nassau Literary Magazine* and

that would soon be cannibalized for *This Side of Paradise*) in their September 1919 issue. *The Smart Set*, edited by this time by H.L. Mencken and George Jean Nathan, who would both become firm supporters of Fitzgerald's talent, was a respected literary magazine, but not a high payer; Fitzgerald received $30 for this first appearance. Buoyed by this, and frustrated by his job, Fitzgerald elected to leave work and New York and return to his parents' house in St Paul, where he would make a concerted effort to finish his novel. As none of the early drafts of *The Romantic Egoist* survive, it is impossible to say with complete certainty how much of that project was preserved in the draft of *This Side of Paradise* that emerged at St Paul. It was, at any rate, more attractive to Scribner in its new form, and the editor Maxwell Perkins, who would come to act as both editor and personal banker for Fitzgerald, wrote on 16th September to say that the novel had been accepted. Soon after he would hire Harold Ober to act as his agent, an arrangement that would continue throughout the greatest years of Fitzgerald's output and that would benefit the author greatly, despite sometimes causing Ober a great deal of difficulty and anxiety. Though Fitzgerald would consider his novels the artistically important part of his work, it would be his short stories, administered by Ober, which would provide the bulk of his income. Throughout his career a regular supply of short stories appeared between his novels, a supply that became more essential and more difficult to maintain as the author grew older.

Newly confident after the acceptance of *This Side of Paradise*, *Success* Fitzgerald set about revising a series of his previous stories, securing another four publications in *The Smart Set*, one in *Scribner's Magazine* and one in *The Saturday Evening Post*, an organ that would prove to be one of the author's most dependable sources of income for many years to come. By the end of 1919 Fitzgerald had made $879 from writing: not yet a living, but a start. His receipts would quickly increase. Thanks to Ober's skilful assistance *The Saturday Evening Post* had taken another six stories by February 1920, at $400 each. In March *This Side of Paradise* was published and proved to be a surprising success, selling 3,000 in its first three days and making instant celebrities of Fitzgerald and Zelda, who would marry the author on 3rd April, her earlier concerns about her suitor's solvency apparently eased by his sudden literary success. During the whirl of 1920, the couple's *annus mirabilis*, other miraculous portents of a future of plenty included the sale of a story, 'Head and Shoulders', to Metro Films for $2,500, the sale of four stories to *Metropolitan Magazine* for $900 each and the rapid appearance of *Flappers and Philosophers*, a volume of stories, published by Scribner in September. By the end of the year Fitzgerald, still in his mid-twenties, had moved into an apartment on New York's West 59th Street and was hard at work on his second novel.

Zelda discovered she was pregnant in February 1921, and in May the couple headed to Europe where they visited various heroes and attractions, including John Galsworthy. They returned in July to St Paul, where a daughter, Scottie, was born on 26th October. Fitzgerald was working consistently and well at this time, producing a prodigious amount of high-quality material. *The Beautiful and Damned*, his second novel, was soon ready and began to appear as a serialization in *Metropolitan Magazine* from September. Its publication in book form would have to wait until March 1922, at which point it received mixed reviews, though Scribner managed to sell 40,000 copies of it in its first year of publication. Once again it would be followed within a few months by a short-story collection, *Tales of the Jazz Age*, which contained such classics of twentieth-century American literature as 'May Day', 'The Diamond as Big as the Ritz' and 'The Curious Case of Benjamin Button'.

1923 saw continued successes and a first failure. Receipts were growing rapidly: the Hearst organization bought first option in Fitzgerald's stories for $1,500, he sold the film rights for *This Side of Paradise* for $10,000 and he began selling stories to *The Saturday Evening Post* for $1,250 each. *The Vegetable*, on the other hand, a play that he had been working on for some time, opened in Atlantic City and closed almost immediately following poor reviews, losing Fitzgerald money. By the end of the year his income had shot up to $28,759.78, but he had spent more than that on the play and fast living, and found himself in debt as a result.

The Fitzgeralds' high living was coming at an even higher price. In an attempt to finish his new project Fitzgerald set out for Europe with Zelda and landed up on the French Riviera, a situation that provided the author with the space and time to make some real progress on his novel. While there, however, Zelda met Édouard Jozan, a French pilot, and began a romantic entanglement that put a heavy strain on her marriage. This scenario has been read by some as influencing the final drafting of *The Great Gatsby*, notably Gatsby's disillusionment with Daisy. It would also provide one of the central threads of *Tender Is the Night*, while Gerald and Sara Murphy, two friends they made on the Riviera, would be models for that novel's central characters. Throughout 1924 their relations became more difficult, their volatility was expressed through increasingly erratic behaviour and by the end of the year Fitzgerald's drinking was developing into alcoholism.

Some progress was made on the novel, however, and a draft was sent to Scribner in October. A period of extensive and crucial revisions followed through January and February 1925, with the novel already at the galley-proof stage. After extensive negotiations with Max Perkins, the new novel also received its final title at about this time. Previous titles had included *Trimalchio* and *Trimalchio in West Egg*, both of which Scribner found too obscure for a mass readership, despite Fitzgerald's preference for them, while *Gold-Hatted Gatsby*, *On the Road to West Egg*, *The High-Bouncing Lover* and *Among Ash Heaps and Millionaires* were also suggestions. Shortly before the novel was due to be published, Fitzgerald telegrammed Scribner with the possible title *Under the Red, White and Blue*, but it was too late, and the work was published as *The Great Gatsby* on 10th April. The reception for the new work was impressive, and it quickly garnered some of Fitzgerald's most enthusiastic reviews, but its sales did not reach the best-seller levels the author and Scribner had hoped for.

Fitzgerald was keen to get on with his work and, rather misguidedly, set off to Paris with Zelda to begin his next novel. Paris at the heart of the Roaring Twenties was not a locale conducive to careful concentration, and little progress was made on the new project. There was much socializing, however, and Fitzgerald invested quite a lot of his time in cementing his reputation as one of the more prominent drunks of American letters. The couple's time was spent mostly with the American expatriate community, and among those he got to know there were Edith Wharton, Gertrude Stein, Robert McAlmon and Sylvia Beach of Shakespeare & Company. Perhaps the most significant relationship with another writer from this period was with Ernest Hemingway, with whom Fitzgerald spent much time (sparking jealousy in Zelda), and for whom he would become an important early supporter, helping to encourage Scribner to publish *The Torrents of Spring* and *The Sun Also Rises*, for which he also gave extensive editorial advice. The summer of 1925 was again spent on the Riviera, but this time with a rowdier crowd (which included John Dos Passos, Archibald MacLeish and Rudolph Valentino) and little progress was made on the new book. February 1926 saw publication of the inevitable follow-up short-story collection, this time *All the Sad Young Men*, of which the most significant pieces were 'The Rich Boy', 'Winter Dreams' and 'Absolution'. All three are closely associated with *The Great Gatsby*, and can be read as alternative routes into the Gatsby story.

Paris

With the new novel still effectively stalled, Fitzgerald decamped to Hollywood at the beginning of 1927, where he was engaged by United Artists to write a flapper comedy that was never produced in the end. These false starts were not, however, adversely affecting Fitzgerald's earnings, and 1927 would represent the highest annual earnings the author had achieved so far: $29,757.87, largely from

Hollywood

short-story sales. While in California Fitzgerald began a dalliance with Lois Moran, a seventeen-year-old aspiring actress – putting further strain on his relationship with Zelda. After the couple moved back east (to Delaware) Zelda began taking ballet lessons in an attempt to carve a niche for herself that might offer her a role beyond that of the wife of a famous author. She would also make various attempts to become an author in her own right. The lessons would continue under the tutelage of Lubov Egorova when the Fitzgeralds moved to Paris in the summer of 1928, with Zelda's obsessive commitment to dance practice worrying those around her and offering the signs of the mental illness that was soon to envelop her.

Looking for a steady income stream (in spite of very high earnings expenditure was still outstripping them), Fitzgerald set to work on the "Basil" stories in 1928, earning $31,500 for nine that appeared in *The Saturday Evening Post*, forcing novel-writing into the background. The next year his *Post* fee would rise to $4,000 a story. Throughout the next few years he would move between the USA and Europe, desperate to resuscitate that project, but make little inroads.

Zelda's Mental Illness By 1930 Zelda's behaviour was becoming more and more erratic, and on 23rd April she was checked into the Malmaison clinic near Paris for rest and assistance with her mental problems. Deeply obsessed with her dancing lessons, and infatuated with Egorova, she discharged herself from the clinic on 11th May and attempted suicide a few days later. After this she was admitted to the care of Dr Oscar Forel in Switzerland, who diagnosed her as schizophrenic. Such care was expensive and placed a new financial strain on Fitzgerald, who responded by selling another series of stories to the *Post* and earning $32,000 for the year. The most significant story of this period was 'Babylon Revisited'. Zelda improved and moved back to Montgomery, Alabama, and the care of the Sayre family in September 1931. That autumn Fitzgerald would make another abortive attempt to break into Hollywood screenwriting.

At the beginning of 1932 Zelda suffered a relapse during a trip to Florida and was admitted to the Henry Phipps Psychiatric Clinic in Baltimore. While there she would finish work on a novel, *Save Me the Waltz*, that covered some of the same material her husband was using in his novel about the Riviera. Upon completion she sent the manuscript to Perkins at Scribner, without passing it to her husband, which caused much distress. Fitzgerald helped her to edit the book nonetheless, removing much of the material he intended to use, and Scribner accepted it and published it on 7th October. It received poor reviews and did not sell. Finally accepting that she had missed her chance to become a professional dancer, Zelda now poured her energies into painting. Fitzgerald would organize a show of these in New York in 1934, and a play, *Scandalabra*, that would be performed by the Junior Vagabonds, an amateur Baltimore drama group, in the spring of 1933.

His own health now beginning to fail, Fitzgerald returned to his own novel and rewrote extensively through 1933, finally submitting it in October. *Tender Is the Night* would appear in serialized form in *Scribner's Magazine* from January to April 1934 and would then be published, in amended form, on 12th April. It was generally received positively and sold well, though again not to the blockbusting extent that Fitzgerald had hoped for. This would be Fitzgerald's final completed novel. He was thirty-seven. *Final Novel*

With the receipts for *Tender Is the Night* lower than had been hoped for and Zelda still erratic and requiring expensive medical supervision, Fitzgerald's finances were tight. From this point on he found it increasingly difficult to produce the kind of high-quality, extended pieces that could earn thousands of dollars in glossies like *The Saturday Evening Post*. From 1934 many of his stories were shorter and brought less money, while some of them were simply sub-standard. Of the outlets for this new kind of work, *Esquire* proved the most reliable, though it only paid $250 a piece, a large drop from his salad days at the *Post*. *Financial Problems and Artistic Decline*

March 1935 saw the publication of *Taps at Reveille*, another collection of short stories from Scribner. It was a patchy collection, but included the important 'Babylon Revisited', while 'Crazy Sunday' saw his first sustained attempt at writing about Hollywood, a prediction of the tendency of much of his work to come. His next significant writing came, however, with three articles that appeared in the February, March and April 1936 numbers of *Esquire*: 'The Crack-up', 'Pasting It Together' and 'Handle with Care'. These essays were brutally confessional, and irritated many of those around Fitzgerald, who felt that he was airing his dirty laundry in public. His agent Harold Ober was concerned that by publicizing his own battles with depression and alcoholism he would give the high-paying glossies the impression that he was unreliable, making future magazine work harder to come by. The pieces have, however, come to be regarded as Fitzgerald's greatest non-fiction work and are an essential document in both the construction of his own legend and in the mythologizing of the Jazz Age.

Later in 1936, on the author's fortieth birthday in September, he gave an interview in *The New York Post* to Michael Mok. The article was a sensationalist hatchet job entitled 'Scott Fitzgerald, 40, Engulfed in Despair' and showed him as a *Suicide Attempt and Worsening Health* depressed dipsomaniac. The publication of the article wounded Fitzgerald further and he tried to take his own life through an overdose of morphine. After this his health continued to deteriorate and various spates in institutions followed, for influenza, for tuberculosis and, repeatedly, in attempts to treat his alcoholism.

His inability to rely on his own physical and literary powers meant a significant drop in his earning capabilities; by 1937 his debts exceeded $40,000, much of which was owed to his agent Ober and his editor Perkins, while Fitzgerald still had to pay Zelda's medical fees and support his daughter and himself. A solution to this desperate situation appeared in July: MGM would hire him as a screenwriter at $1,000 a week for six months. He went west, hired an apartment and set about his work. He contributed to various films, usually in collaboration with other writers, a system that irked him. Among these were *A Yank at Oxford* and various stillborn projects, including *Infidelity*, which was to have starred Joan Crawford, and an adaptation of 'Babylon Revisited'. He only received one screen credit from this time, for an adaptation of Erich Maria Remarque's novel *Three Comrades*, produced by Joseph Mankiewicz. His work on this picture led to a renewal of his contract, but no more credits followed.

Sheila Graham   While in Hollywood Fitzgerald met Sheila Graham, a twenty-eight-year-old English gossip columnist, with whom he began an affair. Graham, who initially attracted Fitzgerald because of her physical similarity to the youthful Zelda, became Fitzgerald's partner during the last years of his life, cohabiting with the author quite openly in Los Angeles. It seems unlikely that Zelda, still in medical care, ever knew about her. Graham had risen up from a rather murky background in England and Fitzgerald set about improving her with his "College of One", aiming to introduce her to his favoured writers and thinkers. She would be the model for Kathleen Moore in *The Last Tycoon*.

Among the film projects he worked on at this time were *Madame Curie* and *Gone with the Wind*, neither of which earned him a credit. The contract with MGM was terminated in 1939 and Fitzgerald became a freelance screenwriter. While engaged on the screenplay for *Winter Carnival* for United Artists, Fitzgerald went on a drinking spree at Dartmouth College, resulting in his getting fired. A final period of alcoholic excess followed, marring a trip to Cuba with Zelda in April and worsening his financial straits. At this time Ober finally pulled the plug and refused to lend Fitzgerald any more money, though he would continue to support Scottie, Fitzgerald's daughter, whom the Obers had effectively brought up. The writer, now his own agent, began working on a Hollywood novel based on the life of the famous Hollywood producer Irving Thalberg.

Hollywood would also be the theme of the last fiction Fitzgerald would see published; the Pat Hobby stories. These appeared in *Esquire* beginning in January 1940 and continued till after the author's death, ending in July 1941 and appearing in each monthly number between those dates.

In November 1940 Fitzgerald suffered a heart attack and was told to rest, which he did at Graham's apartment. On 21st December he had another heart attack and died, aged just forty-four. Permission was refused to bury him in St Mary's Church in Rockville, Maryland, where his father had been buried, because Fitzgerald was not a practising Catholic. Instead he was buried at Rockville Union Cemetery on 27th December 1940. In 1975 Scottie Fitzgerald would successfully petition to have her mother and father moved to the family plot at St Mary's. *Death*

Following Fitzgerald's death his old college friend Edmund Wilson would edit Fitzgerald's incomplete final novel, shaping his drafts and notes into *The Last Tycoon*, which was published in 1941 by Scribner. Wilson also collected Fitzgerald's confessional *Esquire* pieces and published them with a selection of related short stories and essays as *The Crack-up and Other Pieces and Stories* in 1945.

Zelda lived on until 1948, in and out of mental hospitals. After reading *The Last Tycoon* she began work on *Caesar's Things*, a novel that was not finished when the Highland hospital caught fire and she died, locked in her room in preparation for electro-shock therapy.

F. Scott Fitzgerald's Works

Fitzgerald's first novel, *This Side of Paradise*, set the tone for his later classic works. The novel was published in 1920 and was a remarkable success, impressing critics and readers alike. Amory Blaine, the directionless and guilelessly dissolute protagonist, is an artistically semi-engaged innocent, and perilously, though charmingly unconsciously, déclassé. His long drift towards destruction (and implicit reincarnation as Fitzgerald himself) sees Blaine's various arrogances challenged one by one as he moves from a well-heeled life in the Midwest through private school and middling social successes at Princeton towards a life of vague and unrewarding artistic involvement. Beneath Fitzgerald's precise observations of American high society in the late 1910s can be witnessed the creation of a wholly new American type, and Blaine would become a somewhat seedy role model for his generation. Fast-living and nihilist tendencies would become the character traits of Fitzgerald's set and the *This Side of Paradise*

Lost Generation more generally. Indeed, by the novel's end, it has become clear that Blaine's experiences of lost love, a hostile society and the deaths of his mother and friends have imparted important life lessons upon him. Blaine, having returned to a Princeton that he has outgrown and poised before an unknowable future, ends the novel with his Jazz Age *cogito*: "'I know myself,' he cried, 'but that is all.'"

Flappers and Philosophers

Fitzgerald's next publication would continue this disquisition on his era and peers: *Flappers and Philosophers* (1920) is a collection of short stories, including such famous pieces as 'Bernice Bobs Her Hair' and 'The Ice Palace'. The first of these tells the tale of Bernice, who visits her cousin Marjorie only to find herself rejected for being a stop on Marjorie's social activities. Realizing that she can't rid herself of Bernice, Marjorie decides to coach her to become a young femme fatale like herself – and Bernice is quickly a hit with the town boys. Too much of a hit though, and Marjorie takes her revenge by persuading Bernice that it would be to her social advantage to bob her hair. It turns out not to be and Bernice leaves the town embarrassed, but not before cutting off Marjorie's pigtails in her sleep and taking them with her to the station.

The Beautiful and Damned

The Beautiful and Damned (1922) would follow, another novel that featured a thinly disguised portrait of Fitzgerald in the figure of the main character, Anthony Patch. He was joined by a fictionalized version of Fitzgerald's new wife Zelda, whom the author married as *This Side of Paradise* went to press. The couple are here depicted on a rapidly downward course that both mirrored and predicted the Fitzgeralds' own trajectory. Patch is the heir apparent of his reforming grandfather's sizable fortune but lives a life of dissolution in the city, promising that he'll find gainful employment. He marries Gloria Gilbert, a great but turbulent beauty, and they gradually descend into alcoholism, wasting what little capital Anthony has on high living and escapades. When his grandfather walks in on a scene of debauchery, Anthony is disinherited and the Patches' decline quickens. When the grandfather dies, Anthony embarks on a legal case to reclaim the money from the good causes to which it has been donated and wins their case, although not before Anthony has lost his mind and Gloria her beauty.

Tales of the Jazz Age

Another volume of short stories, *Tales of the Jazz Age*, was published later in the same year, in accordance with Scribner's policy of quickly following successful novels with moneymaking collections of short stories. Throughout this period Fitzgerald was gaining for himself a reputation as America's premier short-story writer, producing fiction for a selection of high-profile "glossy" magazines and earning unparalleled fees for his efforts. The opportunities and the pressures of this commercial work, coupled with Fitzgerald's continued profligacy, led to a certain unevenness in his short fiction. This unevenness is clearly present in *Tales of the Jazz Age*, with some of Fitzgerald's very best work appearing beside some fairly average pieces. Among the great works were 'The Diamond as Big as the Ritz' and the novella 'May Day'. The first of these tells the story of the Washingtons, a family that live in seclusion in the wilds of Montana on top of a mountain made of solid diamond. The necessity of keeping the source of their wealth hidden from all makes the Washingtons' lives a singular mixture of great privilege and isolation; friends that visit the children are briefly treated to luxury beyond their imagining and are then executed to secure the secrecy of the Washington diamond. When young Percy's friend John T. Unger makes a visit during the summer vacation their unusual lifestyle and their diamond are lost for ever. The novella 'May Day' is very different in style and execution, but deals with some of the same issues, in particular the exigencies of American capitalism in the aftermath of the Great War. It offers a panorama of Manhattan's post-war social order as the anti-communist May Day Riots of 1919 unfold. A group of privileged Yale alumni enjoy the May Day ball and bicker about their love interests, while ex-soldiers drift around the edges of their world.

In spite of the apparent success that Fitzgerald was experiencing by this time, his next novel came with greater difficulty than his first four volumes. *The Great Gatsby* is the story of Jay Gatsby, born poor as James Gatz, an *arriviste* of mysterious origins who sets himself up in high style on Long Island's north shore only to find disappointment and his demise there. Like Fitzgerald, and some of his other characters, including Anthony Patch, Gatsby falls in love during the war, this time with Daisy Miller. Following Gatsby's departure, however, Daisy marries the greatly wealthy Tom Buchanan, which convinces Gatsby that he lost her only because of his penuriousness. Following this, Gatsby builds himself a fortune comparable to Buchanan's through mysterious and proscribed means and, five years after Daisy broke off their relations, uses his new-found wealth to throw a series of parties from an enormous house across the water from Buchanan's Long Island pile. His intention is to impress his near neighbour Daisy with the lavishness of his entertainments, but he miscalculates and the "old money" Buchanans stay away, not attracted by Gatsby's *parvenu* antics. Instead Gatsby approaches Nick Carraway, the novel's narrator (who took that role in one of the masterstrokes of the late stages of the novel's revision), Daisy's cousin and

The Great Gatsby

Gatsby's neighbour. Daisy is initially affected by Gatsby's devotion, to the extent that she agrees to leave Buchanan, but once Buchanan reveals Gatsby's criminal source of income she has second thoughts. Daisy, shocked by this revelation, accidentally kills Buchanan's mistress Myrtle in a hit-and-run accident with Gatsby in the car and returns to Buchanan, leaving Gatsby waiting for her answer. Buchanan then lets Myrtle's husband believe that Gatsby was driving the car and the husband shoots him, leaving him floating in the unused swimming pool of his great estate.

All the Sad
Young Men

Of *All the Sad Young Men* (1926) the most well-known pieces are 'The Rich Boy', 'Winter Dreams' and 'Absolution'. All three have much in common with *The Great Gatsby*, in terms of the themes dealt with and the characters developed. 'The Rich Boy' centres on the rich young bachelor Anson Hunter, who has romantic dalliances with women, but never marries and grows increasingly lonely. 'Winter Dreams' tells the tale of Dexter Green and Judy Jones, similar characters to Jay Gatsby and Daisy Miller. Much like Gatsby, Green raises himself from nothing with the intention of winning Jones's affections. And, like Gatsby, he finds the past lost. 'Absolution' is a rejected false start on *The Great Gatsby* and deals with a young boy's difficulties around the confessional and an encounter with a deranged priest.

'Babylon Revisited' is probably the greatest and most read story of the apparently fallow period between *The Great Gatsby* and *Tender Is the Night*. It deals with Charlie Wales, an American businessman who enacts some of Fitzgerald's guilt for his apparent abandonment of his daughter Scottie and wife Zelda. Wales returns to a Paris unknown to him since he gave up drinking. There he fights his dead wife's family for custody of his daughter, only to find that friends from his past undo his careful efforts.

Basil and
Josephine

Between April 1928 and April 1929, Fitzgerald published eight stories in the *Saturday Evening Post* centring on Basil Duke Lee, an adolescent coming of age in the Midwest, loosely based on the author's own teenage years. A ninth story, 'That Kind of Party', which fits chronologically at the beginning of the Basil cycle, was rejected by the *Saturday Evening Post* because of its description of children's kissing games, and was only published posthumously in 1951. These stories were much admired by both Fitzgerald's editor and agent, who encouraged him to compile them in a book with some additional stories. Fitzgerald did not act on this advice, but between April 1930 and August 1931 he published, again in the *Saturday Evening Post*, five stories focusing on the development of Josephine Perry, a kind of female counterpart to Basil Duke Lee. In 1934 Fitzgerald then considered collecting the Basil and Josephine stories in a single volume and adding a final one in which the two would meet and which would transform the whole into a kind of novel, but he shelved the idea, as he had doubts about the overall quality of the outcome and its possible reception. He was still favourable to having them packaged as a straightforward short-story collection, but this would only happen in 1973, when Scribner published *The Basil and Josephine Stories*.

Tender Is the Night

The next, and last completed, novel came even harder, and it would not be until 1934 that *Tender Is the Night* would appear. This novel was met by mixed reviews and low, but not disastrous sales. It has remained controversial among readers of Fitzgerald and is hailed by some as his masterpiece and others as an aesthetic failure. The plotting is less finely wrought than the far leaner *The Great Gatsby*, and apparent chronological inconsistencies and longueurs have put off some readers. The unremitting detail of Dick Diver's descent, however, is unmatched in Fitzgerald's oeuvre.

It begins with an impressive set-piece description of life on the Riviera during the summer of 1925. There Rosemary Hoyt, modelled on the real-life actress Lois Moran, meets Dick and Nicole Driver, and becomes infatuated with Dick. It is then revealed that Dick had been a successful psychiatrist and had met Nicole when she was his patient, being treated in the aftermath of being raped by her father. Now Dick is finding it difficult to maintain his research interests in the social whirl that Nicole's money has thrust him into. Dick is forced out of a Swiss clinic for his unreliability and incipient alcoholism. Later Dick consummates his relationship with Rosemary on a trip to Rome, and gets beaten by police after drunkenly involving himself in a fight. When the Divers return to the Riviera Dick drinks more and Nicole leaves him for Tommy Barban, a French-American mercenary soldier (based on Zelda's Riviera beau Édouard Jozan). Dick returns to America, where he becomes a provincial doctor and disappears.

Pat Hobby Stories

The "Pat Hobby" stories are the most remarkable product of Fitzgerald's time in Hollywood to see publication during the author's lifetime. Seventeen stories appeared in all, in consecutive issues of *Esquire* through 1940 and 1941. Hobby is a squalid Hollywood hack fallen upon hard times and with the days of his great success, measured by on-screen credits, some years behind him. He is a generally unsympathetic character and most of the stories depict him in unflattering situations, saving his own skin at the expense of those around him. It speaks to the hardiness of Fitzgerald's talent that even at this late stage he was able to make a character as amoral as Hobby vivid and engaging on the page. The Hobby stories are all short, evidencing Fitzgerald's skill in his later career at compressing storylines that would previously have been extrapolated far further.

The Last   Fitzgerald's final project was *The Last Tycoon*, a work which,
Tycoon   in the partial and provisional version that was published after the
author's death, has all the hallmarks of a quite remarkable work.
The written portion of the novel, which it seems likely would
have been rewritten extensively before publication (in accordance
with Fitzgerald's previous practice), is a classic conjuring of the
golden age of Hollywood through an ambiguous and suspenseful
story of love and money. The notes that follow the completed
portion of *The Last Tycoon* suggest that the story would have
developed in a much more melodramatic direction, with Stahr
embarking on transcontinental business trips, losing his edge,
ordering a series of murders and dying in an aeroplane crash. If
the rewrites around *Tender Is the Night* are anything to go by,
it seems likely that Fitzgerald would have toned down Stahr's
adventures before finishing the story: in the earlier novel stories
of matricide and other violent moments had survived a number
of early drafts, only to be cut before the book took its final form.

– Richard Parker

Select Bibliography

Biographies:
Bruccoli, Matthew J., *Some Sort of Epic Grandeur: The Life
of F. Scott Fitzgerald*, 2nd edn. (Columbia, SC: University of
South Carolina Press, 2002)
Mizener, Arthur, *The Far Side of Paradise: A Biography of F.
Scott Fitzgerald*, (Boston, MS: Houghton Mifflin, 1951)
Turnbull, Andrew, *Scott Fitzgerald* (Harmondsworth:
Penguin, 1970)

Additional Recommended Background Material:
Curnutt, Kirk, ed., *A Historical Guide to F. Scott Fitzgerald*
(Oxford: Oxford University Press, 2004)
Prigozy, Ruth, ed., *The Cambridge Companion to F. Scott
Fitzgerald* (Cambridge: Cambridge University Press, 2002)

ALMA CLASSICS

ALMA CLASSICS aims to publish mainstream and lesser-known European classics in an innovative and striking way, while employing the highest editorial and production standards. By way of a unique approach the range offers much more, both visually and textually, than readers have come to expect from contemporary classics publishing.

LATEST TITLES PUBLISHED BY ALMA CLASSICS

www.almaclassics.com